Christmas at Camp Cedarwood

By Holly Welland

Contents

Prologue

The sun was just inches above the horizon and glowing in bright red-and-orange. Its warm late-summer rays reflected off the thick, fluffy clouds above and the shimmering lake waters below. Everything visible to the eye was illuminated in a golden tinge. It was like being in the middle of some grand painting.

Ashley sighed and leaned back on her hands. This would be the last time she'd watch this sunset. Sitting on the dock, legs dangling over the edge, toes just tapping into the cool lake water, she once more took in the feeling of the sun on her face as it made its way out of the sky. Soon would come night and its millions of stars.

She idly kicked her right foot and splashed water up into the air. She was going to miss this. Not so much that she was sad to be leaving, but these sorts of sunsets were almost impossible to come by in the city. Here at Camp Cedarwood, they were a daily — well, nightly — occurrence.

Footsteps came from behind her. They were heavy, lumbering steps that sounded like they belonged to a linebacker or burly woodsman. But she knew that neither of those sorts of people were coming to see her. Just a lanky boy with an awkward gait.

"I was wondering when you'd get here," she said, not turning around. Not when she had just minutes left of this last sunset.

"Sorry, Ash." The voice was soft and low. "I had to get the boys all packed up. I think I was at least a bit successful."

She laughed and kicked at the water again. "My girls were ready this morning. But we are the more-organized gender."

"No argument here." He sat down to her left, his hand nearly touching hers. They were quiet for a few seconds, with the only sound being the waves gently crashing onto the dock. Then he spoke. "I guess this is our last sunset, huh?"

"I guess it is," she said, still keeping her eyes on the sun. It was now touching the horizon.

"It's been a great summer. I mean, I've had great summers here before, but this one seemed extra special."

She smiled. "I'm glad. I had a good one too. I didn't know what to expect when I came up here, but it turned out pretty decent." She took a deep breath. The sweet, refreshing air was another thing she would miss. "Camp Cedarwood is a pretty special place."

"Yeah, it is." His fingers brushed against hers. "Which is why you need to come back here next year."

She shook her head. "I can't. My program has internships every summer." It was one more reason it was the top in the country.

"And you can't do those internships here?"

A third of the sun was now covered by the horizon. The part the remained seemed to glow even brighter. "Not unless Cedarwood becomes a top marketing firm."

"You could do marketing for the camp." In her peripheral vision she could see him looking right at her. "Or you could choose a different program. One that lets you take your summers off."

"I could." She shrugged. "But I want to go where the money is."

"What about where I am?"

The question caught her off-guard. Now she turned and looked at him. His soft, boyish face that made him look younger than his age of 18. His crystal-blue eyes. His shaggy blonde hair, which had been shorter and neater when they'd met at the start of the summer, two months earlier. She put her hand on top of his. "I'm never going to forget you, Marc. You're such a great guy and you're smart and caring and you make me laugh, like, so hard." Her hand gripped his more tightly. "But this isn't—it wouldn't—it won't work. I'm going off to school, you want to work here year-round. Let's both do what matters to us. We'll always have the memories we made here this summer."

His eyes were watering, but he nodded and smiled. "I get it. I just…" He looked out at the lake, then back at her. His eyes closed slightly and he leaned in, bringing his lips towards hers.

She gently put her hand against his chest. "Marc," she whispered.

He backed away, looking upset. "I want to kiss you."

Now she could feel her own eyes becoming wet. All the time they'd spent together, all these sunsets on the dock, all their talks and jokes as they walked through the camp's forest trails, and now they were going to have their first kiss, 12 hours before she was set to leave camp forever? "I... I..." She sighed. "I want to too. But let's not make this harder than it already is." She turned and looked back at the sun. It was now just a semi-circle, and sinking quickly.

He said nothing, but interlocked his fingers with hers. They both sat on the dock as the sun continued to fall. A third of it remained. Then a quarter. Then just its peak.

And then it was gone.

Marc stood up and helped Ashley onto her feet. He opened his arms for a hug. She embraced him without second thought. "I'm going to miss you," he whispered.

"Me too," she said. She squeezed him tightly. "Thanks for making this summer bearable for me."

They let go of each other and started back down the dock and up the winding path, towards the sound of children's shouts and laughter. "Hey," Marc said, his voice even softer. "Do you think, like, if circumstances were different, we could have made it work?"

She thought for a second. "Maybe. You never know. If we're meant to be, then we're meant to be."

December 21

Chapter 1

"Chestnuts roasting on an open fire…"
Click.
"O'er the hills we go…"
Click.
"Holy infant so tender and mild…"
Click.
"Yuletide carols being sung by a choir…"

Ashley Tidings pushed the radio's power button so hard she thought she might break it. There were only three radio stations in the area and all of them played Christmas songs. Did no one care about classic rock, or 90s pop, or Top 40? Heck, at this point she would have taken classical music or jazz. Anything but the same holiday drivel that plagued the airways at this time every year.

She focused her attention back to the highway, or what she could see of it. The snow that had been a light dust when she'd left the city had been getting heavier and heavier as she drove, and now she could barely see more than twenty feet beyond the windshield. She flicked her sedan's headlights to high beams. It was just a curtain of white in front of her.

Her phone rang, causing her to jump in surprise. It was George, her boss. She put it on speaker so she could keep her eyes on the road and both hands on the wheel. "Hey," she said. "Did you hear from them?"

"Just got off the phone." He sounded loud and giddy. "They loved what you presented and want to bring us on immediately. They specifically requested you as the lead for the project."

"Uh huh? And what did you say?"

"I said that you cost an extra two hundred bucks an hour. They said yes."

She grinned. That sort of price increase meant her own base rate would go even higher. "Guess I need to get to work then."

"Or you can take a few days off. Christmas is, what, five days away?"

"Four," she said. "It's the 21st. Happy winter solstice." The darkened sky despite the early evening made it clear that this was the shortest day of the year.

"Same to you. I'm about to leave the office and we'll be reopening it after New Years. You can start working then. Go enjoy the holidays."

"I would if I could, but I can't say I have any plans." Maybe a few fitness classes, a couple of drinks with friends and then spending Christmas Day in her pajamas with Netflix and popcorn. Sounded like a fine time to her.

There was a chuckle on the other end of the line. "Why am I not surprised? Well look, the office is closed, so if you really want to work from home you're welcome to, but a few days to yourself won't kill you."

"I'll try. Thanks George."

"Merry Christmas, Ashley. Get home—" Her phone beeped. Low battery. "—safe."

"Will do." She hung up and tossed the phone back on the passenger seat. The snow was getting even heavier, especially now that the sun had set. The cars she passed—while few and far between—were coming out of nowhere, their taillights only visible once she was fifty feet behind them. These were dangerous driving conditions for anyone, especially someone in a smaller car, on an unfamiliar highway, with a near-dead phone.

And she still had at least another two hours to go. When she'd made the trip north two days ago, it had been sunny skies and the drive had been a quick and easy three hours. Today she'd left the client's office at around three in the afternoon, and now it was passing five and she knew she was nowhere close to home.

Keeping her eyes on the road, or what she could see of it, she grabbed her phone and tried to pull up the weather app. As she pressed on it, the phone beeped again and went black. She looked around for her charging cable before remembering she'd brought it into the hotel room, and she couldn't remember taking it back when she'd left.

"Shoot," she muttered. Now she really had to get home. She turned the radio back on and switched to AM. There had to be a news station broadcasting nearby.

"*Hang a shining star upon the highest bow…*"

Click.

"*He sees you when you're sleeping…*"

Click.

"You're listening to ENAD Radio. Coming up, two uninterrupted hours of your favorite Christmas hits—"

CLICK.

"…which the President fervently denied. And now let's go back to the weather." Oh, thank God, she thought. "Blizzard conditions continue across the area. Authorities have advised everyone to stay home and keep warm. Weather services predict the snow will keep up for at least another day. Sounds like we're going to have a white Christmas after all!"

She once again pounded the power button. A white Christmas? All she wanted was to get home, pour herself a warm bubble bath and soak for the rest of the evening. This snow was keeping her from doing that.

Another beep, this time from her dashboard. The "low fuel" indicator lit up. She rolled her eyes. She had filled it up before starting the journey two days earlier, and normally a full tank would have been more than enough to get her there and back, but she had been blasting the heat the last two hours as the temperature had plummeted. It was just one more strain on her car.

"Just great," she said. She looked up at the sky. "Okay universe, any other way you want to make this trip even worse?"

Her question was answered a minute later, as a slew of police lights came into view across the highway. She slowed down and stopped in front of an officer who was waving his flashlight back and forth. She rolled down the window a few inches. Freezing air filled the car, as did thick, wet snowflakes.

"What's going on?" she asked.

"The bridge ahead has iced over," the officer shouted from within his thick blue parka. It occurred to her that she'd packed nothing remotely close to that when she'd left—just a light jacket. She hadn't expected to be outside much. "You'll have to detour around. The side roads will take you there, but if I were you I'd find shelter as soon as you can. It's not safe to be out here right now."

You're telling me, she thought. "Thank you," she said, smiling out of politeness. She rolled the window back up and followed the trail of lights leading off the highway and onto the side road. She could hear gravel under the tires. She didn't know if this was more or less reassuring. Would the car be more prone to skidding with all this snow?

The road took her into the countryside. She passed farms and fields, all blanketed in a good foot and a half of snow, and cozy brick farmhouses decorated in lights and with smoke coming from their chimneys. Ashley looked at them with envy. They were all warm and lit in golden light, and she was out here in the dark and cold, gripping onto her steering wheel for dear life at every turn.

The dashboard beeped again. The fuel meter was now well in the red. What were the odds that she'd be able to find a gas station on these backroads? Next to none, she reckoned. She needed to stop. "Okay," she muttered to herself. "Just choose a house, pull in and ask if they had a charger." Then she could get her phone working, call for help—her work had a strong insurance package that would get her everything she needed—and then wait in warm comfort for it to arrive. Easy peasy.

Except that now she seemed to be on a stretch of road without any houses nearby—just thick clusters of trees on either side, with the occasional break for a river or small field. She kept going, her eyes scanning for any sign of life, while glancing down at the fuel gauge every thirty seconds. She could feel her heartrate picking up and her breaths going shallow. This wasn't good. For the first time in a long time, it occurred to her that her safety may be at risk.

The snow seemed to be coming down even harder as she pulled out from a small forest and went past a wide field. She looked down it, hoping that she'd see some light at the end, but it was only snow and darkness, the same thing she'd seen for the last ten minutes of driving. Ashley knew she had to turn around and head back to the houses she'd seen earlier. The only question was whether her car had enough gas to make it.

She started to put her foot on the break when two things happened. First, her dashboard dinged again, the low fuel light seeming to shine even brighter. At the same time, a billboard sign along the side of the road suddenly lit up in front of her. Under the glare of the bright lights, she saw a massive photo of trees and cabins in front of a blue lake, with words on top: "Camp Cedarwood, next right!"

She brought the car to a full stop right in front of the sign and stared up at it, mouth agape. "You have got to be kidding me," she said. Camp Cedarwood, the camp she'd worked at, what, fifteen years ago? She had completely forgotten about it. And yet here it was, a refuge in the middle of this storm. She could park, break into the office, call for help, and wait out the blizzard indoors. It wouldn't be luxury, but it was better than staying on the road.

She pressed back on the gas and drove slowly, looking for the turn. None of it was familiar to her. She'd only driven to camp once, and a decade and a half—a lifetime—had passed since.

After a few minutes she saw the road. She turned onto it, feeling the wheels skid under the ever-falling snow, and kept going. The road sloped downward, with no light except her high beams. She tried to remember the way. If she recalled correctly, the camp would be at the end of the road. However long that went.

She took her foot off the gas, grateful that the hill was more than enough to guide her car down. After what felt like an hour of gliding, the road leveled off and branched off in three different directions. The ones to her left and right led into darkness. The one in front of her had two large trees on either side, with a banner hanging between them: "Welcome to Camp Cedarwood!"

Ashley drove under it and onto the camp's long, winding driveway. This she remembered. They used to have races from the camp's entrance to the lake. It could take five minutes to run it. She wasn't sure her car had that much fuel left.

Somehow, though, the vehicle kept going through each twist and turn, until she knew she was close to the cabins. She thought through her plan: park outside the office. Grab a wrench from the small toolbox in the trunk. Break a window. Go into the office. Find a way to turn the power on. Call for help. Write a check for the window.

It was the perfect plan, except that as she turned the final corner she realized that it would never happen. Because she saw lights.

Lots of lights.

"What on earth?" she asked herself. Beyond the driveway and camp's parking lot sat the office and a handful of cabins — new cabins — all shining light from within. A multitude of Christmas lights flashed from their roofs. A large wreathe hung from the office's wall. Several bright streetlights above the parking lot illuminated about a dozen cars and trucks.

There were people here. There were people at Camp Cedarwood.

Someone came running out from between the cabins towards her, waving their arms towards a gap in the parked cars. They were decked out in a thick winter coat and mittens, with a knitted cap on their head and a scarf wrapped around their face. Ashley followed their directions and slowly maneuvered her car between the others. She turned off the engine and rolled down the window as the person walked up to the door. "Hi, I'm having—"

"We're glad you could make it!" The voice was a bit muffled by the scarf. "We were afraid the storm would have kept you!"

"Make it?" Ashley said. She rolled the window down more. All the heat in the car dissipated in seconds.

"But don't worry, your cabin is all ready for you!"

The window opened fully and Ashley stuck her head out. Thick, wet snowflakes blanketed her hair. "No, you don't understand. I got detoured and my car is almost out—"

"What the…" The person took a step back. "No! No way!"

"I'm sorry? What's wrong?"

"Ash?" The man pulled off his hat, revealing neatly trimmed blonde hair. "Is that you?"

For the second time in half an hour, Ashley's jaw dropped. "Marc?"

Chapter 2

"What are — how did — " Marc stared at Ashley in wide-eyed amazement, before giving his head a quick shake. "No, tell me in a minute. Let's get you inside."

"I'd like that," Ashley said. Her hands were already starting to feel the bite of the cold air. She raised the window back up and reached into the backseat to grab her purse and the one duffle bag she'd brought with her for the trip. A few changes of clothes and some toiletries were typically all she needed. In this case, she had greatly underestimated things.

She opened the door and stepped out of the car, into what now had to be two feet of snow. She regretted wearing heels instead of boots. And a skirt and leggings instead of pants. And not wearing socks at all.

Ashley managed to get out of the car and close the door before her feet slipped and she toppled forward. She would have fallen face-first into the snow had Marc not linked his left elbow with her right and held her in place. "Thanks," she said.

"You're welcome," he said with a chuckle. "C'mon. This way."

Taking big steps to get through the thick, heavy snow on the ground (and very thankful that her shoes somehow stayed on as she did), Ashley walked alongside Marc through the parking lot and onto a pathway with significantly less snow on it. "I think I've shoveled this path four times today," Marc said. "And I'll probably do it two more times before the day ends."

Ashley nodded but said nothing. Her teeth were already starting to chatter. Marc led her past several of the cabins, giving her a better look at them. They were definitely new. Unlike the traditional cabins at Camp Cedarwood, which were made of wood, had no heating or insulation, and had thick canvas flaps for doors, these appeared to be constructed from metal and concrete and each had a little deck with an awning above. She saw several pairs of boots sitting next to the doors.

They were also decorated like they'd just been dropped in from the North Pole. One had what had to be a thousand Christmas lights on its roof and going down its walls like vines, shining colors of red, green and white. Another had four reindeer on its roof and another four placed in front of the deck. Each plastic animal wore a collar of flashing white lights.

The next cabin over had a half-completed Nativity next to it: two life-size mannequins dressed as shepherds, wearing brown shawls and holding crooks in their hands, and another two dressed as wise men, with fine robes adorning their bodies and golden crowns on their heads. Ashley could only stare in bewilderment at these scenes.

"And here we are." Marc stepped onto the deck of a darkened, undecorated cabin and opened the door. He flicked a light on as Ashley followed him in. "What do you think?"

"Wow." She was genuinely surprised. The one summer she'd spent at Cedarwood she'd been in a cramped cabin with half a dozen girls for campers. But these cabins were nothing like that one. On her immediate right, in the corner of the room, was a double bed, covered in a thick red-and-yellow quilt and with three fluffy pillows resting at the head, right under a four-pane window. A wooly rug lay next to it, covering the concrete floor, obviously for bare feet in the morning and at night.

At the foot of the bed, pressed up against the side wall, was a dresser with several shelves. Along the back wall was a small sofa, able to fit two people comfortably, with a miniature fridge to its side. To her left were two open doors, one leading into a small bathroom with a shower, the other to a closet with a variety of hangers along the beam. "This is great. How long have these been here?"

"Seven years now. I had them built to attract people to camp year-round."

"You had them built?" Ashley tossed her suitcase onto the bed and put her purse in the dresser's top drawer. Big clumps of snow fell from her shoes and legs as she walked, but the cabin was warm and she was confident it would melt and evaporate in no time.

"I did." Marc unwrapped his scarf, revealing a chiseled face that had clearly changed, and only for the better, with age. His eyes were still their striking blue, but now they seemed even more bright and emphasized than when she'd last seen him. His round face at 18 years had given way to one that was narrower and more defined. She hadn't remembered him having such a strong jawline when they'd last been here, and the light scruff along it certainly didn't hurt things. That summer 15 years ago she had thought he was cute. Now, she could only admire how handsome he was. "After I was hired as Cedarwood's director eight years ago—"

"You're the camp director?" she exclaimed, cutting him off. "That's amazing! That was always your dream, right?"

He grinned and looked down at the floor. "It was. It is. I love doing this." He looked back up at her and shook his head. "Wow, we really have a lot of catching up to do, huh? But before that, what are you doing here? I take it it's not for some impromptu reunion?"

"Believe me, I wish this had been planned." She sat down on the bed. The mattress sank down under her. "I'm just trying to get home." She filled him in on her day so far—how a sunny afternoon had turned into a blizzard on the highway, leading to a detour through the farmlands, and then how her car had run out of gas and her phone died. "I honestly thought I was going to be stranded. When I found the camp I wasn't expecting anyone to be here. My plan was to break into the office and call a tow truck." She raised an eyebrow. "Sorry about that."

"All good. I probably would have done the same if I were in your shoes." He gestured to the soaking wet heels still on her feet. "Well, maybe not those shoes."

Ashley put her hands on her lap. "Now that I've told you what I'm doing here, it's your turn. What's going on and why are so many people at camp?"

He leaned against the closed door. "This is our Christmas family camp. It started today," he said. "When I became director here I really wanted us to expand our year-round programs. We had the summer, obviously, and a few weeks in the spring and fall, but once the weather got too cold no one wanted to stay in the cabins. So I borrowed some money and had five year-round cabins built. They caught on and soon we were booked at least twice a month. Church groups, corporate retreats, family camps, things like that. I was able to convince the camp's Board of Directors to add another five, and now we're here."

Ashley took another look around the cabin. "I am impressed. But a Christmas camp? I'm surprised people want to spend Christmas here." She paused before adding, "No offense."

"None taken. This is actually one of our most-popular weeks of the year. We'd had every cabin booked, but there were some last-minute cancellations. When you first arrived I thought you were one of our guests. I guess he wasn't able to brave the storm as well as you."

"Well in case he does show up, I don't plan to be here too long. If you'll show me where a phone is, I can call for assistance and be out of your way."

Marc's smile seemed to waver. "Of course. If that's what you want."

She felt her face go hot. "I—it is—I mean—you know, I just—"

Sleigh bells rang from outside. Marc looked out the window. "That's the signal for dinner. Why don't you come join us, and then you can call a tow truck afterward? Give the storm a bit of time to pass through anyway."

"Oh, thank you, but I couldn't. I'm not one of your guests. I shouldn't even be here."

He cocked his head to the side. "I'm not so sure about that. Besides, once a Cedarwood guest, always a Cedarwood guest."

It was hard to turn down such an invitation, especially since the last thing she'd had to eat was a fiber bar just after she'd finished her presentation to the client. "That's a pretty good argument." She pushed herself up off the bed and readjusted her jacket.

Marc once again offered his arm. She linked it with hers and he opened the door. A blast of cold air hit her, along with several large snowflakes. "We'll hurry," Marc said.

She had no issues with that. They stepped outside and walked across the deck and onto the pathway, which looked like it had accumulated a good two inches of snow in the ten minutes they'd spent inside. Ashley was able to walk with a bit more ease, though her heels still lacked any of the traction of a boot. Or even a sneaker.

Marc led her to the right, away from where they'd walked in from the parking lot. As they moved, Ashley took a look around. The ten year-round cabins were placed in a large oval, all on the outside of the pathway. At one tip of the oval was the camp's office — the one building that had been there when she was a counselor — with the parking lot beyond it, while at the other tip was a larger building that was several stories high, which they were now heading towards. In the center of the area stood a massive cedar tree, though Ashley was surprised to find it undecorated. "Kind of sparse for a Christmas tree, huh?"

"Maybe for now," Marc said wryly.

They passed another cabin, this one glowing particularly brightly in the dark night. Ashley slowed down to look at its decorations. Strings of Christmas lights in purple and gold circled around the eaves multiple times and crisscrossed over the awning and down the two wooden pillars that held it up over the deck. A large plastic Santa, wearing a dark sweater with a logo she couldn't make out, sat in the middle of the awning, held in place by the lights. "What is this?" she asked, in equal parts awe and confusion.

"They're school colors," Marc said. "Someone's a proud alumni."

"No, I mean, what's with the decorations in general? Did you do them?"

"Nope. They were done by the guests. They bring all the materials up and really go to town, as you can tell."

"They did this?" She looked around again, from the cabins close by to the ones on the other side of the circle, about fifty feet away. Of the ten, six were decked out, one was lit up from within but had no decorations on the outside, and three—including her temporary accommodation—were dark. "But I thought you said the camp just started today."

"Yep."

Her mouth fell open for the third time that day. "They did this all today?" she nearly screamed. Her voice echoed off the surrounding trees. "My goodness, it's like Whoville out here! Are they all professionals or something?"

"Nope!" a voice said from behind them. An older man and woman walked up, looking appropriately dressed for the weather. He had a bulky grey jacket around his wide frame, with thick blue gloves on his hands, black winter boots on his feet and green earmuffs around his partially bald head. She wore a long pink coat that went all the way down to her ankles, with a hood pulled over her head. Ashley could see a plump face with rosy-red cheeks underneath. The man waved in salutation. "We just love Christmas!"

"They sure do," Marc said. "Ash, this is Bill and Carol Fischer. Bill and Carol, this is Ash. She used to be a counselor here."

"You don't say," Carol said, in a Southern drawl. She gave Ashley a wink. "Is this your first time at Christmas camp? I can't say I've seen you here before."

"Oh, I'm not staying," Ashley said quickly. "I'll be leaving as soon as the storm clears up."

"I was going to say," Carol said, giving her a look up and down, "you don't exactly look dressed for the season. No worries, I can loan you a few things. You're about as tall as I am round, so it should fit!" She laughed heartily.

"Why don't we get inside so you can get acquainted over dinner?" Marc said. Still linking arms with Ashley, he continued walking to the large building. Ashley was grateful for it. It didn't take long to feel the cold out here. "I guess I should point out that we're heading to the Wilcox Lodge. It's where we do all our year-round indoor activities. I think you'll like it."

"Wilcox," Ashley said as they reached the Lodge's stairs. "Why does that name sound familiar?"

"Henry Wilcox. He was the founder of Camp Cedarwood, seventy-five years ago now. We thought it'd be appropriate to name the building after him."

They took the stairs slowly. Her shoes slid on the wood under the foot of snow, but Marc's arm kept her from falling over. "Right. I guess when you found a camp you don't have to worry about paying for the naming rights."

He scoffed. "Yeah, well…" His voice trailed off. "Anyway, here we are!" He grabbed the door and opened it, revealing a small meal hall.

As soon as Ashley saw, and smelled, it, her stomach rumbled.

Chapter 3

The four stepped inside and Ashley was again grateful for the warmth in the room. She looked over the hall, feeling like she'd been transported to some sort of quaint, traditional Christmas setting that only existed in movies.

There were four tables, with six chairs each, closer to the front doors, while along the far wall was a small stage with a microphone and two speakers. In the back-left corner was a large window from which came sounds of steam and the clinking of metal utensils, while several other closed doors along the left wall led to rooms unknown. In the middle of the right-side wall was a large stone hearth, with a roaring fire crackling inside.

Much like the cabins, the hall was decorated for Christmas, except in a much more traditional (and in Ashley's mind, less gaudy) fashion. Long streams of gold and silver tinsel hung from the walls about ten feet up, with paper bells covering the nail or tack that held up their highest points. Flashing white Christmas lights bordered the kitchen window and green garland, with a big red bow on top, was placed on either side of it. There were two wreaths, made from pine branches, on either side of the hall — one at the back, behind the microphone and stage, and one hanging above the door Ashley had just walked through.

Surprisingly, there were no Christmas trees, though as Ashley walked into the middle of the room she saw two tree holders on either side of the stage. It was odd, but she thought nothing of it as she sat down along with Marc, Bill and Carol. The tables were the same wooden ones she remembered eating at when she was a counselor, though the decorations on top made them look much nicer. A fine red linen tablecloth covered it, and two snowmen candleholders, each with electric tea lights flickering in them, sat at either end. In the middle was a small poinsettia plant. The whole setup felt like something out of a fancy restaurant, not a camp in the middle of nowhere.

Ashley's chair faced the front door, and she watched as other guests streamed in. First was a middle-aged couple with two daughters, who waved at Marc as they took seats at another table. Then a younger man—maybe around 25 or so—walked in, holding the door open for a young woman of about the same age. They greeted the family happily and sat down with them.

The door had barely closed when it opened again, revealing a man and woman, maybe a few years older than Ashley, dressed in designer winter wear: him, a three-button wool jacket that seemed to just cover his broad shoulders, and her, a slim white coat that left none of her dark skin exposed from her neck to her knees. Ashley's eyes went wide. She recognized the coat from window displays in the city.

The woman caught Ashley staring and walked over. "Please tell me I don't have something on my face."

"O-oh, no," Ashley stammered. "It's just your coat. I love it."

The woman laughed and looked over at the man. "See, this is the sort of things you should say more!"

Marc spoke up. "Janice, this is Ash. Ash, this is Janice Hope and her husband Roger."

Ashley reached out and shook both of their hands. "A pleasure," Janice said. "Mind if we join you?"

"Not at all." The two sat down opposite each other, with Janice next to Ashley. She took off her jacket and hung it from the back of her chair.

Marc looked around the room. "Let's see, that's six cabins accounted for. Two more to go. Then we can eat!"

"Let's hope they get here soon," Janice said. "Ash, what brings you to Christmas camp?"

"Oh, I'm not really a guest. I'm here accidentally." She once again explained how she'd been diverted off the highway and found the camp just as her car was running out of gas. "Honestly, I feel bad for even eating with you. You've paid to be here. I haven't!"

"Don't worry about that," Roger said. "There's always more than enough food. Christmas is all about excess, especially here."

"I'm starting to see that." Ashley looked outside through the large windows facing the cabins. "Speaking of excess, which cabin is yours?"

Roger grinned and held up a finger. "Oh oh, not so fast. You have to guess."

Janice sighed. "Really Roger?"

Ashley leaned in and looked from Roger to Janice. "It's okay. You want me to guess? Game on." She already felt relaxed around them and was happy to have a bit of fun. "Let's see. Roger, you seem really excited about the whole decorating thing, while Janice, I saw you roll your eyes when I asked about your cabin. But you both seem pumped up about Christmas camp, so it's not the decorating itself you don't like. It's what the decorations are." Her eyes darted between them again. They both seemed amused. "I doubt it'd be the cabins with the traditional Christmas lights or reindeer, and you two seem to mesh well enough that I doubt you would clash over religious expression, so it's not the Nativity scene. That leaves the really, really weird cabin with the purple and gold Christmas lights." She raised her eyebrows. "Did I get it?"

Roger sat back, shaking his head. "That obvious, huh?"

"I told you!" Janice said. "Those are his alma matter colors. Doesn't matter that he graduated fifteen years ago, he still reps them any chance he gets. He even tried to paint our bedroom with them."

"Like a good alumnus should." He reached out and took his wife's hands. "Maybe one day, when we have a nursery, the purple and gold will look great on a crib." Janice rolled her eyes again.

The doors opened and a man and two kids—a boy and a girl—walked in. The man brushed snow from his shaggy brown hair and looked at both of the full tables. "See, this is what happens you take too long to get ready," he said to the boy, who looked to be around ten. "Now we have to sit by ourselves."

"Don't say that, Harvey," Marc said. "We can move people around. You never sit alone at Camp Cedarwood."

Harvey touched his nose. "You're not making it easy for me to teach my kid a lesson, Marc."

Marc held his hands up in surrender. "My bad. Go sit by yourselves."

The three sat down at one of the empty tables. Marc looked over at the kitchen. "We still have one cabin left, but I know we're all hungry and we don't want the food to go cold, so I say we eat!" This elicited cheers from the other diners. "But first, it's not a meal at Camp Cedarwood without a song, so…" He took a deep breath. "*I'm a knife, fork, spoon, spatula, a cha-cha-cha.*"

Ashley buried her head in her hands. That song. Why was Marc singing a kid's song—to the tune of "If You're Happy and You Know It"—with a group of adults? She lifted her head up and saw that they were all singing along. "*I'm a knife, fork, spoon, I'm a knife, fork, spoon, I'm a knife, fork, spoon, spatula, a cha-cha-cha!*"

"Alright, let's eat!" Marc walked over to the kitchen window, as did an adult from each of the other tables.

Janice nudged Ashley with her elbow. "Not much of a singer, huh?"

"Not of kids songs," Ashley said.

"Maybe that will change."

Marc returned with a large metal tray. He placed it in the middle of the table, next to the poinsettia. It was divided into three sections, each filled to the brim with a different food: fried chicken, thick potato wedges and steamed vegetables.

"Wow," Ashley said. The food when she was a counselor had been decent at best, but this was a whole other deal.

"What would y'all like?" Carol asked, grabbing a pair of tongs that sat on top of the food.

"Who, me?" Ashley asked. "Please, you all go first."

"That's not how it works here," the older woman said with a smile. "Now can I fill your plate or would you like just a little?"

Ashley shrugged and handed Carol her plate. "As long as everyone else gets enough, I'm fine." But boy, did that chicken look appetizing.

Carol put two chicken thighs on the plate, then surrounded them with a heaping serving of wedges and a pile of vegetables. She handed it back to Ashley and then moved on to Janice's plate. Ashley pulled her knife and fork from the napkin—which bore a pattern of boughs of holly—and dug in. "Oh my goodness," she said after one bite. "This is delicious!"

"I knew you'd like it," Marc said.

Carol put two drumsticks and two thighs on his plate. "You're still a growin' boy, right?" she asked playfully.

Ashley quickly picked the first thigh down to its bones, and followed it with a few of the wedges—crispy, but not burnt; salty, but not overdone—and the vegetables, which tasted like they had been picked that day. Normally she never ate anything quickly, especially in the presence of others, but when she saw the other women at the table eating like no one was watching she went along with it. The food was just too good, and she was too hungry, to try to savor every bite.

She was just finishing off the last carrot when the front doors opened and three people walked in: a man and a woman, looking rather haggard, and a boy of about ten between them, holding on to each of their hands. The kids at the other two tables jumped up and ran over to the boy.

Carol's face contorted in apparent confusion and she gave Marc a look. "Is he... should he be here?"

The camp director nodded. "He really wanted to come. I wasn't going to say no. I think... never mind. Let's talk about this later."

Ashley shifted her attention back to the newcomers. They had sat down at the same table as the shaggy-haired man and his two kids. As they removed their jackets and hats, she saw that what she thought had been a scarf the boy was wearing was actually a red medical mask. It was odd, but she didn't give it any more thought, and instead grabbed the tongs and gave herself another helping of everything in the deep tray, before offering Carol some more.

Twenty minutes later, with the tray empty and the table having gone through a few rounds of small talk about the weather and the challenges of the drive up, Marc grabbed each person's plate and cutlery and loaded them into the metal tray, then carried it all back to the kitchen window. Shortly afterward, the other two tables did the same. Ashley looked back at the boy who had been wearing the mask. A slightly picked-at meal sat in front of him.

When the tables were cleared, Marc went up to the stage and tapped on the microphone several times. "Good evening everyone and welcome to Christmas at Camp Cedarwood!"

Everyone cheered and Ashley found herself clapping. "It is so good to see all of you here," Marc continued. "We have five amazing days planned and I'm sure this is going to be our best Christmas camp ever! I hope you all brought plenty of warm winter clothes, because you and the snow are going to be best friends by the time this is over."

Ashley looked over at Carol. She was just about ready to take her up on her offer. "Now, normally at the end of dinner we would have dessert, and I do promise we have a delicious treat for all of you, but you're going to have to wait a little while for it, because it is going to be part of the…" He took a deep breath, his broad chest jutting out from under his plaid shirt. Then, in a loud, dramatic voice, he shouted, "Christmas Cup!"

There was another round of cheers and applause. "Christmas Cup?" Ashley repeated to herself.

"Be back here in half an hour!" Marc continued. "And get ready to have fun!"

The others began to get up and put their coats on. Marc hopped down from the small stage and walked over to Ashley. "So," he said, once again flashing her a bright smile, "I guess you have a phone call to make, huh?"

Chapter 4

There were a million things for Marc Rollier to think about. The start of Christmas Camp at Cedarwood and the dozen-odd guests he needed to keep entertained. The thick, heavy snow that kept falling from the sky and how they would impact the activities he'd planned. The thousands of worries that came with running a camp and how he would address them. The meal he'd just eaten and whether it had the right blend of carbs and protein to keep him in shape.

But none of those things were able to hold his attention. Only one thing could: the beautiful woman from his past, who had pulled up to camp a few hours earlier and who he was now guiding across the snowy, slippery path towards the camp's office.

Ash Tidings. He'd been barely 18 when they'd met and spent a summer — the best summer of his life — together. And at the end of it, just when he'd finally worked up the nerve to kiss her, she'd left, disappearing from his life like a vapor in the wind. He had never, ever expected to see her again.

Until two hours ago.

There was nothing else that could distract him from her. The sun could suddenly rise and melt all the snow, the Lodge could catch fire, Santa could show up in person and give him a red Ferrari, and he'd still just want to stare at her. Her unblemished skin that seemed to glow in the cabins' Christmas lights. Her light green eyes that reminded him of Cedarwood's forests in the height of the summer. Her flowing dark hair as it was blown back by the wind.

Fifteen years had passed since they'd last seen each other. So why did she still feel so familiar to him?

"This way," he said, opening the side door into the office. He flicked the lights on. During the summer months the four cubicles in the room would have staff managing camper registrations, ordering food and supplies, and answering questions from concerned parents. Now it was cold and empty, used only when he had to look up particular files on the computers or needed to get out of his cabin to do work.

He pointed to the closest phone. "It's all yours."

"Thanks." She picked up the receiver and dialed a long number from what appeared to be memory. She waited a few seconds and pushed a few more numbers.

He felt surprisingly calm as he watched her. One of two things were going to happen: either she was going to find out that the roads were far too snowed-in to get out of Cedarwood any time soon, or she would leave and he'd have this strange and wonderful memory of her to get him through the rest of the winter.

She pushed her hair back and sighed, looking over at Marc and then rolling her eyes. He tried to conceal a smile. Ash would at least be staying the night. "Bad news?" he asked, trying to sound concerned.

Ash looked down and pressed the phone's Speaker button. "Thank you for calling City Insurance's VIP Support line," the robotic voice on the other end said. "Your call is important to us. Please note that there is an approximate four hour wait to speak with an agent."

"I guess I'm going to be waiting for a while," Ash said. She grabbed a chair and sat down.

"You could do that. Or you could enjoy the evening here and call them tomorrow." Did he sound too eager? He didn't want to sound too eager. "It's just, you know, even once you get on the phone with them, who knows how long it will take for them to actually send help?"

She leaned back in her chair and looked at him with those brilliant green eyes. "You have a point," she said. His heart leapt. "Also, I'm a bit curious about this Christmas Cup. It sounds corny and silly. Let me guess: you came up with it?"

"You know it, Ash." He regained his composure and took a deep breath. Her perfume filled his nostrils.

She chuckled. "You know, I don't think anyone's called me Ash in ten years. I kind of ditched the shortened name when I started working full-time."

"Uh huh? Do you want me to call you Ashley, then?"

She thought for a second. "Nah, it sounds weird coming from you."

"Well then, Ash, if you want to find out more about the Christmas Cup, be back in the Lodge in twenty minutes."

She stood up and held her elbow out again. "I'm not going anywhere unless you escort me." He tried his best not to show his excitement.

He led her back to her cabin, cherishing every step they took with their arms locked together. "I'll see you in twenty," she said before she closed the door.

Marc took a second to collect his thoughts. Then he cut across the small field in the middle of the cabins, his legs sinking into a good two feet of snow, and made his way to the cabin that was lit on the inside but had no decorations on the outside. He could hear several voices as he knocked on the door. "Come in!"

Marc opened the door and stepped inside. This one was the same size as all the others, but its layout was different: there was still a double bed in the corner and a dresser along the wall, but where Ash's cabin had a small sofa there was instead a bunk bed. On the top of that bunk was a boy with sandy blonde hair and big hazel eyes. "Well hello there!" Marc said. "Are you new to Christmas Camp?"

Though he wore a red medical mask over his mouth, Marc could see his cheeks forming dimples. "No!" he said. "It's me! Adam!"

Marc looked over at the boy's parents, who sat on top of the thick wool quilt on their bed. "Is this Adam? I don't think it is. Last time I saw him he was a good two inches shorter and had green hair."

Adam grabbed a pillow and threw it at Marc. "I did not!" he shouted. "I was here in the summer and my hair was the same color as now!"

Marc caught the pillow and lobbed it back. "I'm still skeptical," he said. He walked up to Adam's bunk. "There is one way to prove that this is Adam, though. The Adam I know is very, very…" He reached across Adam's chest. "…ticklish!" He grabbed the boy's sides and started tickling.

"Stop!" Adam howled as he laughed. "It's me! I promise!"

Marc let go and rubbed his hair. "I guess that proves it. It's good to see you again." He looked back at Adam's parents. "And I suppose it's good to see your parents again too."

"That's because I'm better than them!" Adam got up on his knees and wrapped his arms around Marc's shoulders. Marc returned the hug, noticing how skinny and frail his body felt. "I told them that this is the year we're going to win the Christmas Cup and that they better be ready to go all the way!"

"That's what I like to hear." Marc lifted Adam up and out of his bunk and placed him on the floor. "Why don't you go and wash up so you're ready to go?"

The boy scampered into the bathroom and closed the door. Marc walked over to his parents. "It's so good to see you guys here." He lowered his voice. "How's he doing?"

Paige, Adam's mom, shifted on the bed. "There are good days and bad." It sounded canned, like something she'd said a thousand times before. "We're just taking it as it comes."

"He's so happy to be here, though," David, Adam's father, added. "He has been talking about it ever since the first snowflake fell in November. After what happened over the summer, I think he wanted to come back here even more."

Marc nodded. "I'm glad. And I guess this is the year you win the Cup?"

David chuckled. "That's the other thing he won't stop talking about. He made us memorize every Christmas carol known to man, so that better be one of the challenges again."

"You'll see," Marc said. The bathroom door opened and Adam walked out. "And I will see you all in a few minutes. Get ready for some fun!"

He left the cabin and stopped for a moment at the edge of the small porch. This was the seventh Christmas Camp he had run, and yet already it felt different. It was like someone had attached a hundred-pound weight to his heart. Could it have something to do with the boy in the cabin right behind him? Or the woman in the one fifty feet in front of him?

Whatever it was, he knew that it would be a week unlike any other. Taking a deep breath, he stepped back out into the snow and headed towards the Lodge. The Christmas Cup was about to begin. He had to be at his best.

Chapter 5

Ashley was surprised to find a complete winter outfit waiting for her on her bed as she entered the cabin. Thick grey boots that went halfway up her calves sat on the rug, while on top of the mattress was a poofy white-and-orange jacket, a knit cap with a pom-pom on top, a three-foot long scarf and grey woolen gloves. A note on a piece of scrap paper next to everything read "Hope this helps! – Carol".

She slipped out of her heels and light jacket and tried each thing on. The gloves, scarf and hat fit perfectly and warmed her up in seconds. The coat, on the other hand, was more suited for Carol's stature than her own. It hung off her shoulders like a poncho, but it ended a few inches above her waist and the sleeves barely went past her elbows.

The boots were also not exactly a perfect fit, with her feet having plenty of room to move around inside them. Still, it was far better than what she'd shown up in, and at least now she wouldn't need to slip and slide with every step she took in the snow... even if she did enjoy having a handsome man to keep her from falling over.

She smiled as she sat on the edge of the bed and thought of Marc. Before she left in the morning, she'd have to take some time to talk with him and catch up. To find out what he had been up to in the last fifteen years. Had he worked outside of Camp Cedarwood for a time, or had the camp always been a part of his career? Had he done any travelling or met some interesting people? Had he dated or been married? She hadn't seen a ring on his finger, but maybe he had a girlfriend who lived beyond the camp's walls. It wouldn't surprise her. He was a good-looking man. That was one thing that hadn't changed.

She shook her head slightly and snorted. Not that it mattered. She would be gone in just a few hours. There was no point in ruminating over his chiseled jaw, or those ocean eyes, or what his chest looked like under his shirt...

"Stop it," she chided herself. She did this to herself way too often. Meet a cute guy, obsess over him for a few days, and then after a date or two realize he wasn't what she was looking for and end things. It was the same old story.

The bells jingled outside. She jumped off the bed, glad she didn't have to go any deeper in self-reflection, and left the cabin. The cold air greeted her, but this time she didn't mind it. Her hands and face were protected from it, as was most of her upper body, and the boots had all the traction that her shoes didn't. She was able to walk into the Lodge without a single slip.

The meal hall had been rearranged so that the tables were all pushed to the side and two rows of chairs had been place in front of the small stage. Ashley spotted Janice sitting in the second row. "Mind if I join you?"

"Not at all." Janice looked up at her and laughed. "I take it you borrowed some winter clothes?"

Ashley removed the outerwear and sat down. "They were loaned to me and I appreciate them. Though the fit leaves a bit to be desired."

The other guests began to enter and take seats around them. "Fortunately for you, I happened to bring a few extra coats," Janice said. "You're welcome to use them. Just stop by my cabin. You know which one it is." She said the last sentence with disdain.

"That is too kind, but I plan to be gone by tomorrow morning."

Janice frowned. "So soon?"

Ashley shrugged. "I have to get home."

Roger sat down next to Janice. "I finally got the last decoration up!" he said excitedly. His hands were clenched and pulled close to his chest. He looked like a kid who had just ridden a bike for the first time.

"Ooh, last decoration?" Ashley asked, half out of interest and half as a tease towards Janice, who seemed none-too-pleased with her husband's announcement.

"You'll have to see it for yourself," Roger said.

"You won't miss it," Janice muttered. "No matter how hard you try."

Just about all the seats had filled up. Ashley spotted Carol a few chairs away and mouthed "thank you" towards her. The older woman grinned and waved. Next to her was Bill, and next to him were the young man and woman who Ashley had seen earlier. The kids were all there too, fidgeting in their seats, including the boy in the medical mask. He wore a red hooded sweatshirt with the words "Super Kid" on the front.

The one person Ashley couldn't see was Marc. As she turned to look behind her, the lights suddenly cut out, throwing the hall into complete darkness. There were a few shouts in surprise. Ashley wagged her tongue against her lip. What was Marc planning?

The lights above the stage turned on, illuminating it in red and green. "Ladies and gentlemen," Marc's voice boomed from the speakers. "Are you ready to start the Christmas Cup?"

The others cheered. Ashley looked around, bemused. "I can't hear you!" Marc shouted. "Are you ready to start the Christmas Cup?"

The cheers got even louder. "Run Rudolph Run" played over the speakers as Marc ran onstage, clapping his hands. He wore an oversized Christmas sweater with Santa's face knitted into it, and there was red foam bulb on his nose. Ashley couldn't help but cringe in embarrassment for him.

After a few seconds the music cut out and the house lights came back on. "Alright!" Marc said. "Welcome everyone to the Camp Cedarwood Christmas Cup! For those of you who are new —" He gave a quick look right at Ashley —"the Christmas Cup is just about the best tradition we have at Cedarwood. Two teams will compete in ten events to be crowned the Christmas Champs and receive all the glory and prizes that come with it!" More cheers. "But first, we need teams! As always, teams will be chosen via captains, and kids can be on any team that one of their parents is on. Beyond that, anything goes!"

He reached down and picked up a felt top hat. "This year's captains are…" He reached in and scrummaged his hand around. Ashley was impressed with his showmanship. It was like being at a cheesy gameshow.

Marc pulled out a slip of paper. "Carol and Bill Fischer! Come on up, guys!"

There was more applause as the couple walked up next to Marc. "This is going to be done like a schoolyard pick. And Carol, since we are all gentlemen here, you will pick first."

"Oh, that's easy," Carol said without hesitation. She pointed both her hands forward. "I want my girl Janice!"

"Yes!" Janice shouted. He leapt up from her chair and embraced Carol before facing the crowd. "You are all going down!"

"Well, half of them will be your teammates, but we appreciate the enthusiasm!" Marc said. "Okay Bill, who do you want?"

"If she's taking Janice, I want Roger!" He pointed both fingers at the husband, who rose joined Bill on stage with a fist bump.

The choice went back to Carol, who called up Harvey and his son and daughter. Bill chose Jack, the man who had come with his wife and two daughters. He picked up his younger daughter and brought her up with him.

Ashley sat back and enjoyed the show. Carol and Janice were whispering back and forth about the next pick. She figured they'd take the young man or woman, or maybe Jack's wife to even things out. Instead, Carol pointed right at her and said, "We want Ashley!"

"Wait, what?" Ashley sat up.

Marc grinned, showing every one of his pearly white teeth. "Ash Tidings, come on up and join your team!"

Ashley tried to protest and state that she wouldn't be staying much longer, but it was drowned out by cheering. She reluctantly pushed herself out of her chair and walked up to the stage. Janice wrapped her arms around her shoulders. "Welcome to the team!"

The remaining campers were chosen, with Bill taking Drew and Sally, the young man and woman, and David, the father of the boy in the mask. Carol took Emma, Jack's wife, and her older daughter, and Paige and her son Adam, the kid in the mask.

"Excellent!" Marc said once the teams were chosen. "Next we need team names. You have exactly one minute to come up with a name, so choose well! And… go!"

Carol reached her arms out and pulled her teammates into a huddle. "We need something good," she said, her voice low and hushed. "Last year we called ourselves 'Santa's Elephants' and it stopped being funny after an hour."

"How about 'The Snowmen'?" Paige asked.

"That's kinda sexist," Janice said. "We could at least say 'Snowpeople.'"

"Ooh, ooh!" Adam shouted, his voice slightly muffled by the mask. "Let's call ourselves the 'Ice Dinosaurs!'" He formed his hands into claws and roared. Next to him, Harvey's son nodded in agreement.

"That's not all that Christmasy, is it?" Emma said. She had her arms wrapped around her daughter. "What if we went with 'The Running Reindeer?'"

From between the two teams, Marc shouted, "Thirty seconds!"

"Y'all, we need to choose," Carol said. "Janice, you got anything?"

She shook her head. "There's a reason I hire a marketing team for my job."

"Twenty seconds!" Ashley looked over at Marc. He was completely focused on his watch, but his wide blue eyes and bright smile showed all of his glee. He was having a blast. Of course he was. He lived for these events. It was another thing about him that hadn't changed.

"I work in marketing," Ashley said, turning back into the huddle. All eyes were suddenly on her. "I can tell you right now what the best name is."

"Ten seconds!" Marc shouted.

"Uh huh?" Carol said. "And what would that be?"

"Easy," Ashley said. "The name we should use is…"

"Five seconds! Get ready to share your name!"

Ashley raised her hands in claws. "The Ice Dinosaurs!" She made a roaring noise to mimic Adam's.

The boy's face lit up, and he again formed his hands to match hers. The others joined in, with the adults looking amused, save for Emma, who looked to the side and pulled her daughter in closer to her legs.

"That's time!" Marc pointed to Bill's team. "What are your names, competitors?"

Bill clapped his hands together. "We are the Frost Bites!" He snarled his teeth out.

"Love it! And Carol, what is your team name?"

"We are the Ice Dinosaurs!"

"Okay then! Frost Bites and Ice Dinosaurs. Definitely a departure from the more traditional names, but intense names means intense competition! And speaking of competition…" Marc waved to the kitchen. Two of the chefs, who were older men dressed in big white aprons, came out, each pushing a cart with a dozen large slices of chocolate cake on them. "It's time for your first event!"

Chapter 6

"If you will all gather around your carts, please," Marc said. Ashley and her team did just that. She glanced back at him. Just what sort of mischief was hiding behind that smirk of his? "In each slice of devil's cake, there is a small, plastic candy cane. Don't worry, I washed them all before they were put into the batter. Each member of your team is to eat a slice of cake until they find the candy cane, and then put it in the middle of the cart. The first team to have all their members do this wins and gets a point for the Christmas Cup!"

Ashley positioned herself behind a slice. It looked delicious — triple layers of dark brown cake, separated by a creamy filling, with ripples of icing on top. Dessert at Camp Cedarwood was always great, even when the rest of the food wasn't. This cake didn't break that trend.

She reached for a fork, only to see that there weren't any on the cart. "Oh, and one more thing," Marc said, his grin as devilish as the cake. "You're not allowed to use your hands. And three… two… one… go!"

"Wait, what?" Ashley asked. Her teammates dove their faces into their slices and began eating. She stared at her piece, suddenly feeling not all that hungry. It was the kind of cake that was supposed to be eaten in small bites, with sips from a cup of coffee or espresso between, not one that you'd plow your face into with fury.

"Ash!" Janice looked up, her mouth and nose covered in frosting. "Hurry up! Let's go!"

Ashley looked at the other team. They had all buried their faces in their cakes. As much as she didn't want to look like them, she also didn't want to let her team down, even if this would be the only event she did. She sighed and lowered her face into the cake.

It was as delicious as it looked. The frosting was sweet but not too sugary and the chocolate was rich but not overbearing. The cake itself was moist and light, making it easy for her to bite into it, chew twice and swallow. She worked her way through the top layer quickly, being careful not to take too big a bite and crunch down on the candy cane.

She raised her head to get a breath and saw that Carol, Paige and Harvey had all fished their treasures out and dropped them in the center of the cart. Harvey's kids were trying to pull their canes out with their teeth. She had to speed things up.

She opened her mouth wider and bit in again. From the other cart came cheers. Were they already done? She took another bite, chewed, swallowed, and opened her mouth again. She could now barely taste the strong chocolate or rich icing. Another bite, and she felt her teeth brush against something hard. She worked her mouth around it, biting off chunks of cake, until the top of the candy cane was visible. Then she wrapped her lips around it, pulled it out, and flung it into the middle of the cart.

Ashley looked up and saw that all of her teammates were done and had been watching her finish. Marc stood just behind them, wearing that same mischievous smirk. "And now team Ice Dinosaurs is done, but the Frost Bites finished first, so they get the first point!"

The other team cheered, while Ashley's team politely applauded. "Sorry everyone," Ashley said. "Guess I needed to eat a bit faster."

She caught a few side-eyes from the others, but Carol spoke up. "It's all fine. We have plenty of competitions left. You'll just need to make it up to us!"

"I'll do my best," Ashley said, as though she planned to be around for any more of them. Maybe her leaving would be the best benefit she could give to her team.

Marc announced that the rest of the evening would be free time, and that breakfast tomorrow would be at 8am. He also cautioned all of the guests to be careful as they walked back to their cabins; the snow was still coming down and would likely keep coming all through the night. Ashley shuddered at the thought.

The kitchen doors swung open and now the cooks brought out a metal urn of hot chocolate. A line quickly formed in front of it.

Ashley grabbed a napkin and wiped her mouth, and then her nose. She was a bit concerned by how much cake came off.

"Hey." Marc came up to her. "You, uh, got something here." He waved his hand all over his face.

"Ha ha," she said. "I suppose you enjoyed watching me give myself a cake facial?"

"It was one of the better parts of the day." He pointed over to Ashley's new coat. "I see you've gotten some new clothes?"

"I've got something to last me until tomorrow. But then I'll be out of here. I don't care if I have to wait on the phone for half the day. You have your camp to run and I have a city to get back to."

"Of course you do." He brushed his hand back through his hair. It was the first time she'd noticed how big his arms were. His biceps seemed to be trying to burst right out of their sleeves. "Until then, enjoy your evening here. I'm glad to see you've made some friends."

"Well, they're nice, but I'm not sure I'd call them friends just yet."

"It's camp," he said, gesturing around the room. "Everyone is friends here. That's the best part of it. And sometimes they get to be even more..."

He was cut off as Harvey's kids grabbed his legs and started asking if he'd be telling bedtime stories again this year. He lifted them up, one in each arm (yes, they were definitely big arms), and told them he'd only be telling them a story if they were super-good, and that he'd heard from Santa that maybe they hadn't been as good as they thought. They protested, but quickly realized he was joking.

Ashley watched him with the kids and saw a part of Marc she hadn't seen before. The Marc she had known as a counselor had always been a bit uncomfortable and awkward with his campers, acting more like a babysitter than a friend. It was as though they had scared him a little bit.

But this Marc, he seemed so comfortable with them he may as well had been their father.

As he held them both up over his shoulders and spun them around while making airplane noises, she couldn't help but think of how different he was from all the men she'd gone on dates with in the last two years. Almost all of them were handsome, successful and often kind and funny, but they were all more focused on their job and careers, and they gave off an air that they had been stuck in the city's rat race for a bit too long. She couldn't remember the last time she'd dated a man who was genuinely fun, or who gave any indication that he wanted to have kids. Heck, she couldn't remember the last guy who gave any indication that he had once been a kid.

No, they weren't like Marc, who was clearly having a blast this evening. From the over-the-top competition announcement to the cake eating competition to the way he was playing with kids who weren't even his own… he was different.

That's enough, she thought to herself. She would be leaving tomorrow. There was no sense in dwelling on the past, or on a guy who she was about to depart from once again. Even if he was very handsome.

Her focus drifted to the rest of the room. A jazzy version of "Jingle Bells" played from the speakers as the other guests drank hot chocolate and chatted. Janice and Carol stood to the side, speaking quietly and pointing at the other Ice Dinosaurs. Strategizing for the rest of the competition, probably. Roger, Bill and Harvey were laughing about something one of them said, and then even harder when another one added to it. Paige and Emma served each of the kids a cup of cocoa. All the while, the streams of tinsel glowed under the lights.

It was nice. Cheesy, like she'd stepped into a Christmas card, but still nice. All these people had turned this into their holiday tradition and it clearly meant a lot to them. Marc had built up a lovely little thing, here in a camp in the middle of nowhere.

But it wasn't her thing. And she was tired. She gave a quick wave to the group, put on Carol's ill-fitting jacket, and headed back into the night air.

The snow had not let up at all. The path leading back to the cabins must have had a good foot of the white stuff on it, but her oversized boots held firm as she trudged back. As she passed Janice and Roger's cabin, she looked up and saw a giant star, made up of purple and gold Christmas lights around a wire frame, sitting at the top of the roof. Janice was right: it was hard to miss. And yet despite it, she kind of liked it.

Ashley reached her cabin and left her boots on the porch, right next to the door. She changed out of the clothes she'd been wearing all day and into her pajamas, which were the one set of non-business professional clothes she had with her. She turned out the light and climbed under the covers, feeling her body sink into the soft mattress and the warmth of the thick covers over her.

She was asleep in minutes.

*   *   *

Marc finished spinning the kids around and place them back on the floor. They scampered off to join the hot chocolate line. He wiped sweat from his forehead. Playing with kids could be tiring. Especially when he was wearing a heavy Christmas sweater.

He looked to the front of the hall to see Ash just walking out the door. There was a twinge of pain in his chest as he watched. He was tempted to run after her, but what good would it do? She had made it clear that she was leaving tomorrow. Anything he tried would just look foolish.

"She's nice." Bill was beside him, holding a plate with a slice of cake in his hand. "You say you two used to know each other?"

"We were both counselors here when we were teens." And I let her get away back then too, he thought.

"Musta been a long time ago," Bill chuckled. "She doesn't seem like the camp type. I'm surprised she didn't ask for a soy mocha latte Frappuccino or the like."

Marc snorted. "She's not that much of a city dweller. If she stayed longer I bet… never mind."

"Well, she's going to miss out on the fun. Let's just hope the snow stops at some point. I love the winters up here, but it's going to be hard to do anything if the snow is six feet high!"

"Yeah," Marc said, as he thought about the circumstances that had brought Ash back to Cedarwood. "Too much snow. Wouldn't that just be awful?"

December 22

Chapter 7

The sounds of a noisy motor and metal being scraped across concrete woke Ashley up. She sat up in confusion, wondering what she was doing in this soft bed with its array of sheets and covers, before remembering that she was at camp. "Right," she said to herself. She spent another minute enjoying the comfort of the bed before hopping out of it. She had an important phone call to make.

Her feet landed on the warm carpet and she enjoyed the gentle fibers against her bare skin before they hit the cold concrete that lay beyond it. She showered in the small stall and was pleasantly surprised that the water was warm and the pressure strong. Though she may not have been prepared for the wintery weather, she had very much been prepared for good hygiene, even in the middle of nowhere: her duffle contained all the toiletries she needed to keep her hair, face, and body clean and fresh. It also contained a plush, oversized towel, because hotel towels were always a gamble.

She was just walking out of the steamy bathroom when the jingle bells sounded outside. She grimaced. Her plan had been to go to the office, call the insurance company and then leave the call going and grab breakfast in case she was hit with another long wait time. That ship had sailed. She'd have to get breakfast first and then head to the office. Marc had asked her to be their guest, and the last thing she wanted was to show up just as everyone was finishing their food. Even if she was never going to see them again.

She got changed into the one pair of jeans she had brought with her and pulled Carol's jacket over her blouse. Then came the hat, scarf and gloves. She opened the door and was immediately met with a blast of cold air and a flurry of snowflakes.

The snow was now falling lightly, but the damage had been done. It rose a good foot above the deck, except for a plowed path that led from the deck to the main path in the middle of the cabins. There had to be at least three feet of snow on the ground. Her stomach dropped. This was going to make getting home much harder.

She slipped her feet into the boots. They were cold, but little snow had gotten in and they warmed up quickly as she walked down the path to the Lodge. She marveled at just how high the snowbanks were on either side of her. It was like the parting of the Red Sea.

Ashley walked into the Lodge and was met with the sweet aromas of eggs, butter and syrup. She knew immediately what was being served. At each of the three tables—after not being used for dinner, the fourth still sat along the wall—were plates stacked high with French toast. She licked her lips.

Marc, sitting at a full table with Bill, Carol, Harvey and his kids, looked up and smiled at her. She waved and took her place at another table, putting her in the middle of Paige and David on one side, Drew and Sally on the other, and Adam in the middle, his mask pulled down to his chin as he ate. "Good morning," Drew said. He was already using the tongs to put three thick slices of the crispy toast on Ashley's plate. "Sleep in a bit late?"

"That, and I enjoyed my shower a bit too much," she said. She unwrapped her knife and fork from another festive napkin—this one with white snowflakes on a light blue background—and dug in.

After several days of reheated frozen waffles and runny scrambled eggs in the hotel restaurant, any decent breakfast would have been heavenly. But this… this was way beyond that. Her teeth bit through the crunchy outer shell and was met with gooey textures of eggs and sugar that seemed to melt in her mouth. There was no better French toast than Camp Cedarwood French toast.

"Oh, so you were showering?" Paige asked. "What do you think about that, Adam? Maybe you want to try it some time?"

The boy scowled. "I showered last night and you know it!"

"Uh huh?" Ashley asked, finishing another forkful of French goodness. "And when you shower, do you measure it in seconds or milliseconds?"

Adam glared at her. "You don't know what you're talking about."

"I know that you're a boy. And I know that boys are smelly. So…"

Paige reached over and squeezed her son's shoulder. "Adam has actually been very good at staying clean. We told him that one of the conditions to coming to Christmas camp was that he washes his hands before and after every meal and activity, and he's been doing just that."

"That's great!" Ashley exclaimed. She looked briefly at his mask and wondered what it was for. Was he fighting an illness? Or maybe taking a medication that made him more susceptible to being sick? "If he's as good at washing his hands as he is at coming up with team names, he'll have the cleanest hands in the country!"

Adam beamed, his rosy-red cheeks jutting out above his dimples. "It is a great name, isn't it? The Ice Dinosaurs are going to eat up the other team!" He chomped the air with his mouth.

"I'm sure you will!" She cut off a bigger piece of the toast and had it down in two chews.

"I will?" Adam asked. "But you're on our team too! You need to help us win, especially after we lost last night because of you."

"Adam!" Paige scolded. "That's a very rude thing to say. It's just a game."

"No, no, it's okay. Last night was on me," Ashley said. "But unfortunately, I'll be leaving today. I have to get back to the city for work." It wasn't full truth, but it was true enough.

The boy's expression dropped. "Really? That stinks."

"Are you sure you have to go?" David asked. "You're missing out on a lot of fun here."

"Believe me, I know. But I just… I have to go…" She decided it was best to change the subject. "Hey Adam, what's your favorite course in school?"

For the next five minutes the boy went on about how much he enjoyed Math and solving number problems, but how he hated English because "all the books are so boring." A few times he mentioned being away from school for a time and then coming back, with all the casualness of if he were talking about playing basketball at recess. Ashley found it curious, but didn't pry. She was too busy digging into her fifth slice of French toast.

Ashley volunteered to clear the table, but David was already up and grabbed the cleaning tray and cloths. Once the dishes were cleared and the tables wiped down, Marc took to the microphone and went into the plan for the morning: free time until 10, and then the second competition would take place. He didn't say what it was, but he told everyone to "Be prepared to be outside for an hour or two. And to spend a lot of time in the snow."

He dismissed them—as much as a grown man could dismiss other grown adults—and Ashley quickly got up and left the Lodge. As much as she wanted to say hi to Janice and Carol, she had to get the call going. She could speak with them after.

She trekked down the snowy path to the office and went inside. The door was unlocked, because of course it was. She flicked the light on, lifted the receiver and dialed the insurance company's number. "Thank you for calling City Insurance," came the overly-cheery voice. "Please enter your customer num—" She punched in the 10-digit code, a number she'd committed to memory for events such as this.

There was a brief pause, and then the robotic voice: "Thank you for calling City Insurance's VIP Support line. Your call is important to us. Please note that there is an approximate five hour wait to speak with an agent."

Ashley huffed and sat down in the creaky office chair. Five hours now. This storm must have really wreaked some havoc.

But if she had to wait a few hours before she'd be able to speak with an agent, at least she didn't have to spend it here. She put the receiver next to the phone and stood up. Hopefully the camp had an unlimited minutes plan.

The office door opened and Marc walked in. "Thought you'd be here," he said as he dusted the few snowflakes off his shoulders.

"I just wanted to get my place in the queue. Hope that's okay."

"Of course. How long's the queue?"

"Five hours."

"Jeez. Do they only have one person working the phones?"

"Honestly, it's probably something close to that. But I can wait. At some point they're going to come and get me. Then I can finally get out of here."

Marc's gaze fell to the floor. "Yeah, for sure. You can do that." He exhaled loudly and looked back up. There was a look of determination on his face—his eyes were narrowed and his lips pursed. "Or you can stay."

She stood up. The chair creaked again. "Marc, I need to get home and—"

"I know, I know. You want to get back to the city. But look how it is outside." He pointed to the window. "The snow is still coming down. Your car isn't going to make it more than a few miles, especially along these back roads. Why not just stay here?"

"I couldn't… I can't… I don't…"

"You don't what? We have a cabin here for you and I'm sure we can get enough clothes that fit you to keep you warm for the next four days. You may have noticed, but everyone here is super friendly and they all really like you. Besides, what do you have to do in the city that's so important?"

Ashley thought back to her plans. Netflix. Popcorn. A hot bubble bath. How did they compare to spending time up here at Cedarwood? "But I… I just…" She sighed. Was this the first place she wanted to spend Christmas? Not even close. But the thought of trying to navigate the snowy roads and blizzard conditions again was enough to make it look at least somewhat appealing. She smiled. "I guess I do owe it to the Ice Dinosaurs to win the Christmas Cup."

A massive grin came across Marc's face for a second, before he seemed to push it down. "There you go. I think you're really going to enjoy yourself here."

"Not the first time I've heard that about Camp Cedarwood," she said. "But there's one condition."

"Name it."

"I'm paying the full price to be here. I want you to charge me whatever you charge all the other guests."

Marc shrugged. "I mean, you can write me a check if you want, but don't expect it to be cashed for a month or two."

"I'm not going to stay here for free, Marc. I'm sure the camp could use the money."

His eyes briefly glanced sideways. "How about you help out around here, like with meals and whatnot? Our head chef is just a local who enjoys cooking and he'd appreciate some assistance."

"Deal." Cooking wasn't her strongest suit, but she could make it work. "I'm still going to leave a check, though. And if you don't cash it, I will mail you a stack of bills."

"I know you will. Remember when we'd go into town for lunch on our days off? You never, ever let me pay for you. Not even fifty cents for a coffee."

She smirked at him. "That was less out of principle and more because of how funny it was to annoy you."

He cocked his head up. "You were always very good at that."

She moved past him, to the door, allowing her arm to brush up gently against his. "And now you get another four days of it. Aren't you lucky?" She opened the door and walked outside.

Ashley paused, looking out at the circle of cabins, most of them heavily decorated, all of them covered and surrounded with snow. This was going to be her home for the next few days. As strange and unexpected as it was, there was something about it, deep down in her heart, that just felt right. Her shows and popcorn could wait. Her bathtub would still be there when she got back to her condo. But Christmas at Camp Cedarwood? This was something different, something she would never have thought of doing. She may as well make the most of it.

A gust of wind blew under her coat. She pulled it tighter and started down the plowed path, heading not to her own cabin, but to the one covered in purple and gold lights.

If she was going to stay, she was going to need a better jacket.

Chapter 8

Ashley knocked on the small part of the door that wasn't covered in a pin-up of Santa holding a football. From inside she heard, "Coming Ash!" A few seconds later the door opened. Janice, wearing grey sweatpants and a beige sweatshirt, invited her in.

"How did you know it was me?" Ashley asked.

"Because everyone else would just come right in," Janice said. "You're new here, so of course you knocked." When Ashley raised her eyes, she grinned. "You're not the only one who can play detective."

She motioned to a worn-out easy chair in the corner of the room. Ashley took a seat and gave the cabin a quick look around. She was surprised to find the interior looked almost identical to hers. "And now you're wondering why none of Roger's school paraphernalia is in here, right?" Janice asked. "I managed to get a compromise out of him: he can put whatever he wants on the outside, but nothing on the inside."

"Sounds like a fair arrangement. Where is he now?"

"He and Harvey are still in the Lodge, talking football or something. Or he's offering to take Harvey's kids off his hands for a few hours."

"That's a nice thing to do."

"It's all for his own pleasure. The man loves children. I'm surprised he didn't go into pediatrics."

"Uh huh?" Ashley decided it was okay to pry a bit. "He mentioned painting a nursery earlier..."

Janice rolled her eyes. "He's not exactly subtle about it, is he? But yes, we're trying to become parents at this point." She tilted her head back to the bathroom behind her. "There may be a few pregnancy tests in my toiletries bag."

"Oooooh. Are you expecting, you know, to be expecting?"

"Maybe," Janice said, smiling wryly. "Don't tell him, please. But you know, I just kind of have a feeling."

"My lips are sealed. I won't even comment on how well Roger plays with Harvey's kids."

"Yeah, well, I think he's mainly just checking in on Harvey to make sure he's okay."

Ashley opened her mouth to ask why, but caught herself. She didn't want to come across as a gossiper. Janice noticed and said, "Harvey's wife died early last year. Skiing accident. It was really bad. They'd been coming to Christmas camp for quite a few years, since the kids were very small, and we were all crushed by it. Harvey and his kids missed last year's session, which, you know, you can't really blame them for, so seeing them here this time is really nice."

"Wow. That's heartbreaking."

"It is. But that's the beautiful thing about this place. We can all be here for each other. Whether it's Harvey and his kids or Adam and his parents…" She trailed off. "But that's what Christmas is all about, right? Which is why I guess you have to head home. Were you able to get a tow truck for your car?"

"Actually, Marc convinced me to stay for the session. Probably safer than trying to drive home in this weather."

"Good! I'm sure Marc was very persuasive." Janice clapped her hands together. "And now, I believe I have some things to give you!"

She walked over to the small closet and pulled out a long, sleek black jacket. "You've got, what, one or two inches on me? This should fit you fine."

Ashley walked over and let Janice put it on her. It was soft and warm on the inside, while the outside appeared to be made of some sort of synthetic fur that felt incredibly smooth as she rolled her hands down it. She was able to raise the zipper all the way up without issue. It came down to just below her waist, making it a far better fit than Carol's coat.

"This is… amazing," she said, feeling the material again. It had to cost a few thousand dollars, at least. "I'm honored that you'd share such a, um, valuable jacket with a person you just met."

"Are you that surprised? I thought you and Marc used to work at this camp together. You know how camp works—you share everything with everybody."

Not four-thousand dollar designer jackets, Ashley thought. "You're clearly a woman of style. Do you work in fashion?"

Janice giggled. "Fashion? Please. No, I'm a lawyer. And before you get too excited, I'm not the fun kind of lawyer. I'm a tax lawyer. And you said you work in marketing?"

Ashley unzipped the jacket. She was already starting to heat up in it. "Yes. I'm a consultant. Companies hire me to come in and make people want to buy their products."

"Sounds like fun. Though I'm a bit surprised. After you used your powers of deduction on me and Roger last night, I figured you were a detective or something."

"Heh. Very funny." She patted the coat. "Thanks again. I promise to keep it in tip-top shape."

Now Janice raised her eyes. "Here? At camp? That is wildly optimistic of you."

Jingle bells sounded outside. "Guess we've got a competition to get to." Ashley zipped the coat back up. "But if you knew your coats were going to get damaged, why would you even bring them here?"

"Mainly because it annoys Roger," Janice said. "And if he's going to put up those embarrassing lights, it's the least I can do."

*   *   *

Five minutes later, Ashley and Janice had gathered with the rest of the campers in front of the Lodge. Marc stood on the small deck, his scarf pulled down over his chin so he could speak. "Welcome to the second event of the Christmas Cup! I hope you all had a big breakfast, because this one is going to require a lot of strength, endurance and creativity!"

Ashley looked around at the other guests. Aside from Janice and Carol, she could not easily make out who all the others were. Everyone wore thick jackets, with either hoods or hats or both pulled over their heads and scarves covering their mouths. A few even wore sunglasses or ski goggles, making their identities completely unknown. Was the guy in the red-and-blue puffy coat and brown scarf David or Harvey? Was the woman in the purple jacket Paige or Emma? Who was the kid weaving in and out of the others, wearing a one-piece snowsuit?

"When I say go, you'll trek up to the summer camp cabins, where you'll find a carton for each team—green for Ice Dinosaurs, red for Frost Bites—with a top hat, pipe, carrot, scarf, and two pieces of coal. Your goal is to build the biggest snowman that you can and put the items in its face. Your snowman must consist of just three snowballs, which can be as big as you wish, but remember that you'll have to stack them on top of each other. The team with the tallest intact snowman at the end of two hours will win!"

Ashley shifted in place. She couldn't remember the last time she'd built a snowman. Heck, she couldn't remember the last time she'd played in the snow, period.

"Any questions?" Marc asked. Hearing none, he shouted out, "Then we will begin in three... two... one... GO!"

The competitors all started moving around. "Ice Dinosaurs, gather around me!" Carol shouted. Ashley walked over and joined with the rest of her team. She was able to make out Harvey, wearing green biker glasses and a red hat, along with his two kids, as well as Paige and Adam. The boy ran up to her.

"I thought you were going home!"

"And make you all lose? Not a chance!" She gave his hat a rub. "You ready to build a snowman?" He nodded excitedly.

"Are y'all here?" Carol asked. She looked over at Ashley. "Looks like y'all are. And some of you have finally found some good snow clothes to wear." She pointed her hand forward. "Now let's go!"

The group walked past the Lodge and into the adjoining field, heading towards the summer cabins. Ashley tried to recall the camp's layout. When she had been a counselor, and the winter cabins hadn't been built, the area had housed a playground for the youngest campers. It sat at the southern-most point of the camp, with the lake just beyond it.

The actual summer cabins were to the northwest, beyond this large field that was used for just about any sport. The cabins were clustered in three age groups: Juniors, Intermediates and Seniors. Ashley's campers had been Intermediates, around 11-12 years ago. She coughed a laugh as she realized that meant they'd be around 26-27 now. How time flies.

To the east of the winter cabins and the camp's office was a large, deep woods. She remembered doing a few nature walks with her campers to listen for bird calls and look for any woodland animals. There had been days when they'd walked a good 45 minutes and not hit the end of the forest. Back then, it had seemed like the trees would just go on forever.

Despite the deep snow, the walking wasn't too bad. The flakes were heavy enough that they crunched beneath Ashley's feet, causing her to sink just a foot or so in. "This is good packing snow," Harvey declared. He rolled up a small snowball in his hands and tossed it out in the field. "We're going to make a big snowman today. I can feel it."

"We're going to make a big snowperson," Janice said. "No reason that our creation has to be a man." Ashley nodded in agreement.

The cabins came into view. Next to them was Tamarack, which was the Lodge where all the summer camp's meals, games and indoor activities were held. Even though everything was covered in snow, Ashley could tell not much had changed. There were no new cabins or modern amenities that had been added—just a bunch of old wooden buildings with no heating, insulation and, in at least some cases, electricity.

She smiled under her scarf as the memories came back to her. The last time she'd walked this field it had been in the late-August heat, when she'd made one last trip back to her cabin to get all of her things. Her cabin had been further back and wasn't visible from the field. At some point she'd have to visit it and reminisce.

"Let's hurry up!" Carol shouted. Ahead of them, the Frost Bites had reached their carton and were setting up a space to begin construction.

Ashley snapped out of her memories and focused on the task at hand. "Have you done this before?" she asked the team captain. "I mean, has snowman, or snowperson, building been a part of the Christmas Cup in the past?"

"No it hasn't, hun," Carol said. "Marc likes to mix the events up. But if that's your roundabout way of askin' if I have a plan for how we're going to build this thing, well, I can't say I do."

Just ahead, against the brown wood wall of one of the cabins, was a bright green milk carton. Carol picked it up. "Alright y'all," she said, in between heavy pants. "Let's get to work. How do you think we should build this thing?"

A bunch of ideas were shouted out at the same time. Someone suggested rolling three balls up and then putting them on top of one another. Another said they should start with a small snowperson and just keep adding more and more on. One of the kids asked if they could climb up on the cabin's roof to build from there.

Harvey raised his hands up. "Hold up everyone," he said, in a deep, baritone voice. "Why don't you trust the engineer to oversee this?"

"Sounds good to me," Janice said. "What do you think we should do, Harv?"

"We start with one big ball," Harvey said. "And I mean massive. We'll roll it up. Then we can get a few of the kids to climb up. We'll hand them snow and have them build the second and third balls by hand."

It was a good idea to Ashley, and the others seemed to agree. "Great," Harvey said. "Then if you don't mind, I'm going to put on my Project Manager hat and assign roles. Carol and Emma, can you and the kids work on making a very, very big pile of snow for the top two parts of the snowperson?"

The women agreed and ushered the kids away to start working. "Now the rest of you, roll up your sleeves," Harvey said. "We've got a great big butt to make for our snowdude."

Chapter 9

Half an hour later, Ashley stood at the other end of the field, gasping for breath. Despite the cold air and noticeable wind, she was drenched in sweat. She pulled her scarf from her mouth and yanked her thick hat off to let the warmth out of her body.

She'd expected Harvey to want a base for the snowperson that was maybe four or five feet tall. The colossal snow boulder she stood next to made it clear that it had not been his plan. He'd started by packing some snow together to form a ball of about a foot or so, and then he'd placed it on the ground and started pushing.

And pushing. And pushing. And pushing.

Soon the ball had grown to two feet. Then three. Then he'd no longer had to bend down as he rolled it along the snow. Then he'd called the others to join in. Ashley had come up next to him while Janice and Emma had gone to either side to guide it. After a few minutes, the ball was as tall as her. And they'd just kept pushing.

Now, with the ball at the far end of the field, it was a good eight feet in diameter. "I'd say this is looking pretty good," Harvey said. He leaned against one of the trees that separated the field from the camp's driveway. "Ready to head back?"

"No," Janice groaned. "But why do I get the feeling I don't have much of a choice?"

"It won't be too hard." He pushed himself off the tree and walked over to the snow boulder. "Same positions as before. Once we get momentum going it should be easy enough."

Ashley walked over and stood next to Harvey, while Emma and Janice stood on either side of the giant snowball. Harvey counted to three and they all began to push. It took about ten seconds of pressing up against the hard, cold snow with all her might before Ashley felt the ball begin to move. She dug her oversized boots into the snow and pushed from her core to keep it going. Her fitness class instructor would have been proud.

Soon the base was rolling again, following the same path in the snow. This made the task much easier.

"Having fun?" Harvey asked after about a minute of pushing.

"Just a great time," Ashley said. "After all this work we're putting in, we better win the event. And the Christmas Cup, for that matter."

"That's what I like to hear. This is our year to win it. I can feel it in my bones."

"You haven't won it before?" The snowball hit a bump in the path, causing it to abruptly stop. Janice told them all to push to the left. It took a bit of struggling, but they were able to get around the bump and continue their journey.

"I haven't," Harvey said, once the ball was rolling again. "This is our fourth year here. The first two years Marc ran it in four teams, and we just weren't good enough to take first place. Then two years ago he reduced it to two teams competing, and we lost by just a point. And then last year, uh, I wasn't here." He was quiet for a second, never ceasing to push the snowperson's lower third, now even bigger and heavier. "Did anyone tell you about me and my family? I just ask because, you know, you're new here."

"It was mentioned," Ashley said. "I'm so sorry about your wife."

"Thanks," Harvey said, sounding genuinely appreciative. "The kids were really excited about coming back here, which has made it easier. This camp means the world to them."

Ashley nodded. "All the more reason to win the Cup, huh?"

The path began to get steeper as the group approached the cabins. In front of them, Carol, Paige and the kids had assembled a large pile of snow, easily a good foot taller than Carol's head.

"Wow!" Adam exclaimed. He had ditched his hat and scarf and his red winter jacket was half-unzipped. "That thing is massive!"

With a final push, Ashley and Harvey brought the snowperson's lower third to rest in front of the snow pile. Ashley looked over at the Frost Bites' work, about a hundred feet away. They were in the process of rolling three balls. The biggest one was maybe a foot or two smaller than theirs.

"Okay, I need two kids to help me out!" Harvey said. Every hand shot up instantly. He pointed at Adam and his own son. "Adam and Ian, you two climb up on top. We're going to pass you snow and you're going to build the remaining sections of our snowman."

"Snowperson," said Janice.

"Snowbeing," Harvey said. Janice snickered. "Adults, let's give the boys a boost up."

Paige grabbed her son under the arms and lifted him up to the snowball. She was able to get him about halfway. Ashley crouched down and pushed up on Adam's feet. Though it was awkward, the two were able to get him on top of the ball. Harvey, meanwhile, picked up Ian and threw him up.

"Be careful!" Emma said. She pulled her own daughter back a few feet.

Once the boys had found their footing, Harvey grabbed a chunk of snow from the pile and handed it up to them. Ian grabbed it and placed it on top of the base. "I'll put the snow down and you can build it up," he said to Adam.

"That's a good idea!" Adam said. He looked down. "Hey mom, I can see our cabin from here!"

"I'm sure you can, honey," Paige said. She took a handful of snow and passed it up to Ian.

From the winter cabins came an amplified voice. "Attention Christmas competitors! You have one hour left to construct your snowperson!"

"Let's keep moving," Harvey said. He glanced over at the other team, still rolling up their snowperson's parts. "We don't have a moment to lose."

*   *   *

Mark's watch beeped, indicating that it was quarter to noon and there were fifteen minutes left in the snowman — snowperson — building competition. He sighed and gave one final look over the bills, invoices and bank statements that covered the table in his cabin. "You haven't solved this in the last two months," he muttered to himself. "I'm not sure what you thought another hour would do."

He grabbed his measuring stick, threw on his winterwear and boots, and walked out into the cold. The snow had all but stopped falling, with just a few flakes blowing through the air, and the sky was clear, bright and sunny. He took in a deep breath of the frosty air through his nose. No matter how many years he'd spent up at Cedarwood, he never, ever got tired of the fresh air in his lungs. It probably had something to do with how it changed with each season: in the winter the air was crisp and refreshing; in the spring, warm and fragrant; in the summer, hot and sweet; and in the fall, cool and smokey.

Marc walked from his cabin, located on the other side of the camp's office, and marched through the snow to the camp's field. At the other end of it he saw two massive snow structures, both looking close to completion. On the right, closer to the camp's summer Lodge, the team was attempting to lift up a snowball that was a good four feet in size on top of one that was about six feet wide. Next to them was a smaller ball, clearly this snowperson's head.

On the left was a snowperson with a base that had to be ten feet in diameter. On top of it were two more balls, both much smaller and more mishappen than the base. Two kids were walking around, adding snow to make them bigger.

"Wow," he said once he'd reached the teams. "This is impressive, to say the least. I don't think I've ever seen bigger snowfolk in my life!"

"Ours is bigger!" Adam shouted from on top of his team's snowperson. He pointed over to the other team. "They can't even get theirs all built up!"

"Yes we can!" the boy's father shouted. He was bent down next to his team's base, the second snowball resting on his shoulders. With a grunt, he stood up and slumped forward, onto the top of the snowperson's lower third. His teammates reached forward and rolled the ball off of him and onto the base. "See! Told ya!"

Marc looked at his watch. "You've got five minutes, so hurry up, and make sure your snowperson has a face!"

The Ice Dinosaurs continued to pass snow up to the boys, who in-turn added it to the snowperson's head. Marc's attention focused on Ashley. Her hat and scarf were on the ground and her smooth brown hair was flying back and forth as she moved around, shining whenever the sunlight hit it. She had a massive smile, those pearly white teeth flashing out from between her plump red lips. She was having a good time, and that was what Marc wanted to see.

As he watched, she passed a bit of snow up to Adam, and then reached down, formed a small snowball in her hands, and threw it at Janice. It hit her shoulder and she gave Ashley an incredulous look before laughing and reaching down to make her own ammo.

"Two minutes!" Marc yelled. He looked back at the Frost Bites. David had climbed up on the snowperson's base, similar to what his son was doing, and was reaching down to grab the head, which was being held up to him by Drew and Roger. With a heavy groan, David pulled the head up and planted it on the snowperson's torso.

Marc glanced between the two snowpeople. With the naked eye, it was challenging to tell which one was taller. He thought the Ice Dinosaurs had a bit of an edge, thanks to their massive base, but his measuring pole would have to say for sure.

"One minute!" he yelled.

Carol and Emma grabbed the snowperson's decorations from the crate and passed them up to the boys. Drew picked up his team's crate and handed it to David, who was still standing on his snowman, his feet on the lowest section and his legs and arms straddling each side of the snowperson's torso and head. David held the crate in one hand and reached in with the other. He pulled out a carrot and shoved it into the middle of the top snowball.

"Thirty seconds!" The Ice Dinosaurs were just about done. The snowperson had a full face and Ian wrapped the scarf around its neck while Adam reached up to put the top hat on. On the other side, David frantically tried to get the coal to stick in his snowperson's head. "And five, four, three, two, one… TIME!"

Adam and Ian jumped down from their completed snowperson as their teammates clapped and cheered. Drew, seeing that his snowperson's face had yet to be completed, attempted to hop up on the other side of it and help David finish the face.

That's when disaster struck. The snow David had been standing on suddenly gave way, causing him to slip and fall from the top of the four-foot ball. Drew, seeing David fall, leaned forward and tried to grab at him. He missed, but his force caused the top two snowballs to come loose and topple in the same direction David had fallen, bringing Drew with them.

"No!" Marc shouted as David landed in the snow on his back with a thud. A second later, the two large snowballs fell on top of him, exploding into a thick white pile that covered his entire body, while Drew managed to kick off of the snowperson's base and land on his left leg, just next to the man.

His cries of pain echoed through the field.

Chapter 10

Marc dashed over to David and began clawing the snow away. He was joined by Roger, Bill and Jack, the four of them digging through the snow like mad dogs. In seconds, David's jacket had been uncovered, and then his scarf and the rest of his face. He took several deep breaths, but didn't move.

"David, you okay?" Roger asked.

"Y-yeah." His voice was shaky. "Just feeling a little dazed."

"Can you sit up?" Roger offered his hand. David grabbed it and slowly sat up. "How's everything feel? Can you move your legs for me?"

Marc stepped back at let Roger have his space. He breathed a small sigh of relief. A doctor was definitely the right sort of person to have around.

David shook both legs and wiggled his arms and midsection. "I feel fine. Just like that I'm going to throw up."

Roger nodded knowingly. "Sounds like a concussion. We should get you to the ER just to be safe."

"I can drive him," Paige said. She and the rest of the Ice Dinosaurs stood a few feet back. She had her arms around Adam.

"Okay, great." Roger spun around and faced Drew. The young man lay on his back, both hands grasping his left leg. "Your turn, Drew. Where does it hurt?"

Drew seethed in air. "My ankle," he said. "I landed on it and I think I felt it snap."

Roger looked at Marc. "Do you have a stretcher or something we can carry him on?"

"There's one in the first aid station. I'll go get it."

"I'll come with you," Ashley said.

Marc nodded and started toward the station. He knew there was a stretcher there—it always seemed to be used once or twice during the summer — but it'd been a while since he'd seen it. He hoped it wouldn't take long to find.

"Hey," Ashley came up next to him. "You okay?"

"Oh, yeah," he replied. "Can't say I was expecting this to happen, but it could have been a lot worse." He'd seen a lot worse. At least this one had no blood.

"If it helps, everyone was having a great time up until then. I don't think I've ever seen such big snowpeople."

"That's good." At least Ash was enjoying herself.

They reached the Lodge — locked and shuttered up for the winter — and Marc gazed up at the snow hanging over the high roof. "Bring back any memories?"

"A few," she said. "It's a bit hard to remember things when it's all covered in snow."

"It's kind of nice though, isn't it? Do you remember how hot it could get here during the summer? We'd just cancel all the activities and spend the day in the lake."

She gently elbowed him in the ribs. "I also remember spending a few nights in the lake too."

"Right! We snuck off a few times to go swimming so that we'd be able to sleep." He shook his head. "You know, if I ever caught any counselors doing that now, they'd be fired immediately."

"Then I guess it's a good thing you never caught us."

The first aid station was adjacent to the Lodge, sharing part of the larger building's wall. Marc reached down his shirt and pulled out a lanyard with several keys on it. He walked up the slight ramp and unlocked the station's door. It creaked loudly as he pulled it open.

The station was divided into three rooms: a small waiting room that normally had a few chairs, but was currently empty; a main treatment room with just about all the amenities of a doctor's office; and a sleeping quarters for the doctors or nurses who volunteered at the camp. Walking through it now, when all medical equipment, supplies and drugs had been removed, felt a bit eerie. It was just a room with a bunch of bare cabinets.

"I think it's back here," Marc said. He opened the door leading into the sleeping quarters. Sure enough, propped against the wall next to the bed, was the stretcher. Though it was used 99% of the time for campers, it was adult-sized and would more than support Drew's slender frame. He pulled it off the wall and carried it out of the room. Ashley grabbed the front end and helped navigate it back to the front door.

"What's the worst thing you've ever seen in here?" she asked.

"Hoo, that's a question. Let me think. There was a kid with a snakebite, but it turned out to be harmless. A kid took a soccer ball to the face and had two teeth knocked out. Lots of blood. And then... ooh yes, that one."

They walked out the door and down the ramp. Marc stopped to close and lock the station up. "Which one?" she asked.

"You don't want to know. It was bad."

"C'mon, tell me. I'm not a little girl anymore."

You never were to me, he thought. "Fine," he said. "A few years ago, one of the counselors tied a really bad knot for a kid who was doing the high ropes course."

"Oh no."

"The kid climbed up and was doing one of the tightropes or something. And he slips, and the knot comes undone, and he falls like thirty feet. Lands on his feet and breaks both of his legs. Bones were sticking out and everything."

They kept walking, moving past the Lodge. "Was he okay?"

"I mean, he is now. Broken bones heal and everything. But those screams I heard, they will stay with me for the rest of my life. I have never heard such pain and agony from a twelve-year-old." He hoisted the stretcher up a bit higher. "Still happy you asked?"

"Of course. Makes me glad for all the minor problems my campers caused." She looked out into the distance. "You know what's really weird? I barely remember them. Like, anything about my campers. Their names, personalities, activities we did… none of that has stayed with me."

"It's been a long time. Memories fade."

She looked back at him. "I guess. I do remember other things though."

Before he could ask what those things were, they turned around the cabin and the group came into view. Drew was sitting up, supported by Sally and Carol, while Roger was standing on the base of the fallen snowperson, cellphone in his hand, trying to get a signal. Marc knew it would be no use.

"How are they?" he asked.

Roger hopped down from his snow platform. "They're both okay. Nothing too serious from what I can tell. Paige and I are going to drive them to the hospital in town."

"Sounds like a plan." Marc guided the stretcher over to Drew and laid it down next to him. "Think you can get on it?"

The young man nodded and shuffled onto it, keeping his left leg elevated. His eyes were narrow and his whole face seemed to be clenched up. "Just try to relax," Roger said.

"I am very relaxed," Drew said through gritted teeth. "Can't you tell? I may as well be at a spa right now."

"Good enough." Roger waved over Jack and Harvey to help with the stretcher. Each grabbed an end, then slowly lifted it up.

"I'll go get my car," Paige said. "Can someone help David get across the field?"

Carol gave a thumbs-up with her thickly-mittened hand. "We've got him, honey."

"Wait!" Adam shouted. He was standing a few feet behind his dad. His eyes were big and watery. "What about me? Am I coming with you?"

Roger shot Marc a look. It wasn't a good idea—the hospital wait could take hours, and the two injured men needed all the space in the car that could be afforded them. At the same time, Marc knew all too well how scary sudden separation from parents could be, especially for someone with Adam's needs.

"I'll keep an eye on him." Ashley stepped forward. "That sound good, Adam?"

"N-no!" the boy said. His voice was cracking with nearly every word. "I need to go with my parents!"

Ashley walked over to him and put her hands on his shoulders. "I know this is scary, but your parents will be fine. Besides, we need you here so we can plan the Ice Dinosaurs' strategy for the next event!"

Adam tilted his head up towards her. "Is—is that what we're going to do?"

"Oh, you know it!" Janice piped in. "We have a super-secret meeting at lunch and we'll be looking to you to help us decide how we're going to win."

The boy sniffled and rubbed his eyes with snowy gloves. "Okay, I'll stay here."

"Great," Roger said. "Let's get going. The sooner we get there, the sooner we can get help, and the sooner we can get back."

He leaned over and gave his wife a quick kiss, while Carol helped David to his feet. Marc watched as they started across the field, and then his attention went to Ashley. She held Adam's hand and was laughing with him about something or other. Marc laughed too. Maybe Ashley had forgotten her time as a counselor at Cedarwood. But clearly, her instincts when it came to kids were as strong as ever.

Chapter 11

Camp, Ashley thought, was just a series of calms and storms.

The morning had been a perfect example: the calm and fun of building a massive snowperson, and then the storm that came when two people were injured and had to go for medical help. But like all storms, it had passed, and now they were back in the calm of a delicious lunch of hotdogs and fries, with a side garden salad.

Much like the previous dinner and breakfast, this meal exceeded her standards, with thick, plump dogs that had clearly been grilled, not boiled, and served on freshly steamed buns. Several condiments sat in the middle of the table, in a bottle holder with a festive golden ribbon on top. The fries were fresh-cut and crispy without being too crispy. It reminded her, in the best way possible, of a meal she'd grab from a food truck when she was pressed for time in the city.

It was also the perfect meal for a ten-year-old who'd seen his dad briefly buried by snow and then taken to the hospital. Adam had already scarfed down two of the jumbo wieners and was working on a large plate of fries. Ashley had no doubt that they'd be gone in minutes.

"So," she said, leaning into the table and lowering her voice. "I thought we did pretty well during the snowperson building contest, but we need to up our game if we're going to destroy the Frost Bites. Marc's been quiet about what the next events will be. What do you think we can expect?"

"I have no idea," Janice said, her voice a bit exaggerated. Half of a hotdog lay on her plate and she was slowly forking lettuce into her mouth. "I thought that's what Adam is here for."

"You're right," Ashley looked at Adam dead-on. "What do you think?"

The boy finished chewing and wiped his mouth with a napkin. "There's actually a pattern to the events," he said, his voice also low. His eyes scanned the room, as though to check that no one was listening in. "Marc goes back and forth between indoor events and outdoor ones."

Janice scratched her chin. "You know, in all the times I've come here, I've never thought of that."

Adam went on. "Last night was the cake-eating inside. This morning was the snowperson competition outside. Whatever happens this afternoon will be inside."

Ashley looked over at Janice. "See, this is what a master strategist looks like."

Adam beamed. "In the past Marc has done a mixture of old and new games each year. I think we did the cake eating competition two years ago. We won it that time because none of our teammates were slow eaters." He looked directly at Ashley.

Janice leaned back in her wooden chair and laughed. "The shade! I love it."

Ashley shrugged. "I deserve it. Don't worry, I'm not going to mess it up for our team again."

"That's good," Adam said simply. He took a drink of whatever bright red juice was in his plastic cup. "Do you think my dad is going to be okay?"

"Absolutely," Ashley said. "Roger said he probably just had a concussion, which can be scary, but it's not too serious. The doctors will take good care of him."

Adam nodded. "I know that. The doctors take really good care of me whenever I'm in the hospital. They say I'm their favorite patient too!"

"I don't doubt it." Ashley bit her tongue to keep from asking more. Adam seemed healthy for now, at least. And it wasn't her business, at all, to get him to reveal whatever health issues he was dealing with.

Marc walked up to the microphone on the stage. "Can I have everyone's attention, please?"

The meal hall quieted. Marc smiled. "Thank you. First off, I just heard from Roger, and David and Drew are both waiting to be seen by a doctor, but they're both fully alert and doing well." There were a few positive affirmations from the crowd. "Next, something I obviously forgot to do this morning was announce the winner of the snowperson competition! And since only one snowperson was completed in time, I can safely say that the winning team is the Ice Dinosaurs!"

Carol jumped up from her seat at the other table. "Yes!" she hollered. "We are on the board!"

Marc continued, "The next competition will be at four o'clock. You all have free time until then. If I hear anything more from Roger I will be sure to let you all know."

He started to leave the stage, but Janice called out, "Hey! Any hints for what to expect for this afternoon's competition?"

Marc raised an eyebrow. "It will be indoors, so don't dress too heavily. And it's the sort of challenge you have to take piece-by-piece."

He wished them all a fun few hours of free time and left the stage. Ashley looked back at her tablemates. "Hmm, I wonder what that could be."

"Piece by piece, maybe that means Lego?" Adam asked. He perked up at his own idea. "Oh man, that would be great! I'm the best Lego builder! I have like a hundred sets at home, and I asked my parents if I could bring them up with me but they said no. I bet I'll get a set or two for Christmas though!"

"If it's Lego, I think we've got this one in the bag, then," Janice said. She pushed her chair back and stood up. "I don't know about you two, but I need some quiet time. Ash, are you okay to watch Adam for the next few hours?"

The youngster pouted. "I don't need to be watched. I'm not a baby!"

"Of course you aren't," Ashley said. "Tell you what, think you could spend an hour in your cabin? Then you and I can go do some exploring. It's been a long time since I've been at this camp and I could use someone to help show me around."

He nodded. "You bet! I've been coming here for years, in the summer and the winter! I can show you everything!"

"Then it's a deal." Ashley stood up. "I'll see you in an hour for my tour."

Adam got up and left the hall. Janice pulled her coat — this one dark grey with four stylish, if useless, buttons — and patted Ashley's shoulder. "Yep, I believe it. You were definitely a counselor here. You know how to talk to kids."

"Oh, that has nothing to do with being a counselor," Ashley said. "I just spoke to him the same way I do my male coworkers. Only difference is, he actually listened to me."

Chapter 12

An hour later, after taking some time to relax on her bed and let her coat and gloves dry, Ashley threw everything back on and left the cabin. Not having a phone to play on or text others was an odd feeling, and though she was sure she could borrow a charger from one of the guests she felt no rush to do so. There was no reception at Cedarwood and playing a silly app seemed like the wrong way to be spending time here. If anything, she needed a book or two to curl up with on top of the thick, cozy quilt.

She was just walking away from the cabin when Emma called out to her. She stood on the porch of the cabin to her left, the one with the half-constructed Nativity scene. "I heard you could use some clothes."

Ashley walked over. "It'd be nice. I'd rather not wear the same outfit for the next four days. Even if this is a camp in the middle of nowhere."

"I get it. I have some shirts and pants you're free to use. They might be a tiny bit short but I promise they won't be too tight."

"Wow, thank you, I really appreciate that."

Emma pushed her long, wavy blonde hair back. "Happy to help. I saw how you acted this morning, when we were building the snowman — or snowperson — and then when you helped Marc get the stretcher. It was good to see you so involved in everything. I know it meant a lot to everyone."

Ashley felt her heart go warm. This woman was probably no more than five years older than her, but her praise felt like that from a parent or teacher — like it really meant something. "Thanks."

"I'll leave the clothes on your bed. See you at four. Hope you're ready to win!" Emma waved and went back in her cabin.

Ashley headed across the snowy path to Adam's cabin and knocked on the door. "Coming!" came the squeaky voice from inside. A few seconds later the door opened. Adam was already wearing his coat and hat—or maybe he had never taken them off—and he had a tablet in his hand.

"Ready to go?" Ashley asked.

Adam chucked the tablet onto the bed and stepped into his boots. He grabbed his gloves and scarf and quickly put them on. "Let's go! I have the whole tour planned out for you!"

He led her back down the path to the camp's office and parking lot. Ashley saw her sedan, covered in a foot of snow, as well as a single set of tire tracks in the snow leading up the driveway. It must have been from Paige's car.

"This way." Adam led her to the edge of the camp's massive forest. "You said you used to go to this camp, right?"

"I was a counselor here one summer, but it was a very long time ago," Ashley said. "Well before you were born."

"Then there's a lot I need to show you!" He started into the forest. "Come on!"

Ashley followed after him.

If being at Camp Cedarwood was like stepping into a new world—one without all the distractions of technology and the busyness of city life—then walking into the forest was like stepping into an entirely different universe. The first thing she noticed was the decrease in snow under her boots. There was probably a foot less of it compared to the driveway behind her. It lay completely untouched, save for the occasional animal track. And it felt different too: fresh and powdery. Each step she took was like walking through a pile of feathers or cotton.

She looked up and marveled at the tall pines, spruces, firs, and, of course, cedars, all covered in thick layers of snow across their branches and needles. The sun's bright yellow rays danced in and out from the trees' limbs as they swayed back and forth in the wind. For fun, she reached up and hit one of the lower branches. A pile of snow fell from it, revealing crisp green needles that looked sharp to the touch.

Ashley pulled her scarf down and took a deep breath through her nose. It even smelled different here, just twenty feet in. The cold air mixed with the invigorating scents of pine and frozen sap. It reminded her of something, and after thinking about it for a second she felt her face go red with embarrassment. It was the scented candle she'd light when she took a bath. "Northern Chill" or whatever it was called. Suddenly being in the real thing made her artificial quest for the same scent seem so vain.

"Hurry up!" Adam shouted. He was about fifty feet deeper in the forest. She picked up the pace. The snow was easy to walk through and having half the trees free of leaves made it simple to follow after the boy. It had been a long, long time since she'd last been in these woods, but they felt bigger, the trees taller. Many of the branches that had whacked her in the face as a counselor were now probably thirty feet above the ground.

Adam came to a sudden halt and put his hand up. He stared deeper into the woods to his right. Ashley slowed down and cautiously approached him. "Look," he whispered, pointing his gloved hand ahead.

She followed his hand and saw, about thirty feet away and half-covered by a thick tree trunk, a large deer, its face buried in the snow. "Wow," Ashley murmured. The beast had to be six feet long and four feet high. She wished she'd brought her phone, only to remember that it was in the bottom of her purse with a dead battery.

The deer raised its head out of the snow, revealing two massive antlers. Both Ashley and Adam gasped loudly. The animal turned and faced them, then took off running through the trees.

The two watched it until it had disappeared among the snowy branches. "Wow…" Adam said. "Was that a reindeer?"

"No, reindeer are bigger and furrier," Ashley said. Those were the two things she knew about reindeer. "But I bet he was a cousin, and is probably heading back to them so they can let Santa know that you're here."

"Oh, Santa knows I'm here! I left him a note at my house in case he forgot. I told him to look for my red jacket. Did you know that red is my favorite color?"

"I can't say I'm surprised."

"It's the best color in the world!" Adam exclaimed. He paused and looked around. "Let's keep going. We're almost there."

He took off again. Ashley followed, but found herself slowed down by the denser trees and lower, thicker branches. She tried ducking under a particularly long pine branch, only to accidentally knock into it and receive a dump of snow on her head and down her back. Ahead, she heard Adam snickering.

"You think this is funny?" she asked.

He nodded gleefully and kept walking. She fought the urge to shove some snow down his back and see how much the little punk liked it himself.

After another minute Adam shouted, "There it is!" He started running at a full sprint. Ashley followed him as quickly as she could, trying to avoid getting any more cold snow on her skin. She turned around a large pine tree and saw him standing outside what looked like a teepee-shaped igloo.

It was about six feet high at its tip and probably four feet in diameter. It was entirely covered in snow, save for a two-foot entrance along the ground that faced partly away from her. "What is this?" she asked.

"We built it this summer!" Adam said. "Look!" He brushed some of the snow with his hand, revealing a series of branches, sticks and leaves, all leaning in on each other, that made up the structure. Then he ducked down and crawled in through the entrance. A few seconds later he called out, "Are you coming?"

Ashley didn't particularly wish to crawl through the snow, but she'd come this far and how could she say no to Adam? Plus, she was curious to know what the teepee was like on the inside. She'd never seen something like it before. She stepped over to the entrance, got down on her hands and knees, and moved into the makeshift shelter.

It was quite dark inside, with the snow blocking nearly all the sunlight. Adam sat at one end, looking pleased with himself. Ashley spun around and sat down on the other, putting her legs about six inches from his. The ground here was free of snow but rather wet. She tried not to think about what it would do to her pants.

"What do you think?" Adam asked.

"I love it," Ashley said, playing along. "It's so earthy and close to nature. And I love what you've done with the walls. Do you mind if I move in here for the rest of the week?"

Adam laughed. "I think you might be a bit cold if you do that! When we made it in the summer we wanted to sleep in it but our counselor wouldn't let us."

"Probably a good idea. Not a lot of room in here for a bunch of boys to sleep."

"Then we were going to make it into a clubhouse instead. But I had to go home early so I didn't get to use it."

"Oh no, why'd you have to go home?" The question was out of her mouth before she realized she was asking it.

"I was…" Adam looked down. "I was sick. And everyone thought it'd be good if I went home. It sucked… I mean, it stunk, because I really wanted to be here."

"Well…" Ashley said. "You are here now. And look, your clubhouse is still here. Which means it will probably still be here for next summer." She leaned in closer. "And you know what that means? You are your friends will have a hideout that no one knows about. Not even your counselor."

Adam looked back up and started bouncing in place. "You're right!" he nearly screamed. "That's going to be so cool!"

"You know what you should do?" she continued. "You should leave something here, so when you're back here in the summer it will be waiting for you."

"Yes! That's a great idea!" He clapped his hands together.

Ashley's legs felt cold and wet. As great as this was, she'd had enough. She flipped back onto her hands and knees. "Thanks for showing me this, but I need to get out before I sink right into the ground." She crawled back out into the light of day and stood up, grateful to be able to stretch her legs and back. She twisted her head down and saw that the back of her jeans was covered in dirt and twigs. Ashley scooped up some snow in her hands and rubbed it up and down her pants. Some of the dirt came off.

Adam came out from the shelter. "What do you want to do now?" he asked. "Wanna go deeper in the woods and see what's there?"

Ashley thought back to walking through the forest as a counselor and how the trees had seemed endless. "Not today," she said. "This is a really big forest. I don't want us to get lost."

"Ohh, please?" Adam asked, his voice high and whiny. "I've always wanted to see what's in there! One of my friends told me that there's magical creatures, like unicorns and leprechauns. Don't you want to see if that's true?"

"Of course I do," Ashley said. If he were just a few years older she'd have happily told him that it was highly unlikely such creatures existed, but why ruin such a fantasy for the kid? "My concern is that we'll go too deep, lose our sense of direction, and then have to hunt to survive. And I have no idea how to cook unicorn meat." She winked at him. "Instead, how about we head back to the camp? Maybe we'll spot another deer!"

"I guess," Adam said. "But there's still so much more I need to show you!"

"And you still can! Can you take me to the lake? I've never seen it in the winter."

Massive dimples formed on his cheeks. "You bet!" He started moving back the way they'd come. The kid was just a bundle of energy.

There weren't any other deer sightings on the way out of the forest, which seemed to take a lot less time than the way in. They reached the parking lot and Ashley felt a twinge of sadness at having to leave the forest. There was something peaceful, something serene, about it. She reminded herself that she was going to be at Cedarwood for another few days, and that there'd be plenty of other opportunities to go back in.

Adam led her down a smaller path, forged out of footprints in the snow, that ran from the parking lot toward the lake, going in between the forest and the camp's office. About a hundred feet down, the forest receded slightly, revealing a cabin, twice the size of the other camp cabins. It was made up of large logs stacked on top of each other, with two windows in its side and a chimney sticking out of its snow-covered roof. "Who lives here?" she asked.

"Um, Marc?" Adam said, like it was the most obvious thing in the world. There were no lights on inside.

Just beyond Marc's cabin, another path branched off from theirs, going back into the forest. Ashley vaguely remembered it. "Isn't this the way to Campfire Point?"

"Yeah!" Adam said. "Wanna check it out?"

He didn't wait for an answer and started down the path. Ashley walked behind him. The wide trail wound around a few trees before leading her into a large amphitheater, with rows upon rows of benches (all covered in tall layer of snow), on a large slope. She remembered coming here a few times, always at night. A large campfire would be lit at the bottom and counselors would sing songs and put on skits.

Adam hopped down to the amphitheater's "stage" and looked around. Ashley walked along the earthen steps, trying not to lose her footing, and joined him. At the front of the theatre were a few tall trees, and then beyond them sat the lake. In between two of the cedar trees was a large arch. Ashley remembered it as well. It was made up of a bunch of thick branches that had been twisted together and then apparently petrified to keep them in place. Because of its shape, no snow seemed to be able to accumulate on it.

"Do you know what this is?" Adam asked, pointing to the arch.

"I know it's been here for a very long time," Ashley said.

"Since the start of the camp," Adam said. "I think they use it for weddings and things. Wanna see something cool?" He walked right under the arch and looked up. "Look at this!"

Ashley joined him and tilted her head upward. At the top of the arch were dozens of different colored stones, sparkly brightly as the sunlight passed through. "That's amazing. I never knew those stones were there."

Adam nodded and then pointed out at the lake. "Let's keep going!" He grabbed Ashley's hand and pulled her from the arch, going between the two tall cedars.

They continued along the path and hopped down a small bank. Ashley stared out at what seemed like an endless plain of snow, completely undisturbed. "Where does the lake start?" she asked.

"We're on it!" Adam said. He got down on his knees and brushed the snow away, revealing a smooth sheet of ice. "Pretty cool, huh?"

"That's one way to put it." Her knees suddenly felt shaky. Or was that the ice cracking beneath her? "Is this… you know, safe?"

"Super safe!" Adam hit his hand against the ice. "It's like a foot thick. We always come on here during Christmas camp."

"If you say so. We should probably get going, though." She instinctively reached for her phone to check the time, only to remember, once again, that it wasn't on her.

"Do we have to already? Can't we stay out here a bit longer?"

She looked down at her feet. How deep was the water under her? They were just a few yards from the land, it couldn't be that much, right?

Adam noticed her staring at the ice. "Are you scared?"

"No!" she said. "I was just, uh, thinking about how the last time I was here it was all hot and sunny and I was swimming in this lake."

He grinned. "I know, it's awesome! When I'm here in the summer I tell everyone how I was walking on the lake and they all get really jealous."

"I bet they do." At that moment, swimming in the summer would have felt a million times better than walking in the winter. "Now come on, we need to get back. The next competition will be starting soon!"

That was enough to convince him. He spun around and walked back to the land. They both climbed up the bank and followed another path back to the parking lot. Ashley shot a look back to the lake. She hadn't expected it to scare her so much. The idea of the ice cracking and her falling through it, into the freezing cold lake waters… it wasn't something she wanted to imagine. And up until five minutes ago, never would have.

"Oh!" Adam screamed. Ashley turned back to him, now feeling terror that something had happened to him. Instead, the boy was booking it past Marc's cabin and the camp office. "They're back!"

She chased after him and reached the parking lot to find Paige's silver SUV trying to maneuver into the spot it had pulled out of. Once it was parked, Adam's parents stepped out, along with Roger, supporting Drew, who had two crutches in his hands. Adam ran to his mom and jumped into her arms for a tight hug. "Did you have fun with Ashley?" she asked.

"So much fun!" Adam shouted. "We explored the forest and then we went on the lake. Ashley was scared but I told her it was totally safe!"

"I was not scared!" Ashley said, with mock offense. She gestured to David and Drew. "How was it?"

"Easy," she said. She put her son down. "Got them in front of a doctor in ten minutes. My husband has a minor concussion and Drew has a sprained ankle. The doc recommended rest and relaxation."

"I told her they were already in the perfect place," Roger said. He had his arm around Drew, who struggled with the crutches on the snow.

Jingle bells sounded from the Lodge. Adam looked up at Ashley, who raised an eyebrow in return. "For sure, this camp is all about rest and relaxation," she said. "Except for the next hour."

Chapter 13

"First things first," Marc said from the Lodge's stage. "We are very thankful that David and Drew are both back here and doing great! They're resting in their cabins now but are hoping to join us tonight." Cheers and applause came from the competitors. "And a huge thanks to Paige and Roger for taking care of them and making sure they got the best treatment in the ER. I think we're pretty lucky the storm kept everyone inside, or they may have had a long wait to get help.

"Now," Marc continued, "for your next competition, this one is going to require intelligence, communication and lots of patience."

Ashley focused on the paper bag sitting in the middle of Ice Dinosaur's the otherwise-empty table. On the other side of the room, the Frost Bites had a similar bag on theirs. What was in it? Arts and crafts? Marshmallows and toothpicks? Lego, as Adam had suggested?

"In each of your teams' bags are two puzzles, each with one-hundred pieces. I have no idea what these puzzles are—I asked a friend to buy them for me and put them in the bags so that I wouldn't have any influence on the teams. Your task is to complete both puzzles. The first team to do so wins the event."

Janice, sitting next to Ashley, cocked her head up. "Now this is my kind of game."

"Oh, and one more thing," Marc said. "You are not allowed to talk. At all."

A few people groaned, but Ashley just smirked. Of course this was an added rule. It was such a camp thing to do.

"Everyone ready?" Marc asked. "Three, two—"

"Wait," Ashley said. Marc stopped and looked at her expectantly. "These teams are a bit unfair. The Frost Bites lost two members today who probably won't be able to compete again."

"Okay," Marc said, giving her a playful look with those deep blue eyes. "What do you propose? Are you offering to join their team, Ash?"

"Oh please," she retorted. "I would never betray my Ice Dinosaurs." Across the table, Adam gave her two thumbs up. "But to give our opponents a fighting chance, I think you should join the Frost Bites."

A few "ooohs" came from the other competitors. Marc bit down on his lip. "I appreciate the competitiveness, but someone needs to organize the Cup."

"David can do it," Paige spoke up.

"Drew can help him," added Sally.

Marc snorted. "Is that what everyone wants?" he asked. His question was met with a collective nodding of heads from both teams. "In that case, so be it. I hereby relinquish my title as the Cup organizer, and for the first time ever I am now a competitor!"

He stepped off the stage and walked to his new team's table. "But, uh, since there's no one else here to do it… three, two, one, GO!"

Carol grabbed the paper bag and flipped it upside down. Dozens, if not hundreds, of puzzle pieces fell on the table. Janice grabbed at them and started flipping them over. Ashley and the others did the same, spreading out the pieces as they did. Carol held up a corner piece and put it down in front of her. A few seconds later Paige put another one down with it.

Ashley looked over at Adam. He stared intently at the pieces, his eyes narrow and both hands on his masked chin. He suddenly reached forward and grabbed a few pieces from different parts of the table. Ashley opened her mouth to ask what he was doing before remembering the rule. Adam put the pieces together, creating a two-by-two square, consisting primarily of green and gold colors.

She scanned the pieces and looked for similar ones. It didn't take long to find a few more. She picked them up and handed them to Adam. He looked surprised — he hadn't noticed her watching him — but then his cheeks dimpled and he started trying to fit the new pieces in.

Ashley looked around the table. The pieces were all just about flipped. Carol had collected all eight corners and was trying to figure out which ones went together. Everyone else just stared at the mishmash of pieces. Ashley frowned. What were they trying to do, solve it in their heads?

She grabbed one of the green pieces she'd found for Adam and snapped her fingers at Harvey and his kids. They started looking for more. Janice in-turn nudged Paige and Emma and began pulling black pieces from the pile.

Within a minute Adam had a good twenty pieces to work with. He moved them around, finding the right place for each. Soon a picture began to form: a mixture of different shades of green, with gold, red and blue circles among it. "A tree," Ashley murmured to herself. Adam shot her a look.

She glanced over to the Frost Bites table. They were all moving things around with their hands. Did that mean they were closer to completion? She had to hurry.

Ashley brought her focus back to her table. If this puzzle contained a Christmas tree, what else would be in it? The answer was obvious: presents to go under it. And those presents would likely be covered in shiny, colorful wrapping paper.

It wasn't hard to find pieces that matched it. She grabbed a half-dozen from the center of the table and fit them together to form a small pile of gifts, each wrapped in red or blue paper and with silver bows on top. That made it easier to find the other pieces that went with it, and soon she had a full array of presents. She slid it over to Adam. The boy gave her an impressed nod and fitted her presents under his tree. They snapped together perfectly, forming a picture of a large, fully decorated Christmas pine with a slew of presents beneath it.

All it needed now was a border. Ashley looked back at Harvey and saw that he and his kids had assembled all of the edge pieces. She waved at him and pointed to their near-complete picture. Harvey and his kids carefully slid the matching edges along the table to Adam, who gently connected them with his pieces. He finished by adding on Carol's corner pieces with a satisfying snap. One picture done, one to go.

Clapping erupted from the other table. It looked like they were done one of their puzzles as well. She spotted Marc, leaning way in, both his hands on the table, a serious look on his face. For a second she regretted suggesting he join the Frost Bites. He was good at puzzles... or, really, he was just smart in general. When they'd been counselors together he'd struck her as a bit of a nerd. Kind of like her. Not afraid to do brainy things like word searches or crosswords, or to be challenged with an anagram or brain teaser. Or assemble two puzzles without knowing what either looked like.

Janice slapped the table in front of her, jolting Ashley out of her thoughts, and then looked at her expectantly. In front of her were clusters of pieces that had been put together, in groups of black, white and red, but there was no discernable picture yet. Ashley stared at them and looked at the remaining pieces, most of them the same color. She bit down on her lip and tried to sort it out. Half of all the pieces were black. What Christmasy things were black? Soot, coal, non-Rudolph reindeer noses...

Tension was growing in the room. The Frost Bites were getting close. She could feel it in the air. "Wait..." she breathed. The air. The sky. Night!

She grabbed the cluster of white pieces and tried fitting the black ones around it. It took a few tries, but she was able to get them in place, revealing a bright moon against a black background. Once her teammates saw this, they all jumped in and built the rest of the night sky. Adam and Harvey took the red ones and quickly added the remaining pieces to them to create Santa in his sleigh, just underneath the moon. Carol handed them the bordering pieces, while Emma and Paige filled in the few remaining spots. Ashley looked over at the other table. They were all standing and quickly moving their hands around. Were they close?

Harvey added the bottom row of pieces, completing the picture of Christmas Eve. Then he pounded the table with his fist and shouted out

"Woo hoo!" The rest of the team clapped and cheered. Ashley high-fived Adam with both of her hands.

The Frost Bites looked over. "You guys done?" Marc asked.

"You bet we are!" Carol said. "Come and see."

The two teams switched tables to look at each others' pictures. Marc's table had a completed puzzle of tobogganers on a snowy hill, and a scene of Santa on a rooftop with a big bag of presents on his back that was missing just a few pieces. "Looks good," Marc said. "The Ice Dinosaurs earn another point, putting them up 2-1!"

Ashley and her team cheered again. "Y'all were pretty darn close," Carol said. "I think this is shaping up to be a very exciting Christmas Cup!" Ashley nodded appreciatively. That sort of sportsmanship—being gracious and complimentary in victory—was a staple of the camp experience.

"Dinner is in one hour," Marc said. "See you all back here then!"

The guests headed for the doors. Ashley walked over to Marc. "How was that?" she asked. "Did you enjoy being a competitor for once?"

"It wasn't bad." He put his hands in his jeans pockets and shifted back on his feet. "It was especially fun competing against you. Just like old times."

"And just like old times, I beat you," she playfully punched his shoulder. His cheeks reddened.

"We'll see about that. Until then, see you at dinner?"

"Sure, but I believe you and I had an agreement." She motioned to the kitchen. "I told you I want to earn my keep here, and I meant it."

"Uh huh? You want to help out with the cooking?"

"You know it, boss," Ashley said, giving him a smirk. "Give me an apron, a chef's hat, and put me to work."

Chapter 14

Fifteen minutes later, Ashley stood over a large sink, moving a
colander full of mini potatoes around under a stream of cold water.
Though she'd initially tried to stay as dry as possible, after getting
splashed multiple times she'd decided that water wasn't so bad and
stopped trying to avoid it. It had sped the work up, even if her shirt was
now soaked.

"They look good!" Gunter, the camp's cook, said. He motioned over
to a large pot on the gas stove. "Drop them in!"

Ashley lifted the colander and tipped it over the pot. The potatoes
fell into the boiling, foamy water. She dropped the colander back in the
sink and wiped the condensation from her face. Next to the pot was a
large saucepan, with a thick brown gravy gently simmering. Gunter gave
it a stir and looked back at her. "You're a natural," he said. "Do you do a
lot of cooking at home?"

"Oh no," Ashley laughed. "It's delivery for me just about every
night. The most cooking I do is when I heat up popcorn in the
microwave." It had always been something in the back of her mind — her
condominium had stainless steel appliances, including a really good
convection oven — but her days were always so busy that it was difficult
to find the energy to cook when she'd get home.

"Well maybe you'll learn a few things here, then," the older man
said. Ashley liked him already. He was probably in his late sixties, with a
ring of wispy white hair running along his otherwise-bald head, but a tall
body that moved around without any difficulty. He had a warmth that
reminded her of her grandfather, back when she was a kid and he was
still alive. "Those potatoes won't take long to cook, so let's get the
meatballs in."

He went into the walk-in fridge and pulled out a metal cooking tray,
covered in cellophane. Under the plastic wrap were dozens of small,
round balls. He handed the tray to Ashley, who carried it over to the

large industrial oven, next to the stove. She pulled open the door and was met with a blast of hot, dry air.

"You might want to take the plastic wrap off first," Gunter said. He walked over with a second tray.

Ashley set the tray down and pulled off the cellophane. "These look delicious," she said, taking a closer look at the meatballs. They were slightly misshapen, as though they had been crafted by hand. "Where did you get them?"

"I made 'em this morning."

"No way." She slid the now-plastic-free tray into the oven. He added his tray and closed the door. "That must have taken you hours."

"Twenty minutes," he said, looking mighty proud of himself. "When you've worked here as long as I have, you get pretty good at these sorts of things."

"And how long have you worked here?"

"Well, ten years now. I started volunteering with the summer camp's kitchens and then when we moved up here full-time I offered Marc my help and he gladly took it." He pointed out the small window. "I live on the other side of the lake, so in the winter it's really easy to get here. Just a ten-minute walk."

"You... you walk across the lake?" She felt her stomach drop.

"Oh yeah. Pretty neat feeling, really, to be walking on top of the same places you go swimming in the summer." He reached over to the gravy pan and stirred it again. "Marc told me you two used to work here together?"

Ashley was grateful for the change in subjects. "Yes, years and years ago. I actually am here now by a freak chance. But it's been nice to see what Marc and Cedarwood have been up to since I was last here."

"I'm sure. This camp is a pretty special place. And, of course, Marc is a pretty special guy. Everyone who comes here just seems to love him, you know? That girlfriend of his sure is lucky."

Her heart stopped. "His... his girlfriend?"

Gunter howled with laughter. "I'm just kidding. The guy never seems to want to be with anyone. Not that he has the best pickings around here, but still." He pointed up to one of the cabinets, where a set of gravy boats sat. "Can you grab those and fill them up? We'll be eating in five minutes."

She took each boat and filled it using a ladle. Only a bit of gravy spilled on the stove, which she felt pretty proud about. Maybe she really could do more cooking at home.

She put the three boats on a tray and started heading for the meal hall.

"Oh, by the way," Gunter called after her. "You said you're here by freak chance. Based on the way your face fell when I joked about Marc's girlfriend, I can't help but wonder if maybe it wasn't a freak chance after all."

*   *   *

Her second dinner at Cedarwood was just as delicious as the first. The meatballs were moist and flavorful, with just the right combination of spices, so much so that the gravy was almost unnecessary—not that it stopped her from slathering it all over her food—and the potatoes were tender to the point of nearly falling off of her fork as she ate them. A side of corn, which Gunter must have cooked when she wasn't looking, made it a perfect meal, and she didn't even mind having to sing about a great big moose when Marc led them all in a pre-dinner song.

After a dessert of ice cream bars (there were enough for each guest to take three, but Ashley stopped herself after two), Marc walked up to the stage and tapped on the microphone. "Good evening everyone! We have had one heck of an eventful day, and again I want to thank you all for supporting each other and maintaining our Camp Cedarwood cheer. I just spoke with David and Drew, and they are doing well and are going to try to be at tonight's Christmas Cup event!"

Ashley glanced at the other tables. Sally and Paige both looked relaxed, even happy. That was a better sign than anything Marc could say, even if he did have a way of always sounding reassuring. "Speaking of tonight's event," Marc said, "we will be back outside, so bundle up. It will take place at the archery range at eight, which means you have about an hour to prepare. See you there!"

He stepped off the stage and walked towards her while she got up from her seat. "How was cooking your first camp meal?"

"It was fun," she said. "Though I want to wait and see if anyone gets sick before I make a final judgment on my skills."

"I think we'll be okay. Can't remember the last time someone got sick because of boiled potatoes," he chuckled. His eyes, deep and blue, met hers and for a second all they did was stare. Then he broke away and said, in an overly cheery voice, "Anyway, I'll see you at the range! You remember how to get there?"

"I think so. I'll just follow everyone else."

There was a twinkle in his eye. She could see it. She knew what was going to come next. "Great. Now you do have to promise not to try to kill me this time."

She sighed dramatically. "I knew you'd bring that up. It was one time!"

"I know. And yet somehow I've never forgotten it." He raised his eyebrows at her. "See you there, Ash."

He stepped away and started talking to Paige and Adam. Ashley slowly exhaled, letting her momentary annoyance with him pass, and then walked back to her cabin.

She was please to once again find a stack of clothes on her bed, along with a note: "Hope they fit! We'll need you at your best if we want to win the Cup! – Emma"

In the stack were three undershirts, a sweater, two pairs of jeans, and three pairs of socks. Ashley held the shirts and jeans up to her body and was happy to see that they seemed to fit. She carefully put them in the dresser, along with the sparse wardrobe she'd brought with her for the business trip. Then she leaned back and collapsed onto the thick quilt on top of the soft mattress. It occurred to her that she hadn't thought about her phone for nearly the entire day. If she'd been back in the city, she doubted she'd had been able to go more than five minutes without reaching for it. One more thing that was so different about Camp Cedarwood.

At quarter to eight the bells rang outside. She rolled off the bed and got dressed up for the next outdoor activity. Despite night's falling, the air didn't seem so cold as she stepped outside and began to trudge up the camp's driveway. Maybe it had warmed up a bit. Or maybe she was just getting used to the freezing temperatures.

The archery range was about halfway up the winding driveway, past the camp's high-ropes course but before its rock wall. She had probably been there four or five times as a counselor, and all but one of them had been forgettable experiences with her campers.

But it was that last one, the one Marc had oh-so-generously brought up with her after dinner, which had been memorable for all the wrong reasons.

*   *   *

The two were hanging out one evening, while the campers were all doing a campfire and the staff had been given time off, when Ashley complained about how bad she was at archery and hadn't been able to show her campers how to fire an arrow. Marc suggested they go to the range and do some practicing.

Marc grabbed a key to the archery shed and set up three large foam targets, each with a bullseye painted on it, on the range's large wooden stands. She laughed as he lugged the targets around, trying and failing to look like his small, skinny arms could lift them. Once he'd set them up, he handed her a bow and arrow, neither of which she knew how to use.

He smiled and told her not to worry. Then he stepped behind her and put his arms around her body to show her how to string the bow, attach the arrow, and pull back and fire a shot. His breath was in her ear, slow and heavy. It felt intimate, but she felt unsure about it. He guided the string back, aimed the bow and fired. It landed about six inches from the center of the target.

He stepped back and let her try on her own. She tried to follow the same method he'd shown her, but her first shot went straight into the ground, her second fell out of the bow before she let go of the string, and the third sailed well above the targets and into the mesh netting attached to the trees behind them. He laughed and walked out to pick them up for her to try again.

That's when it happened. Marc was picking up the arrow behind the target on the far-right side of the range. Ashley noticed there was one more arrow on the ground next to her and wanted to give one more shot. She strung the bow, added the arrow, closed an eye, aimed at the leftmost target, and pulled back and fired.

And somehow, the arrow flew to the right and hit Marc in the shoulder, just as he was standing back up.

He was fine—the arrows were blunt and could barely pierce Styrofoam, let alone human skin—but his cry of shock made her think she had mortally wounded him. Once his shouting stopped, he'd looked at her with a dumbfounded expression, and then started laughing and laughing. "Ash," he said, wiping tears from his eyes, "I promise, from the bottom of my heart, I am never, ever, EVER, going to let you live this down."

It was the last time she'd shot a bow.

*   *   *

Ashley kicked at the snow as she rounded one of the driveway's many turns. If this was going to be an archery competition, she was in trouble.

Orange light poured out from around the corner. The archery range came into view, illuminated by a dozen torches on each side, their flames casting large shadows against the pine trees that surrounded the area. She spotted Carol and the rest of her teammates to one side. "Good ev'ning Ash," Carol said. "Y'all ready to win another game?"

Ashley looked out at the range. There were no targets. Instead there were two objects, about fifty feet away, each covered in a burlap sack. She shuddered. "I guess we'll see."

The remaining contestants streamed in, including Drew, riding on a toboggan pulled by Sally, Harvey and Ian, and David, walking a bit gingerly alongside his family. Marc emerged from the shed with two bows and a bunch of arrows. He placed each bow in a holder along the shooting platform, and then joined his team.

Once all the competitors were present, Drew slowly sat up and got on his feet, leaning on David for support. "Well, hello everyone!" he said, sounding very cheery despite the circumstances. "David and I are pleased to be your new hosts. Marc walked us through the remaining events, and he's given us full permission to change or modify them as we see fit, since he is now a contestant. We will be doing just that, but for now, let's get to event number four! David, please explain to our competitors what they'll be doing."

"This is going to be an archery competition," David continued. "Each team will have a series of targets to hit. The first team to hit all their targets wins the event and gets a valuable point for the Christmas Cup."

Ashley looked back at the burlap sacks. What kind of targets would be under them, she wondered? They were too small to be the traditional foam targets, and also far too bulky and misshapen.

"Sally, if you would please reveal the targets," Drew said.

Sally walked up to the two sacks, grabbed each, and yanked them off, revealing two small pine trees, each covered in large ornaments. "Oh no," Ashley muttered.

"There are ten ornaments on each tree," David said. "They are made of the flimsiest plastic known to man and will shatter with just a tiny bit of force. Believe us, we tested them. Each team will send up a player to take three shots, and then once they are done they will retrieve their arrows and let the next player go. Everyone must shoot before a player can go again. The first team to have all their ornaments broken wins!"

"Does that sound good to everyone?" Drew asked. There were nods of agreement from each team. "Then let's get started! Teams, send up your first shooter!"

Carol pulled her group into a huddle. "Who wants to go first?" Adam's hand shot up. "I will!" he said from behind his scarf.

There were no objections. Adam stepped up on the platform, while Roger took the same position for his team. "Adam," Paige said, sounding a bit nervous, "do you know how to use that thing?"

"Oh yeah!" Adam said excitedly. "We learned here last summer!"

He grabbed the bow, needing a few seconds to hold it in his gloved hands, and was able to position the arrow along the string. David and Drew gave permission for the archers to fire when ready. Adam raised the bow, pulled the string back, and let it loose. The arrow flew forward and landed in the snow about ten feet in front of the tree. Roger's arrow sailed over its target and hit the netting in the back.

"That's okay!" Ashley said. "You were close! Give it another try!"

Adam strung the next arrow, aimed and fired. This one hit the tree, but not any of the bulbs. Roger's shot skimmed one of the branches and landed in the snow. "That was really close, honey!" Paige said. Any concern she'd had for her son's safety was clearly out the window. "Just a little to the right!"

Adam took the third arrow and held the bow up for a good five seconds before finally firing. The arrow seemed to arc up and then back down before smashing into one of the bulbs. "Yes!" Ashley shouted, joining in with her teammates. She wanted to win. But more importantly, she wanted it to happen before she had to shoot.

Roger managed to pierce the side of a bulb, causing it to crack open. After one shooter, each team had nine bulbs left.

Janice went next for the Ice Dinosaurs, while Bill shot for the Frost Bites. To Ashley's surprise, Janice had a heck of a shot, knocking down two bulbs, while Bill managed to get one. Emma went next and overshot the tree three times; her daughter hit one, tying both teams back with seven ornaments to go.

This continued on until just Carol and Ashley had yet to shoot. The team captain motioned to her. "Alright Ash, how 'bout you get up there?"

"Please, you should go first," Ashley said. There were only two bulbs left on their tree, versus four for the Ice Dinosaurs. Carol could finish things that round.

"If you insist." She climbed up on the platform and strung the bow. Her husband, now shooting a second time, took to the other platform.

Both of their first shots missed, but Carol's second was able to nail one of the ornaments. Ashley breathed a sigh of relief. Just one more. Then she wouldn't even have to risk embarrassing herself.

Carol aimed and let the string go. The arrow sailed through the cold night air and missed the final ornament by half an inch. Her team let out a collective groan, while the Ice Dinosaurs cheered as Bill managed to hit an ornament.

The two Southerners went to retrieve their arrows and Ashley felt her heart begin to pick up. She tried to remember how to pick up the bow, how to load it, how to aim... all the things Marc had taught her fifteen years ago. When his body had been pressed up against hers, guiding her moves...

"Ash!" Carol was back on the platform, bow in one hand and arrows in the other. "C'mon! We need you to take us home!"

Ashley took a deep breath of the chilly air and stepped onto the platform. She held the bow and fumbled with the first arrow as she tried to attach it to the string. It took her a few seconds, but she managed to get it. That gave her a bit more confidence that maybe she could actually do this. Or, at the very least, not embarrass herself.

"Best of luck, Ash." She looked over at the other platform and saw Mark, bow and arrow ready. "Not that you need it. You were trained by the best."

She quickly stuck her tongue out at him and then focused back on her target. Closing an eye, she pointed the arrow's tip at the big red bulb hanging off the left side of the tree. She pulled the string back as far as she could and then let it go.

The arrow went about ten feet above the top of the tree and crashed into the mesh. "Ooh, so close," Marc said, his voice dripping with mock sympathy. "Maybe try this?"

In half a second he'd raised his bow and fired. The rightmost bulb exploded in shards. Ashley glared at him. He hadn't been that skilled the first time he went up to shoot.

She put the second arrow in the bow and aimed again, this time a bit lower than her last shot. She released, and the arrow went wide to the left, not even coming close to the tree but nearly hitting one of the torches. Ashley was sure she heard her teammates sighing in frustration behind her.

"Good try!" Marc sounded like a parent congratulating their child on a t-ball game. He raised his bow. "On the left!" The arrow flew out and hit the left ornament. Marc's team cheered loudly, while Ashley felt a large pit form in her stomach. She had to win this.

Marc looked over to her and winked, then gestured with his hand. "All yours, Robin Hood."

Ashley took a deep breath and raised her bow once again. From behind her came cheers of support and encouragement. She focused the tip of the arrow right at the gold and silver ornament and envisioned it soaring through the air and landing dead-center. She took another deep breath. She could do this. She would prove the jerk wrong.

Her fingers pulled the string all the way back, and then let it go. She felt the force as it snapped and the rush of wind as the arrow left its holder. For a second, time seemed to freeze. Then she heard the sound of plastic breaking, followed by a gasp from one group and cheers from the other.

For a brief moment, relief washed over her. She'd actually managed to do it. She'd proven Marc wrong. She couldn't wait to rub it in his face—his chiseled, scruffy face.

Then she realized that the cheers were coming from the Frost Bites, while the gasps had come from right behind her. She looked over at Marc, who was standing with bow and arrow lowered and a look of pure joy on his face.

She slowly moved her eyes toward her opponent's tree. The last remaining bulb was now shattered, and her arrow was lodged between the two branches where it had hung. Ashley dropped her head in shame and embarrassment.

"Well," Drew said, "I don't think any of us were expecting that! What a finish to a tough competition. The Frost Bites get the point, and the score is now two to two!" The Frost Bites cheered louder and high-fived each other.

"Great work, everyone," Marc said. "But the fun's not over yet! Please join us for cookies and hot apple cider in the Lodge."

He walked over to Ashley and gently took the bow from her hands. "Ash, I gotta say." He was clearly trying to hold back laughter. "You truly outdid yourself. I didn't think you could top our last time here, but you're just full of surprises, aren't you?"

She sneered at him but said nothing, and then hopped down from the platform and followed everyone else back down the driveway. There was no way she could avoid going to this apple cider social. Even if all she wanted to do now was curl up in a ball and sleep for the rest of the week.

Chapter 15

Ashley took her time changing into a fresh shirt in her cabin and then in walking down the path to the Lodge. She entered to find the party in full swing: more festive jazz carols were playing through the speakers, all the guests were gathered around tables in groups of three or four, the Lodge's lights had been dimmed slightly to give the gathering a more sophisticated feel, and a table had been set up in front of the stage with a large coffee urn and multiple plates of cookies.

Janice, sitting at a table with Carol, Paige and Adam, waved at her. "There's the sharpshooter."

Ashley felt her face go hot as she walked over. "I'm sorry guys. I guess that makes two events I've lost for us now."

"Are you kidding?" Adam asked. His medical mask was pulled down to his chin and had several large crumbs on it. "That was hilarious! I've never seen anything like that in my life! It was like, twang!" His hand shot out like an arrow. "And then, BOOM!" His hand curved to the side and "exploded."

"It was pretty funny," Carol said. She stood up. "I promise we're laughing with you, not at you. Can I get you some cider?"

"Sure." Ashley sat down between Janice and Adam. "Got anything to put in it?"

"That comes later," Paige murmured. Carol laughed and walked to the back table.

"You're not all mad at me, then?" Ashley asked. She was surprised at the meekness in her voice. Normally she didn't give a care about what others thought about her, including in the office. She'd learned early on that if she didn't speak up for herself she would simply never be heard, and she'd gone to great lengths to be assertive and vocal in meetings and not take no for an answer when she knew she was right. Had it alienated herself from some of her colleagues? Probably. But it hadn't bothered her, especially when it meant being given bigger projects and promotions.

And yet here, with a bunch of people she'd met just yesterday, she felt a genuine shame for letting them down in what was ultimately a frivolous competition. Camp Cedarwood really was turning her life upside-down.

"Of course not!" Janice grabbed her wrist. "You tried your best and that's what matters. We'll win the next one. And the ones after that."

Ashley put her hand on top of Janice's. "Sounds good to me." She looked over at the rosy-cheeked boy. "Adam, what's the plan for tomorrow?"

He nearly jumped up at being asked for his thoughts. "Obviously, things have changed," he said, clearly trying to lower his voice and sound more mature. "With my dad and Drew out of the Frost Bites and Marc in, we have more people than them, but Marc is like really fast and strong and smart, so we need to keep an eye on him."

Paige and Janice laughed. "Yes, he is fast and strong and smart, isn't he?" Janice said, winking at Ashley. Ashley's felt her face go red again.

Carol returned and placed a mug of cider and a plate of cookies in front of Ashley. She cupped the mug in both of her hands and took a sip. It had been a while since she'd last had any sort of cider, but this was easily the best she'd ever tasted. It was warm and sweet, with more than a bit of cinnamon and nutmeg flavor. That first sip turned into multiple gulps, until she'd already drank half the cup.

"Good?" Paige asked.

"Amazing. How is it that all the food here is just so great?"

"You're telling me! I don't think there's any rational explanation for it."

David walked up to the table and looked at his son. "Alright buddy, I think it's time for bed."

Adam scowled. "Already? Can't I stay up a bit later?" He looked pleadingly at his mom, and then at Ashley.

"You need to be rested for tomorrow," Ashley said. "I'll probably be going to bed really soon too. We need to win all of the events and take a strong lead, and we can't do that if we're tired, can we?"

That seemed to convince him. He hopped up from his chair. "Goodnight everyone! See you tomorrow!" He started to leave, but then stopped and ran back and gave Ashley a hug. "Thanks for making today so fun," he said softly.

She returned the hug. "My pleasure. I'll see you tomorrow!"

He grinned and ran after his dad. Carol looked around the room. "Looks like all the kids are off to bed, so now the real party can start." She stood back up.

"I'll give you a hand," Janice said. The two women pulled their coats on and walked outside.

Ashley watched them leave, then looked back at Paige. "What was that about?"

"Oh, you'll see," Paige said. She grabbed one of the cookies off of the plate. "Thanks again for hanging out with Adam today. He would not stop talking about it. He said you guys went into the forest, but he wouldn't say what you found there."

Ashley's heart swelled. Adam had been willing to share his hideout with her, but not with his parents. "I guess I'm sworn to secrecy then."

"He likes you. I'm glad you stayed for this camp. I know it means a lot to him that you're here."

"He's a pretty special guy."

"He is." Paige looked down and took a bite of the cookie. "I suppose you're wondering about him. Why he wears the mask and everything."

"I... um... it's not like..." She hadn't been expecting that. Of course she had wondered, especially with the cryptic statements the other guests had made, but it never would have been her place to just ask.

"I mean, everyone else here knows. It would be unfair to not tell you." For a second, her voice sounded pained. "That is, if you want to know. I don't want to burden you with it."

"If you're willing to share, I'm willing to listen."

Paige smiled, though there was a sadness behind it. "You're a good person, you know that? But of course you are. Everyone here is a good person." She sighed and looked right at Ashley. "Adam has leukemia."

Ashley gasped slightly and brought her hands to her mouth. "My God. I'm so sorry."

"Thank you. He's had it for several years now, so it's been a journey for us." She said it so casually, like she was talking about the weather outside. Ashley realized that it was probably because of how many times she'd have had to tell people.

"He, uh…" She tried to think of what to say. "He seems to be doing well."

Paige chuckled once as she slowly shook her head. "He's a fighter. He's gone in for who knows how many treatments now and I don't think I've ever heard him complain about it. When he was first diagnosed it was in November, and the doctors told us to make Christmas meaningful, because it might be his last one." She wiped her eye and smiled again. "That was three years ago."

Ashley reached out and put her hand on Paige's. "He's a fighter. Sounds like his mom is, too."

"Thank you." Her voice was now choked, like she was on the verge of crying. "I just… you never know. He's in remission now, but they've told us it isn't gone. It could come back. The last time it did, it nearly took him from us. So I guess…" She wiped her eyes again, and then coughed another laugh. "I'm sorry. I just met you. I shouldn't be unloading all of this on you."

Ashley squeezed her hand. "It's camp. Doesn't matter that we met yesterday. We're best friends now."

Now it was a genuine laugh. "Isn't that the truth?" She sighed and brushed a tear away from her cheek. "I've treated every Christmas here like it was the last one we had with him. It's just that this time, it feels more real. Like it actually will be. He doesn't know it, of course. I'm sure he suspects it somewhere deep down inside, but we've never told him."

"I'll keep my lips sealed," Ashley said. "But I'll also make sure this is the best Christmas ever, for him, and for you."

Paige nodded as more tears fell from her face. Ashley looked around at the other guests. They were all absorbed in their own conversations and paid no attention to the two of them. "Thank you," Paige said. She took a deep breath and seemed to regain her composure. She smiled. "It's going to be the best one because we're going to win the Christmas Cup, right?"

"You know it. So long as there aren't any more archery contests."

Paige laughed. "I still can't believe that happened. I think it's going to become a legend here at Cedarwood."

Carol and Janice came back with a bottle of bourbon, which Carol loudly placed on the table, catching the attention of the other guests. "There it is!" Roger said. He practically danced over to the table. "I've been waiting all year for some southern liquor. Where's this one from?"

"Tennessee!" Carol said, sounding rather proud of herself. "We were in Chattanooga this summer and found a tiny distillery along the river. Best stuff I've ever tasted. We must've bought, what, a dozen bottles? This is the last one left." She held it up. "Who wants some?"

A line began to form, but Carol focused on pouring a few glugs of the liquor into Ashley's and Paige's cups. Ashley raised her mug and toasted her friend. Paige returned it and they both took a sip.

The bourbon was delicious and went perfectly with the cider, giving it an extra warmth and smoothness that she felt all the way into her stomach. Despite the wonderful taste, she had trouble taking any pleasure in it. Not with what she'd just learned about Adam.

It made sense. The mask he always seemed to wear. The hushed whispers when his family had arrived the day before. The cryptic things they'd said about his health. But still, knowing that he had cancer, and one that his mother seemed to think would be terminal... it was a lot to take in. And despite her work in the corporate world, Ashley had never seen drinking as much of a crutch. This sweet, rich cider only tasted sour.

She looked back at Paige, who was taking little sips in between talking with Emma and Bill. She was laughing and seemed genuinely engaged in the conversation, just seconds after she had been in tears as she'd talked about her son's childhood leukemia. Behind her, the tinsel hanging along the wall seemed to twinkle in the Lodge's dimmed lights. The light Christmas instrumentals continued to play over the speakers.

Ashley smiled to herself and took another sip. It was amazing, really, how in the midst of this tragedy, Paige and her family had found such joy at Camp Cedarwood. The camp truly was a special place. That was becoming more and more clear to her.

Ashley finished her cider, then got up to get some more.

Chapter 16

Marc surveyed the Lodge and rolled his eyes. The ten or so remaining adults were all slumped in chairs around tables covered in mugs, plates and half-eaten cookies. Two empty liquor bottles stood in the middle of one of the tables, reflecting the light of the flameless candle next to them. A piano version of "Silent Night" was playing through the speakers, giving the atmosphere a classy feel, though it was undone by constant giggling and snorting as the remaining guests found another hilarious thing to talk about. Last Marc had heard, it was a story being told about tripping and falling into a duck's nest.

He walked over to the stereo and turned off the music. "Alright everyone, party's over. Go get some sleep. I don't want to have to deal with any hangovers tomorrow."

A few people groaned, but they all got up and began to put on their jackets and hats. He rolled his eyes again. This was one thing he didn't have to deal with at summer camp. Though drunk adults were still probably better than hormone-filled teenagers.

Marc grabbed a cleaning bin from the kitchen and walked over to the tables to put the dishes away. Ashley had stayed behind and was stacking the plates and cups next to each other. "You really don't need to do that," Marc said. "It's late. I'm sure you want to get to bed."

"I told you I'd help out around here," she said. "It's not like this will take very long."

If anything, he wished it would take longer. Just the two of them under the lights' golden glow? There was something lovely about it. "You have a good day?"

She nodded but kept her eyes down. "Yes. It was a lot of fun. And the people here are great." There was something in her voice. She sounded like she didn't believe what she was saying. Was it just tiredness? Or something else?

"You okay?" he asked. "Let me guess. You're still sore about that archery loss. Look on the bright side, at least you didn't injure anyone this time."

She grabbed the stack of plates and started carrying it to the kitchen. "I guess that's a good thing." Her eyes finally flashed at him, if only for a split second. "'course, you probably would have deserved it if I did." She put the plates on the counter at the kitchen window. "It's not that, though."

"Then what is it?"

She leaned back against the wall. "I talked to Paige."

The heaviness in her voice made it clear what they had spoken about. Marc nodded solemnly. "It's such a sad story. He's a great kid, they're both great parents… you hate to see it happen. He's been coming to Cedarwood for three years now, in both the summer and the winter. I don't know anyone who's more devoted to this place than him."

"Aside from you. At least he leaves here from time to time," she said. "He told me that he had to go home from camp in the summer. What happened?"

Marc briefly debated whether it was the sort of thing that he should share with her, before deciding that it was. If Paige had told her about Adam's condition, this wouldn't be any new information. "He was up here for one of the week-long sessions and he was doing great. Healthy, active, eating well, everything. And then in the middle of the week, during a soccer game, he just collapsed. An ambulance had to take him to the hospital, where they found that the cancer was back." He bit down on his lip. "I felt so bad for him. Here he was, finally able to be a kid again, and then he finds out he still has leukemia. It just didn't seem fair."

"Because it wasn't," Ashley said. "I've known him for all of a day and I can already tell you no one deserves to be healthier than him."

"Heh, yeah. I know I'm supposed to be unbiased as the camp's director, but Adam is my favorite camper. It's not even close."

"At least you're honest about it." Ashley looked down at her feet. "Paige told me she thinks this will be Adam's last Christmas here. Though I guess if I were in her shoes I'd treat it like it was his last Christmas here too."

"Yeah, well, he might not be the only one," Marc muttered, catching himself way too late. "I mean—"

She looked back up at him. "What's that supposed to mean?"

He held his hands up. "Sorry, sorry, it was a bad joke. I've just… it's been…" He sighed and rolled his eyes. No use in keeping the truth from her now. "I may as well tell you this. This is probably going to be the last Christmas Camp at Cedarwood. Because Camp Cedarwood may be about to go out of business."

Her mouth fell open—a reaction of hers that he remembered all too well from their teenage days. "W-what?" she sputtered out. "How?"

His legs suddenly felt weak and wobbly. He grabbed a nearby chair and sat down. "Same reason everyone else goes out of business. We don't have enough money to pay all the bills."

She pushed off the wall and also sat down, sitting about ten feet away from him. "I thought the camp is popular, though. Don't you fill up during the summer?"

"We're normally pretty close, but it isn't that simple." If that wasn't the understatement of the year, he didn't know what was. "You remember how Henry Wilcox founded this place? When he opened Cedarwood, all those years ago, he set-up a large trust fund in the camp's name. The point of the fund was to pay interest and dividends, which goes to the camp's operating funds and allows us to keep our rates low for campers."

"Okay, I follow so far." Ashley leaned in, looking almost intrigued.

"About ten years ago, the camp's operating expenses started to climb, and so the fund started to pay out from the investments in it, meaning its value went down every year. I had no idea this was even happening, until a few months ago when I got a letter saying the fund had been entirely depleted. There's nothing left."

"Yikes. That's bad."

"You're telling me. At this point the only way the camp survives is if we double camper fees or find some way to increase our non-summer revenue by like 500%. I know there are a few members on the camp's Board of Directors who would love to turn us into some big, expensive sports resort for rich kids. The idea of it terrifies me. Camp Cedarwood is for everyone."

"Don't I know it." She looked over at the tables. "I wonder if there's any bourbon left. I think I need another drink now."

"No kidding." He rubbed his forehead. "And there's one other thing. Do you remember the legend of Wilcox's gold?"

She looked up in thought for a moment. "I think so," she said slowly. "It's the story that Henry Wilcox buried gold somewhere on the camp property."

"Exactly. We used to make fun activities out of following a treasure map for it, though all the campers ever found was candy."

She shrugged. "Not the worst prize."

"Here's the thing, though. I've been pouring over the details of the trust fund, and included in Henry's assets was about two hundred thousand dollars worth of gold. No one has any idea where it is. I've looked through all our records. I don't think it was ever in his bank vault or estate."

She cocked her head and looked at him amusedly. "You think there's actually gold buried here?"

"I mean, I like to think there is. A while ago I was at a yard sale in town and I bought a metal detector for twenty bucks. Every so often I'll go around and see if I can get any readings from it."

"Uh huh? And have you found anything?"

"Nothing yet. And maybe there isn't anything to find, but if there was, boy, it would sure help us out financially. Two hundred grand of gold back then would be worth over ten million dollars now."

"Wow." For a second her face lit up, before falling again. "But I guess it's beyond wishful thinking at this point, huh?"

"Pretty much. Which is why I'm not hopeful that there will be another Christmas Camp next year." Despite the dour topic, he felt his shoulders ease up. This was the first time he'd actually told someone about the camp's situation. It was like a weight had been taken off of him. "I trust you'll keep this all to yourself? I don't want the other guests finding out about it before Christmas."

"Of course." She stood up. "And, not that it means anything, but I was planning on this being my last Christmas Camp too."

He knew she was making a joke, but he felt a pang in his chest. It was another reminder that she was only going to be here for a moment, and then she'd be on her way back to the city. Marc stood up. "If we do close down, at least I won't have to try to convince you to come back next year."

They put their coats on and headed out of the Lodge. Marc checked to make sure the doors were firmly closed—a few break-ins from local wildlife had taught him to do so—and then walked Ashley back down the path in the snow. The skies were once again cloudy and moonless, but there were more than enough colored lights shining off the white snow to guide their way.

"You really need some decorations," he said. Her darkened cabin seemed so out-of-place in the middle of all the Christmas lights on the others.

"Sure, I'll just head over to the Walmart next door and get some." They stopped at her cabin. She turned and looked up at him.

For a split second, he was eighteen again, and it was a warm night in the middle of the summer, and the two of them had just finished watching the sunset, and he was bidding her goodnight before she went into her cabin to be with her sleeping campers. He could feel the humid air against his skin, smell the lingering campfire smoke, hear the crickets chirping in the bushes.

Then she spoke, and he was back in the cold, dark night. "I had a really fun day today," she said, her voice soft and appreciative. "And it's thanks to you. You're doing really good work up here." She opened her arms and went in for a hug.

Marc put his arms around her and held her close. He could hear her breath against his ear as she rested her chin on his shoulder. All he wanted to do was squeeze her as tightly as possible, then kiss her cheek. It was the same feeling he'd had those fifteen years ago.

Instead, after holding the embrace for a good few seconds more than a normal hug would have been held, he let go and smiled at her. "Have a good sleep. I'll see you tomorrow. Hope you're ready to see the Frost Bites take a commanding lead in the Cup."

"Don't count on it." She gave his arm a quick rub. "Goodnight, Marc."

"'Night, Ash."

She stood still for a moment, looking at him with those green eyes that seemed to sparkle in the surrounding Christmas lights, and then walked into her cabin. He watched until the door closed behind her and the cabin's interior illuminated, and then he continued on the path to his cabin.

Just before he went past the camp's office, he took one last look at her cabin. "Stop it," he muttered to himself.

She was going to go back to the city in just a few days. She'd once again be out of his life and he would be out of hers. There was no point in trying something, in telling her how he felt, in any of that. It would just break his heart again.

Ash would be gone in less than four days. All he could do was make the most of being with her one more time.

December 23

Chapter 17

Ashley slowly woke up in her soft, comfy bed, this time remembering full-well that she was still at Camp Cedarwood. She gave herself another minute to enjoy the feeling of the thick blankets that covered her body and the tender mattress that supported it, before sitting up and rolling out of bed. She showered and brushed her teeth, then tried on some of the clothes Emma had given her. They fit pretty well — maybe a bit baggy and loose, but it wasn't like anyone was going to judge her for it.

She smiled at the thought of it. When was the last time she'd just gotten up, thrown on some clothes and headed out the door? In the city she could never leave her condo without making sure her clothes matched, her hair and makeup were done and she had given herself a few sprays of perfume. It was so nice to not have to worry about such things up at Cedarwood.

The sun was just starting to rise as she left her cabin. No one else was out and none of the other cabin lights were on. It occurred to her that she didn't actually know what time it was. Her phone still needed charging, and without it she had no access to a clock.

There was light coming from the Lodge, as well as smoke from its tall stone chimney. Ashley headed in and was met with the strong smells of cinnamon, butter and flour. In the hearth along the right wall, several large logs were blazing with flames. Her stomach rumbling, she walked to the kitchen to find Gunter flipping pancakes at the long metal grill. "Frosty the Snowman" was playing through a portable radio that hung on the wall, and the older man seemed to be making the flips in time with the music.

She knocked on the wall. He spun around in surprise but relaxed when he saw her. "You're up early," he said.

The clock on the wall next to the window read 6:45. Normally it would take a loud alarm and a ton of willpower—or the closing of a big client deal—to be up at this time. "I guess I sleep better up here," she said. "Can I help you with anything?"

"That'd be great. You should probably wash up first, though. Bathroom is the first door down."

Ashley stepped back from the kitchen, walked over to the door and pulled it open. She was met with a burst of hot steam and a cry of surprise. "Hey!"

Standing in front of the shower at the back of the sizeable bathroom, towel barely draped around his waist, his body dripping with water, was Marc. "Oh!" Ashley said. "I'm so sorry!"

Marc grabbed the towel with both hands and pulled it up. Beads of water flowed from his wet hair down his chiseled, hairless chest and well-defined abs. He looked at her half-surprised, half-amused. "What are you doing here?"

"I—uh—" She looked away from his bare torso, towards the rack on the wall where all his clothes hung. "I needed to wash my hands. To help with breakfast."

Marc nodded. She found herself looking back at him. Somehow his shoulders seemed broader when he wasn't wearing a shirt. "That's great. But if you don't mind, I kinda need this for another minute or so."

"Right, right, of course." She stepped back and started to close the door. "Wait, what are you doing here? Don't you have your own cabin?"

"It's got a tiny bathroom. The shower's a lot better here." He motioned to his clothes. "Now if you don't mind…"

She nodded and closed the door, then nearly ran back to the kitchen. She stopped just in front of it and gave herself a second to calm down. The Marc she had known fifteen years ago had been as skinny as a beanpole. Clearly, in the time since then, he'd discovered working out.

Gunter was working on another batch of pancakes when she came back in. "Uh, the bathroom was occupied," Ashley said. She went to the sink and used the dishwashing liquid to clean her hands.

Gunter handed her the spatula and went over to make coffee. Ashley flipped the remainder of the pancakes, trying to focus on making breakfast and not on the hunky body she'd just laid her eyes on.

The batter sizzled on the grill. She stuck her finger into the metal bowl next to it and took a taste. It was smooth and sweet, and so unlike the instant pancake mix she used when she'd occasionally make them at home.

"I saw that," Gunter said. He poured a bag of coffee grounds into the urn.

"It's so good," she said. "What's the recipe?"

"It's my secret." He mimed zipping his lips. "If I give it away, no one will want to come back here."

Marc's words the night before, about this possibly being the camp's last Christmas, flashed in her mind. Clearly, Gunter was unaware of it. "I think there are a few more reasons to come here than the pancakes," she said. "Even being as good as they are."

"There are a million reasons to come here," he said. "And probably ten million to stay."

The coffee urn began to percolate, adding the smell of freshly roasted beans to the air. Gunter handed her a large plate and she stacked the pancakes on it. She glanced out the window, at the snow-covered trees between the cabins and the lake, now glowing in the rising sun. Maybe the man had a point. There was something so simple about being up here, away from the rat race of the city, away from the smog and steam, the blaring horns and never-ending construction, the cellular connections and constant alerts and reminders on her phone. Up here was fresh air, wide open spaces, the friendliest of people and the most complex thing she had to focus on was not burning the pancakes grilling in front of her.

"You like it up here?" she asked.

"Love it." There was no hesitancy in his reply. "I wish I'd moved up here thirty years ago. I get that some people find it rather slow and uneventful, but not me. I have everything I want." The pancakes had all been scooped onto the plate. Gunter grabbed a stick of butter and dragged it along the grill, greasing it up for the next batch. "How about you? Are you happy in the big city?"

"I guess," she said. He took the plate from her hands. "There's always things to do and people to see, which is great. But I can see why people like it up here. It's so peaceful and quiet."

He handed her a ladle, which she used to scoop batter from the metal bowl onto the grill. "Easy there, not too much," he said. "You use too much batter and it makes 'em a lot easier to burn." She eased up and he nodded. "There you go. You're going to be a great cook in no time!"

She waited a minute and then flipped the next batch. Each one of them was perfectly round and golden. They looked better than any pancake — or any breakfast food, period — that she'd made in her life.

"White Christmas" began to play from the radio. She checked to see if Gunter wasn't looking, then took another fingerful of the batter. Ashley smiled. A girl could get used to a place like this.

*   *   *

The cooked pancakes tasted even better than the batter. Ashley looked around the room at half-full tables. The guests who were the early risers like her were chowing down on their breakfasts. She felt a swell of pride at her work. Those were her pancakes they were eating. At least, ones she had flipped.

Paige, sitting at a different table with her husband and son, caught her eye and smiled warmly. Ashley gave a little wave and glanced quickly at Adam. The boy was chewing, with his mouth open, on a big piece of pancake, with a little maple syrup dripping down his chin and onto his mask. Ashley looked back at her own plate. The poor kid. Only ten and having already gone through so much.

"No, don't think about it," she said to herself. There was nothing good that could come from feeling sorry for Adam and his family. All she could do was try to give him the best few days here as possible. And fortunately for her, he was a pretty darn easy kid to please.

"Don't think about what?" Sally and Drew approached her table, with her supporting him as they walked. "Mind if we sit here?"

"Be my guest!" Ashley said. "And I was trying not to think about, uh, all the calories I've been eating here these last few days."

They both laughed as they took a seat. "Don't you know?" Sally asked. "Camp calories don't count. Especially when you're trudging through the snow to do everything."

"Tell me about it," Ashley said. She grabbed another pancake from the tray. "How's your leg?"

"It hurts," Drew said. He shrugged. "But what can you do? At some point I was going to injure myself up here, so I guess I'm glad it's just a sprained ankle!"

"Uh huh? Have you been coming here for a while?"

"Ten years," Drew said. "We met as counselors our first year and we did five summers together, and then when we couldn't work here any longer we made a promise to keep coming here once a year. This year Christmas Camp was the only time we were both available, but I think we're both pretty happy we came!"

"That's great!" Ashley said. "I actually used to be a counselor here as well."

"We heard," Sally said slyly. "You and Marc were counselors together."

"I was only here for a year, though," Ashley said. "How you could do five years up here is beyond me."

Sally chuckled. "You're not wrong. It takes certain type of person to want to keep coming back."

Marc walked into the Lodge. He gave a nod and a wave to Ashley and her table, and then sat down with Paige and her family. "Or to live here, for that matter," Drew said. He took his holly-and-ivy napkin and tucked it in his collar, then grabbed a few pancakes and began cutting them up into small pieces before spearing them with his fork and eating them down. "Wow, these are good. Probably the best ones I've had up here."

Ashley deftly pumped her fist in celebration. "Where are you guys from? Is Cedarwood a long way from home for you?"

"Not for me," Sally said. "I'm just a few hours away. But Drew lives on the West Coast these days, which is why it gets harder and harder for us to find a week to meet up here."

Ashley nodded. "Wow, that's quite a long-distance relationship. It's great that you can make it work."

The two young adults looked at each other. Sally tilted her head back and rolled her eyes, while Drew clapped his hands together and laughed. "Yes! I knew it! Pay up!"

Ashley turned her head in confusion. "Sorry, I don't understand. What do you mean?"

Drew was doing some sort of mini happy dance in his chair. Sally raised her hands up and then let them fall. "We're not together," she said. "And we had a bet going that someone would confuse us for boyfriend and girlfriend. Thanks to you, I just lost that bet."

Ashley felt her face go even hotter than when she'd messed up archery the previous night. "Oh my goodness, I am so sorry. I just assumed... you know, you seem so comfortable together..." She tried to clamp her mouth shut to keep from talking, but the words kept spilling out. "Oh no, please don't tell me you're related or something."

Drew leaned over and slapped the table as he laughed. "Oh, that's even better!" He took a deep breath and wiped his eyes. "No, we're not related. Just best friends. I think it's safe to say that we're not exactly each other's type."

Ashley buried her head in her hands. As embarrassed as she felt, there was an odd sense of familiarity to it. Camp was all about awkward conversations: spend weeks on end with the same people, with no privacy and nothing to do but talk, and there was bound to be misunderstandings and inappropriate questions. It was doubly true when kids were involved. When there were no adults around it seemed that any semblance of a filter was out the door, leading to queries and conversations about the most sensitive of topics.

"What's in store for today's Christmas Cup?" she asked, desperate to change the subject.

Drew raised his right eyebrow. "Oh, you'll see. David and I made a few changes to Marc's plans, so it's bound to be fun and exciting. But beyond that, my lips are sealed."

"He won't even tell me," Sally said. "Though maybe if I were dating him he wouldn't keep it a secret, huh Ash?"

They laughed again. Ashley went back to her pancakes. They didn't taste so delicious anymore.

As the meal ended and tables were cleared, David walked up to the microphone and tapped on it a few times. "Uh, good morning everyone. I hope you all had a good sleep and are ready for another great day here!" He paused as the others cheered. There was just never enough cheering up at camp. "There are going to be three events for the Christmas Cup today, with the first one starting in half an hour back here in the Lodge. Please come with clean hands and be ready to do some building!"

Ashley stood up and grabbed her coat from her chair. She said a quick goodbye to Sally and Drew as she headed to the door, and wondered if she would ever feel comfortable eating with them again.

Chapter 18

Thirty minutes later, she was back in the Lodge, gathered around a table with the rest of her teammates, not unlike how they had been organized when they'd raced to complete their puzzles the day before. Janice, dressed in a bright red blouse and dark pants, sat to her right, while Carol, wearing a wool sweater with Santa Claus' face stitched into the front, was to her left. Adam was right across from her, dressed in a blue sweatshirt with a bright red t-shirt underneath, his mask back over his mouth but looking bright and cheery as ever.

Ashley smiled at Adam and tried not to think about what his mom had told her, about the cancer that had sent him to the hospital numerous times and that could be in his body at that exact moment. About how scared he must had been when he'd collapsed at camp that summer. About how unfair it was that such a good, sweet kid had to go through so much so early in his life. At that moment, all she wanted to do was reach across the table and grab him in a tight hug and tell him that everything was going to be okay.

Not that she could do that. She didn't want to make him suspicious about what was really going on and what could happen to him. Paige had made it clear that this was to be the best Christmas Camp ever, and that meant acting like nothing was wrong. Because as far as Adam was concerned, nothing was.

She brought her attention to the large cardboard box in the middle of the table and the long sheet of baking paper that lay under it. David's hint about being ready to do some building had given her a few ideas about what this activity could be. Whatever it was, she was just glad there wouldn't be any more bows and arrows.

David and Drew walked/hobbled up to the front. "Welcome to event number five!" Drew said. "This one involves a classic Christmas tradition, with a twist. In the boxes in front of you are all the pieces and fixings you will need to make the ultimate gingerbread house."

Ashley looked at her teammates. They seemed to perk up at the mention of the house. Good, she thought to herself. This could be a chance for us to get back in the lead.

"You will have forty-five minutes to construct and decorate the biggest and best gingerbread house that you can," Drew continued. "Then your team will have to sell us that house as a place for our gingerbread family to live. Whoever does a better job of convincing us will win a point!"

David cleared his throat. "There's one other thing. The winning team will have their house preserved until Christmas Day, and they will also get to destroy and eat the losing team's house."

Paige rolled her eyes. "This is what happens when you let men plan the events."

"Are teams ready?" Drew asked. "In three, two, one... go!"

Janice stood up and removed the lid from the box, then took out everything in it and placed them on the table. There were numerous planks of gingerbread in different sizes, two large tubes of icing, and a bag of assorted candies. "Okay y'all," Carol said as Janice tossed the empty box aside. "How are we doin' this?"

A bunch of ideas were put forward, including making a three-story gingerbread mansion, doing an open-concept house with decorations inside, and creating a neighborhood of mini gingerbread houses. Carol took the suggestions in before raising her hands. "Lots of creativity here, but we don't have much time and I think we need to focus on making a house that doesn't fall over. I say we do a traditional house, but then we add a backyard with a pool and anything else we can fit in it. Sound good?"

There were no objections and the team got to work. Ashley, Janice and Carol grabbed the different sizes of gingerbread walls and tried to figure out how they all fit together. Paige and Adam poured the bag of candy out on the wax paper and began to separate it into different piles.

Harvey and his kids took the largest pieces of gingerbread and focused on creating a roof for the house.

It didn't take long for the foundation of four walls to be laid out and the candy organized in about ten different piles. Carol took the house's two wall pieces and began to put rows of little icing dots on them, then stuck alternating red and green Christmas mints on them. She passed the icing tube to Janice, who started forming doors and windows on the house's front.

Ashley took the remaining slabs of gingerbread and started working on the house's backyard, consisting of a large piece laid flat on the table, with three smaller ones on its sides to create a fence. She borrowed the icing tube from Harvey to keep everything in place, then looked through the candy piles to find accessories for the space. There were a few green gummies that made for excellent trees, while red, green and white candy corns helped form the outline of the backyard's swimming pool.

As she waited for the icing tube again, it occurred to her just how long it had been since she'd last made one of these. Not since she was a little girl, more concerned with eating the icing and candy than using it to make a house. But she remembered the feelings that came with it, as she and her mom would make the house while the fireplace crackled and Christmas music played on their stereo: feelings of excitement and joy for what was just days away. The gingerbread house was one more sign that Christmas Day was coming.

How much she had changed since then. If she hadn't gotten stuck at Cedarwood, she probably wouldn't have done a single Christmasy thing that entire year. No carols, no decorations, no tree, and definitely no gingerbread house. Heck, her plans for the day itself had been so low-key and uninvolved that it could have happened any day of the year.

No, she thought to herself, being back at camp had at least given her the chance to really experience the Christmas season again. To remember how much fun it could be. Even — or maybe especially — when she was doing it with a group who had been total strangers just two days earlier.

"Uh, Ash?" She snapped out of her thoughts as Janice waved an icing-covered hand in front of her face. "You with us?"

"Y-yeah," Ashley said. "Sorry, just really focusing on the backyard."

"It looks great," Janice said. "We need to start putting everything together now. Do you have steady hands?"

"Like a surgeon." Ashley grabbed two of the decorated wall pieces of gingerbread and held them at a right angle while Janice pressed the tube of icing against them to stick them together. Once the icing had dried she brought the third wall up, and then the fourth.

When the walls were firmly in place, Harvey gently placed the slanted roof on top of the house. Ashley found herself holding her breath as she waited to see if the structure would hold. To her relief, it did. It looked great, too: one side of the roof had miniature chocolates in the shape of stars, while the other had candy canes placed against each other to form hearts. Harvey had also lined the edges with swirls of icing that looked like snow hanging off of the eaves. Combined with the decorating along the front, back and side walls of the house, it looked like a real, professionally-made gingerbread house.

"Five more minutes!" Drew announced. Ashley looked over at the Frost Bites' table, but there were too many bodies standing around it to see what they had done. She focused back on her own table and getting the house's backyard in place. She carefully moved it to the rear of the house. Janice added a line of icing, from a near-empty tube, and Ashley carefully pushed the two parts together. When it became clear that neither was going to move any further, she pulled away and admired her team's handiwork.

"And that is time!" Drew announced. "Teams, be ready to present your houses to our potential buyers. Frost Bites, you're going first! Who is your presenter?"

Marc volunteered himself. He stood up, while the rest of his teammates sat down, finally allowing a view of their house. Ashley heard a few "oohs" and "ahhs" from her team.

Their opponents had gone with the two-story option, creating a house that looked more like a tower. The one side Ashley could see was decorated with small silver balls and M&Ms, which zig-zagged back and forth on the way down. It was good. Very good.

"If you are looking for the perfect place to live, there is nothing better than Gingerbread Tower," Marc said. He had a smarmy, salesman voice. "With its multiple levels, this tower has plenty of room for the whole family, while offering great views of Gingerbread Town. Buy now!"

He swung his arm out dramatically with those last words. Then it happened. His hand hit the tower's second story, which wobbled a few times, came loose, and fell over. It crashed into the table, breaking the gingerbread into numerous pieces and sending candy flying everywhere.

The first story shook and then fell over as well, launching silver candy balls across the table and onto the floor. In just seconds, the entire tower had collapsed into a heap of gingerbread and sweets.

Marc stood frozen in place, his hand hovering where it had made contact with the gingerbread tower, his mouth and eyes wide with shock. A collective gasp emitted from everyone else.

Ashley covered her own mouth as she started laughing. The rest of the Ice Dinosaurs made no such efforts to conceal their joy. Janice was doubled over and holding her sides, while Adam kept screaming "No way! No way!" ecstatically. Marc's teammates, meanwhile, dropped their heads and looked away. Ashley felt a momentary twinge of sympathy for them. All that work, gone in an instant.

David, clearly struggling to maintain his own composure, spoke up. "That was an unfortunate incident, but the game isn't over yet! Ice Dinosaurs, it's your turn to present!"

Ashley nearly leapt out of her chair. "I'll do it." She took a few steps back and addressed the crowd. "What matters most to a family? Stability." In front of her, Carol snorted. "A stable marriage, a stable job, a stable routine, and, of course, a stable house. And with this gorgeous bungalow, complete with a spacious backyard, you can ensure that you'll

be living in a house that won't collapse on you. That's our guarantee!"
She finished with a thumbs-up.

Janice started clapping. The rest of her team joined in. David and
Drew looked at each other and nodded. "I think our winner is clear,"
Drew said. "Ice Dinosaurs get the point!"

Ashley raised her hands and high-fived her teammates. "Now,"
David said, "we did promise that you would get to destroy and eat your
opponent's house, but it seems that they already did the work for you."

Ashley looked back at Marc. He was still standing, staring blankly at
where the tower had been a minute earlier. He looked like a boy who'd
just watched his pet fish get flushed down the toilet. She tried not to
delight so much in his error, but after all the ribbing he'd given her about
the archery competition, it was hard not to.

"Let's eat our own house!" Adam shouted. He raised his hand and
smashed it onto the roof, then grabbed a handful of gingerbread and
candy and shoved it into his mouth.

"Adam!" Paige scolded. She looked mortified at his behavior.

The boy seemed to be in pure joy as he chewed on the confection. It
was the exact state Ashley wanted him to be in. This was meant to be the
best Christmas ever, and how could that be possible without eating a
freshly made gingerbread house?

"He's got the right idea!" Ashley shouted. She broke off a piece of the
wall and put it in her mouth. The combination of the hard gingerbread
with the soft and chewy gummies was certainly an interesting texture,
but it was all so sweet that she didn't mind.

Harvey's kids wasted no time in diving in, and the remaining adults
followed. Paige's mortification fell to annoyance and then happiness as
she split a large piece of the roof with her son. At the other table, the Frost
Bites salvaged and feasted on what they could from their destroyed
tower.

When both structures had been consumed, the competitors cleaned
up and then headed out of the Lodge. Ashley walked over to Marc, who

had broken out of his trance and was now sweeping the bits of candy off the floor. "What a presentation," she said. "You really brought the house down."

He bit down on his lip and shook his head. "I supposed I deserve that after last night, huh?"

"Yes, but there's a lot more where it came from. There's definitely a joke about the Tower of Babel somewhere that I'll find a way to use."

"Uh huh?" He pulled the broom up to his body and leaned on it. "You sure you want to be so mean to a guy who has something you could really use?"

Her arms tingled. For a moment, she once again thought of his bulging chest and rock-hard abs. "What would that be?"

"A truck, and a trip into town," Marc said. "You want to go tonight? You can do any shopping you need. Also, there's cell reception there."

It was an offer that didn't require any consideration. "I'm in."

Marc smiled. "Great. We'll go after we crush you in the evening's competition."

"Don't hold your breath," she replied. "And next time you're taking a shower, maybe try locking the door?"

He raised an eyebrow. "I will, just as soon as someone complains."

She gave him a look and then headed for the door. A few hours in town, to get some necessities and at least check her texts and emails, would be a godsend.

But first, she needed to get a charger. She stepped out into the bright daylight, made even brighter by all the untouched snow surrounding her, and walked over to Janice's cabin. The door opened before she even knocked. "Hey, quick question," Ashley said. "Do you have a phone charger I can use?"

"You bet! What kind?" Before Ashley could respond, Janice stepped away from the door. A few second later she was back with a half-dozen cables in her hand. "Take whatever one you need!"

Ashley found the right kind for her phone. "Thanks. You're the best."

"I do what I can, Ash." Another smile, and then the door closed.

Ashley walked back to her cabin, fiddling with the cable in her hands. She had probably experienced more kindness — more pure, unearned, undemanding kindness — in the last two days than in the full year that had come before it. She grinned and put a hand to her chest.

Her heart felt very warm.

Chapter 19

After another delicious lunch, this time grilled cheese that was perfectly crispy on the outside and filled with gooey cheese on the inside, David announced to everyone that the next competition would start at one and that they would all meet at the Lodge. "Be sure to wear warmth clothes," he added. "This is going to be quite a snowy event."

"What do you think that means?" Ashley asked Carol as they left the meal hall.

The woman only laughed. "Oh, you'll see. I don't want to ruin the surprise."

Half an hour later, Ashley was back at the Lodge's steps, waiting for the rest of her team to join her. She'd taken David's advice seriously and thrown on two of Emma's sweaters and what looked like an older pair of jeans, then zipped up Janice's coat as tightly as possible. If this were going to be a "snowy event," whatever that meant, she was as prepared for it as she could be.

Adam and Paige were the first to join her, with Adam nearly bouncing up to her in his puffy red snowsuit. "Someone's excited," Ashley said.

"My dad told me what we're doing!" he gushed from under his green scarf. "It's the best event yet!"

That did little to calm her. Anything a ten-year-old boy found exciting was bound to be one a thirty-three-year-old woman would hesitate to do. "Can you tell me what it is?"

Adam shook his head. "It's a surprise!"

The others joined them. When both teams were fully present, David and Drew walked out of the Lodge. Ashley was happy to see that Drew's crutches weren't anywhere in sight, even if he did lean on the railing while David spoke. "If you will follow us."

David helped Drew down the steps and onto the toboggan. The others started walking towards the field that led to the cabins.

Ashley came up next to Marc. "Do you know where we're going?"
He looked over at her and smirked. "Of course."

"But you're not going to tell me, are you?"

"And ruin the surprise? Of course not."

The field was a lot easier to cross with all the footprints that were in it, to say nothing of the large paths that had been formed from rolling the snowballs for the previous day's event. The group reached the cabins and kept going. Ashley looked down towards where her cabin had been. She'd need to check it out at some point.

As they walked through the cabin area, Ashley realized there was only one place they could be heading: the camp's beach, which lay at the bottom of a long, winding gravel road. She remembered lining her campers up many times as they waited to get in and go swimming. On hot days, after hours of running around and working up a sweat, there was nothing better than coming around the final turn and seeing the blue water shimmering under the bright sun.

David and Drew (who seemed to be having the time of his life on the sled) moved to the front of the group and stopped at the top of the beach's road. Ashley could see that it had been shaped into what looked like a tobogganing track. The snow was flattened and the turns had massive snowbanks along them. Was that what they were going to do — go sledding?

"Welcome to the Camp Cedarwood Tubing Track!" Drew announced. He stood up, supported by David's shoulder.

"Tubing track?" Ashley asked aloud. Marc glanced over at her and grinned.

"For your next event in the Christmas Cup," Drew continued, "each team will send a played down the track on an inflatable tube. They will soar down this hundred-meter route before reaching the lake, where we have set up markers with different point values. Each player will receive points equal to the furthest marker they pass, and the team with the most points at the end will win the event!"

"Oh no," Ashley murmured, while everyone else cheered excitedly. There was nothing about this she wanted: not flying across snow on an inner tube, not trying to navigate the path without wiping out, and certainly not ending up on the frozen lake. Suddenly, doing archery again didn't seem so bad.

"Since the Ice Dinosaurs are currently in the lead, they will go first," David said. He walked behind one of the cabins and pulled out two massive black inner tubes, each the size of a truck tire. "Who wants to give it a go?"

Without hesitation, Carol raised her hand. "Oh y'all know I've been waiting all year for this!"

David pointed to the left. "If everyone heads over that way, you'll have a full view of the track."

Ashley followed the group to a spot behind the cabins that overlooked the track and lake. Her stomach dropped as she took it all in. The path was steeper than she remembered, with a good five turns—two of them tight, hairpin turns—that led to the beach and lake, all covered in snow and ice, making it impossible to tell where the sand ended and the water started. About fifty feet down was a lit torch, with the number 1 spray-painted next to it. Fifty feet further down was another torch, with a 2 spray-painted. Another fifty feet, one more torch and the number 3. Finally, two hundred or so feet from the shore, was the final torch and the number 5. Anyone who could go the full distance would be a huge boon to their team.

"Everyone ready?" David shouted. He stood at the top of the track. In front of him, lying face-up on the tube, was Carol. She held her mitten up and raised her thumb. "Here we go! Three, two, one... go!"

He gave her a push. The tube started sliding down the path, quickly picking up speed. Carol yelled "Yeehaw!" as the tube hit the first turn and flew up along the steep bank. Ashley gasped and looked at the rest of the group. They were all laughing and cheering Carol on.

The tube continued down the path, hitting the second turn even faster and gliding along the snowbank a good ten feet up. A constant stream of "Whee!" and "Woo!" flowed from Carol's mouth. She was clearly having the time of her life. Ashley could only watch her in stunned silence. How could that be fun?

The tube travelled faster and faster as it sailed down the path and along each turn. Carol ripped along the final curve and flew out onto the lake, her body spinning around like it was on some sort of amusement park ride. She soared past the first torch, then the second, and then slowed down and was barely able to pass the third. When her tube finally came to a stop, she lay there for a few seconds before rolling out onto the ice. She stood up and raised her hands above her head. "Let's do it again!"

"You'll have your turn!" David shouted from the top of the track. His voice carried across the lake. "Okay, Frost Bites, who's next?"

Jack's daughter ran towards him, with Jack right behind. Jack climbed in first, and then his daughter lay on top of him, arms wrapped around his shoulders. Ashley looked over at Emma, expecting to see horror on her face. Instead, she was smiling as her husband and child got ready to race down the tube track. Ashley wondered what was wrong with all these people.

Jack and his daughter flew down the course just as fast as Carol. Every three seconds it looked like the girl was going to fly right off of her dad, but she stayed on throughout, all the way to their stop a few feet past the three-point marker. "Now that's what I call father-daughter bonding," Roger said. He looked over at his wife.

Carol finished climbing up a nearby stairway and dropped her tube in front of David and Drew. Ian went next, while his dad and sister stayed back and watched him. Instead of sitting down in the tube and waiting for a push, he took a running start and jumped onto it on his stomach. He rocketed down the course, seeming to shift his small body at each turn to keep from going too far up the banks, and was absolutely flying as he reached the lake. He cleared the first and second torches in a second, slowed down only slightly for the third and still had plenty of momentum as he reached the last one. He ended a good thirty feet past the five-point torch, drawing lots of cheers and clapping from teammate and opponent alike.

"Wow," Janice said to Harvey. "He looked like a pro out there."

"He loves it," Harvey said. "He built his own track in our backyard and goes down it in a pool floatie." He shook his head and chuckled. "He has his mother's taste for adventure, that's for sure."

There were a few awkward glances as Harvey mentioned his deceased wife, but the tension was broken when Drew called for the next tuber. Roger walked over and was the next one down, getting his team three points.

The teams went back and forth for a few runs before it was Adam's turn. He confidently approached the tube and laid it down at the top of the track. Then he took a few steps back and ran onto it, just as Ian had. Like the other boy, Adam zipped down the track and hit the first two turns with ease, but seemed to lose control at the third, with his tube briefly leaving the ground as he curved along the bank.

"Oh boy," Paige said as her son sped toward the fourth turn, clearly lacking any control of the tube. It hit the bank, climbed all the way up it and flipped in midair. Adam shouted and crashed onto the ground, the big, black inner tube landing on top of him.

"Adam!" Ashley screamed along with his mom. She started toward the track, but stopped as Adam kicked the tube off and stood back up. He jumped back on top of his ride and continued down, taking the last turn with ease and just making it past the first torch.

Paige smiled and rolled her eyes. "What did I tell you?" she said. "He's a fighter."

Chapter 20

Marc, unsurprisingly, soared through the course and cleared the five-point torch like it was nothing. "He probably practices every day," Ashley muttered to no one in particular.

Drew called over to the group. "Who has yet to go?"

Ashley looked around. It was just her, Harvey and Bill. She started to gesture to Harvey, but Janice stopped her. "His daughter doesn't want him to do it," she whispered. Ashley lowered her hand. It made sense why she'd be scared to see her dad go down such a course.

"Guess I don't have much of a choice, then," she said, mainly to herself. She walked over to the start of the track. "I'll do it!"

There was a chorus of "oooh"s from the crowd. She felt her entire body shake as she looked from the big black tube to the track. She sighed. Time to get it over with.

David lay the tube flat and held it as she got on. The large tube felt even bigger with her back and rear hanging over the opening in the middle. Unlike the kinds of inner tubes she'd used on the water a handful of times, this one had no handles or grips. She was at the mercy of gravity to hold her in place during the ride.

"Now remember," Drew said, sounding like a gameshow host, "the Ice Dinosaurs currently lead by two points. If you manage to get five points, you're guaranteed to win the event. If you get three, the best the Frost Bites can do is tie it up. There's a lot riding on this."

"I can see how much is riding on this," Ashley said. She looked down at her body, splayed out like a rag doll on the tube. Getting points would be great, but surviving was the key priority.

David put his hands on the tube. "And three, two, one... have fun!"

He gave it a hard push and the inner tube started sliding down the track. Ashley's stomach lurched as it dropped and quickly sped up. "Wait!" she shouted. "I don't want to—ahh!"

The tube hit the first turn and began to spin around. Ashley reached out and tried to grab something to stabilize herself, but there was nothing for her gloved hands to grasp. Mountains of white snow whirled around her, all while the inner tube continued to speed up. She briefly considered bailing out of the tube, but decided against it, both to avoid the pain of hitting the icy track, as well as the fear of letting her team down once again.

Before she could get her bearings, the inner tube hit the second turn and climbed up the large snowbank. It briefly slowed before sliding back down. The turn caused the spinning to stop, but it stopped with Ashley's head now at the front of the tube. As she continued down the track, Ashley could only look back at where she had already been, with no idea what lay ahead.

Ashley suddenly dropped — with a scream of fright — as the path grew steeper. Not knowing what was coming next making this all the worse. She tried to shift her weight and turn the tube, but it was impossible. Just try to enjoy yourself, she thought. The next turn will be any —

She was suddenly upright, looking at the path that lay ahead. The tube dropped back down, with Ashley now heading feet-first down the track. Having spent the last ten seconds struggling to see where she was going, she now regretted having the view of the drop in front of her. The track was so much steeper in person than when she was watching it from fifty feet away.

The tube blasted down the slope. The next turn, easily the biggest of the entire course, quickly approached. Ashley could feel the cold air and bits of snow whipping against her face. Everyone else had been shouting for joy as they'd done this. What on earth was wrong with them?

She hit the snowbank and jetted upward. Time seemed to slow as the tube climbed higher and higher, until it was completely perpendicular to the ground. For a brief moment, her entire body lost contact with the rubber. Ashley again tried to grab onto something so that she wouldn't end up on the ground like Adam.

Then she felt herself dropping back down and landing on the tube. She was once again spinning and resigned herself to the fact that this would be how her run ended. She felt herself hit the last turn and then the ground flattened out and she gradually slowed down and came to a stop. She could hear cheering as she gave herself a minute for the dizziness to pass.

When the world had stopped spinning around her, she pushed herself off the tube and rolled onto the snow. She was about ten feet past the two-point marker. It wasn't great, but not too bad either. She had made it all the way down, and the ice under her hadn't given way.

She picked the tube up and rolled it up the stairs. "Great work, Ash!" Drew shouted. He turned to the older man standing next to him. "Bill, you need five points in order to win. Think you can do it?"

"Oh, I don't think I can do it," Bill said, directing his voice to the crowd. "I KNOW I can do it! Let's go!"

He took a few steps and dove onto the tube, not unlike the boys who were a fraction of his age. He was at full speed by the second turn, and while he didn't have any of finesse of Ian or Marc, he managed to stay in the tube as it bounced around like a pinball. Ashley could hear him hooting and hollering the entire way down.

He curved along the final turn and was onto the lake with plenty of speed. He sped past the first torch and the second, and by that point it was clear he was going all the way. The Frost Bites shouted loudly as Bill crossed the five-point marker. "Frost Bites win!" Drew shouted. "Great work from both teams! It was a close match!"

Bill came to a stop, hopped off his tube and then lifted it above his head with a fierce cry. Carol laughed and shook her head. "This will be his proudest moment of the entire year," she said. "I wish he went at housework with that kind of intensity."

Marc announced that the tubing track would be open for the rest of the afternoon. Though most of the guests ran to line up for another run, Ashley had no interest in it and was already walking back towards the cabins. There was something she needed to see.

After walking a few feet, she veered off to the right, towards a section that was surrounded by untouched snow. She found herself in front of a semi-circle of ten cabins, all covered in a blanket of white.

The third one from the right seemed to stick out like a sore thumb. There was nothing physically or aesthetically different about it, but after being her home for an entire summer, it may as well have been covered in neon lights and flashing arrows. How many times had she walked these grounds and gone through the green fabric flaps that covered the door? Hundreds of times, at least. Even with all the years that had passed, it still felt a bit like home.

She trudged up to it but was disappointed to find that the flaps had been stapled down and a rope had been tied around the entire cabin, holding the fabric down further and preventing any access to the cabin. She frowned. It made sense that the cabins were sealed up for the winter, but she was disappointed nonetheless.

Ashley walked back into the middle of the section and closed her eyes. She pictured the trees full of green leaves, the ground free of snow, with the sounds of campers laughing and running in and out of the cabins. Her own cabin's flaps were pulled aside, revealing bunks with sleeping bags strewn around, suitcases that were open and had clothes pouring out of them, and more than a few bags of candy and chocolate wrappers laying on the floor.

Her attention moved two cabins to the left. The flaps parted as a tall young man with bleach-blonde hair walked out. He was shirtless, but instead of a skinny frame with little definition, he was rocking a full six-pack and had a bulging chest and shoulders. "Hey Ash," he said. "Ash? Ash?"

"Ash!" Ashley snapped out of her daydream to find Janice standing right in front of her. "Earth to Ash? Anyone home?"

"Um, yeah, sorry," Ashley said sheepishly. She pulled her scarf up higher to hide her red cheeks. "I was lost in thought."

"Reminiscing?" Janice asked, in a knowing tone.

"Something like that." Ashley cleared her throat. "What are you up to now?"

"I'm heading back to my cabin. Need to wrap a present, then probably take a nap."

"A nap sounds like a great idea." Ashley stepped away from the middle of the section and started walking back with Janice. "Though isn't it a bit late to be wrapping presents? Roger might have seen your gift."

"It's not for Roger. I got Drew for Secret Santa and I'd picked out two shirts for him because I didn't know his size. I finally was able to get Sally alone and ask. Now I know which one to wrap and which to give to my nephew."

"Wait," Ashley said. "There's a Secret Santa?"

"Every year. Marc sends out each person's giftee in November and then we all leave our gifts in the Lodge for people to get on Christmas Day."

"That sounds great. But I don't have a gift to give."

Janice shrugged. "I don't think you'd have a person to give it to anyway. But maybe ask Marc?"

She nodded. "We're heading into town tonight, so I can pick something up."

Janice looked at her from the side of her eyes. "You guys are going into town?"

"Yep. There are a few things I need to get. Would probably also be good to respond to anyone who's trying to figure out where I am."

"Well, have fun." They reached the winterized cabins. Janice yawned. "My bed is calling me. I'll see you in a few hours."

"Sleep tight," Ashley said. They parted ways and she went back to her own cabin. After flying down the icy track on an unstable rubber tube, there was no better feeling than kicking off her boots and falling back onto her secure, stationary bed.

Chapter 21

Gunter had enlisted a few neighbors to help prepare dinner, so Ashley wasn't needed in the kitchen. Instead she walked around the meal hall and fixed up some of the decorations — adjusting the streams of tinsel, hanging up the paper bells that had fallen and cleaning bits of food and dirt off of the table trinkets. When she was done she stood in the middle and looked around, feeling surprisingly satisfied. Just a few days ago, any sort of Christmas decorating would have disgusted her. Now, she had a sense of pride and responsibility for these decorations.

She sat with Paige, Adam and David for a dinner of pulled pork sandwiches and corn on the cob, both tasting like they had been imported from genuine southern barbecue joint. Adam talked nonstop about the tubing track and the numerous runs he made down it during the afternoon. Ashley tried her best to look interested and impressed and not give off how terrified she had been of flying down the course. She'd read that most kids didn't develop a full understanding of risk and danger until they were well into adulthood. Adam was proof of that.

After dessert of strawberries and freshly whipped cream, Drew and David walked up to the stage. "Since tomorrow is Christmas Eve, and we know that you all have things to take care of this evening, we are going to get our next competition going right now," Drew said. Ashley glanced over at Marc, who nodded back. "So…" Drew continued. "It's time for the Camp Cedarwood annual Christmas Carol-off!"

Adam started bouncing up and down in his chair. "Yes! Yes! I've been practicing for this one for like a month!"

Paige rolled her eyes. "He really has. I can't count how many times we've woken up to 'Jingle Bells' blasting from his room."

David took the microphone. "Here's how it works. We will call a member from each team up here and give them a song. Both competitors must sing the song at the same time. The first person to miss a word loses the round and their opponent gets the point!"

Ashley rubbed her forehead. Now she wished she'd kept the radio on when she'd been driving.

"Let's start with our team captains, Carol and Bill!" David beckoned the two up. They both faced each other, with him in the middle, like they were on some sort of gameshow. "Let's start with a hard one: 'Santa Claus is Coming to Town.'"

The couple took a breath and began to sing:

"You better watch out, you better not cry,
You better not pout, I'm telling you why,
Santa Claus is coming to town,
He sees you when you're sleeping,
He knows – "

Carol sang, "when you're awake" but Bill belted out, "when you awake." David held his hands up.

"Bill, those are not the correct lyrics. Carol gets the point!" Ashley applauded as the two took their seats. "For our next round, come on up Janice and Roger!"

The two stared each other down – in what Ashley hoped was a joking manner – as David read out the next song: Up on the Housetop. Neither looked particularly at ease with the carol, but they both started:

"Up on the housetop, reindeer paws,
Out comes good ol' Santa Claus,
Down through the chimney with lots of toys,
All for the little ones…"

Roger sang "Christmas joys" while Janice sang "girls and boys." Drew raised his hands. "Roger had the correct lyrics. He gets a point!"

Roger looked over at his wife. "Girls and boys on your mind, honey?"

Emma, Jack and their two daughters all faced off for the next song. They sang "Deck the Halls" surprisingly well, but Emma muffed on the last line of the verse and Jack's team got the point.

When they were done, David said, "Next, since I know they've both been looking forward to this event for months, let's call Adam up to compete against Sally."

Adam jumped out of his chair and ran to the front. Sally walked up, cracking her knuckles and then interlocking her fingers and stretching them in front of her. Adam offered his hand and she shook it. "Alright singers, we know you've been practicing hard, so we're going to give you a real song to sink your teeth into. Here we go: O Holy Night, the stars are brightly shining…"

Adam and Sally locked eyes and continued the song:
"It is the night of the dear Savior's birth,
Long lay the world in sin and ever pining,
Til he appeared and the soul found its worth."

Ashley looked over at Paige in surprise. "How does he know this? I don't even know the first line of this one!"

"He takes this really seriously," Paige replied.

They reached the chorus:
"Fall on your knees, and hear the voices ringing,
Oh night divine, o night when Christ was born,
Oh night divine…"

Adam's next words were "oh night, oh night divine," while Sally's were "oh night, oh holy night."

David stopped them. "Sally, I'm afraid that is not the correct lyrics. Adam wins the point!"

His son threw his hands in the air. "Boo yah!" He skipped back to his mom, beaming under his mask.

"We're all tied up, so let's call our final competitors," Drew said. "Ashley and Marc!"

"Don't expect much," Ashley said to Paige. She walked up and joined Marc at the front.

He offered his hand. "Best of luck."

She shook it with a hard shake. "May the best woman win."

"Your song is..." Drew said. "The Camp Cedarwood Anthem."

Ashley grinned, her smile matching Marc's. After all this time, the words were still fresh in her head. It was bound to happen after singing it every morning for an entire summer.

They both took a deep breath and started singing:

"Hail to Camp Cedarwood, lift your voices high,
Now in song salute her, echoing to the sky,
Trees and mountains surround her, under skies so blue,
Flowing lakes and rivers, calling now to you,
Your magic is forever, clear for all to see,
Oh Camp Cedarwood, how we really love thee!"

Ashley stopped. They'd both completed the song. Was Drew going to give them another?

Marc took another breath and kept singing.

"And when the skies are dark and the moon is full and white,
Look for me to guide you on until the morning light,
I point and reach, continue home, until I speak to you,
For where you find my lasting wealth, your treasure will be too."

Ashley looked at him in confusion. "What was that?" she asked. "Are we allowed to make up verses now?"

Drew shook his head. "That's actually the second verse in the song. It was dropped a while back to make the song shorter, and also because no one understood what it meant." He raised his hand. "Marc gets the point, and the win! Frost Bites now lead with a score of four to the Ice Dinosaurs' three!"

Frowning, Ashley returned to her seat. "That wasn't fair," Adam hissed. "Of course only Marc would know that. They should have you redo it with another song!"

"Honestly," Ashley said, "I doubt I would have done any better."

"Still, he probably paid Drew to use that one."

Paige wrapped her arms around him. "Probably. That's what they need to beat us. Maybe Ash can ask him later tonight." She winked at Ashley.

"Uh, yeah, maybe I'll bring it up." Ashley looked away. What was that comment supposed to mean? Did Paige know the two of them were heading into town? Even if she did, what was she trying to imply?

David wished everyone a good night and the guests began to leave the Lodge. Ashley grabbed her coat and walked up to Marc, trying not to think about Paige's remark. This was just the two of them getting some things and maybe taking some time to catch up. There was nothing more to it than that.

Even if she wanted there to be.

Marc grinned at her. "Before you even say it, I had no idea Drew was going to use that song."

"I'm sure you didn't." She crossed her arms. "Tell you what. You don't bring up any of my Christmas Cup failings tonight, and I won't bring up any of yours."

Marc gave her a pat on the shoulder. "Deal. Now let's hit the town."

Chapter 22

Of all the things Marc had expected for Christmas Camp—inclement weather, power failures, food spoilage, missing presents, unenthusiastic campers—none of them came even close to Ash climbing into his SUV, giving him a big smile and saying, "Let's go."

He found himself just staring at her, taking in this moment that he never thought would have ever been possible. When they'd said goodbye as the sun set those fifteen years ago, he had figured it was the last time they'd ever see each other, the last conversation they'd ever have, and while it took him a bit of time to let go, he'd been able to move on. If he were being honest with himself, it had probably been years since he'd really thought of her, aside from a quick passing memory that may have elicited a smile.

And yet now she was here, and she'd been here for two days, and it was like she had never left, even though in two more days she'd be on her way again. It was a lot to deal with. It felt like the past, present and future were all converging into one moment, here in the truck with her.

"What?" she asked playfully, clearly noticing his stare. "Do I have something on my face?"

"Oh, no, no," he said. He snapped out of his daze and put the vehicle into drive. Just enjoy the moment, he thought. The two of you are together again, just like old times.

He steered the SUV up the winding driveway. The two feet of snow was no match for the all-wheel drive and snow tires. "You have a good day?"

"Really good," she said. "Everyone here is just so nice. A bit weird, but genuinely nice."

He chuckled. "That's the camp effect. It tends to bring out the weirdness in everyone. You're isolated from the rest of the world and living in close community, so of course you're going to let out the side of you that you keep hidden most of the time."

They pulled out of the driveway and started up the hill leading to the country road. This was even easier: there were already multiple tire tracks from the other residents that formed a path for him to follow. "You think camp brings out the kindness in people too?" Ash asked.

"Maybe, but not that much," he replied. He reached the top of the hill and turned onto the road. "I don't think coming to camp makes people nicer. I think it's that nice people are the ones who tend to come to camp in the first place."

He felt her eyes briefly glance over at him. "I'd believe it."

They sat in silence for a minute as Marc drove. The road wasn't plowed, but there had been enough driving on it to form a rudimentary path, with large banks on either side. It was normally a ten-to-fifteen minute drive into town, but with this snow it would probably be closer to twenty. Not that he was going to complain.

He turned on the radio and was met with Bing Crosby singing "White Christmas." Ash groaned and tilted her head back. "Do we have to listen to that?"

"Of course not." He hit over to the next station. A pop song came on. "Had a bit too much Christmas music?"

"Please. One song is a bit too much for me."

"Really? You seemed to be fine at Cedarwood."

She waved her hand in front of her. "That's different. Outside of camp, I'm really not much of a Christmas person."

"Fair enough." He figured there was a story behind it, but he didn't want to press. He inched the volume up slightly higher and continued on towards the town.

*   *   *

The truck crested over a small hill and Ashley suddenly found herself looking down on a valley of light. The town lay about a mile away, nestled between two mountains and with a river running through it. She immediately thought back to her time as a counselor, when she would come here on her days off to stock up on candy, grab a meal that hadn't been prepared for 150 other people, and just spend a few hours away from Cedarwood.

Back then, the town had basically been a Main Street consisting of five or six blocks. Now, as Marc drove down the hill, she could see that it had really hit a growth spurt over the last decade and a half, with rows of streets lit up in bright white and red lights, showing blocks and neighborhoods that had not existed when she had last been there.

Getting closer, she could make out individual buildings that shone against the darkness. The church in the middle of the town, its massive steeple covered in a stream of white lights. The town hall across from it, likely the only three-story building within fifty miles. Her eyes tracked along the town's river, visible only by the numerous lights that followed along either side of its winding banks. She stopped at a large bend. That's where Patty's had been. She must have had ten meals in that diner — sometimes lunch, sometimes dinner, sometimes both. Almost every time, it had been with Marc. She smiled and wondered if the restaurant was still there.

"I hope you can handle all the Christmas spirit here," Marc said. The SUV reached the bottom of the hill and he turned left, onto the Main Street. "It can be a bit much."

He wasn't lying. The entire street was decorated like it was the North Pole, going down as far as Ashley could see. Every streetlamp had a green wreath with a big red bow hanging from it. There were Christmas lights everywhere, from big colored bulbs along shop windows and roofs, to little flashing ones wrapped around street poles and benches, to soft white ones strung over the road, creating the feeling of a tunnel of light as Ashley travelled under them.

Snowmen — snowpeople — seemed to be in front of every shop, each of them decked out to represent their store. The snowperson in front of the grocery store had apples for buttons. The one in front of a clothing boutique had a blouse and scarf. In front of the butcher was a snowperson with a massive stomach. Ashley laughed. Unlike the kitschy

Christmas displays that were so common in the city, this all seemed organic and genuine. Was it a bit much? Sure. But it felt like it came from the heart of a community that loved the holidays, and not from people who were trying to use it to sell more stuff.

Marc parallel parked — rather well, at that — in front of the hardware store with a snowperson wearing a toolbelt and hardhat. They walked across the plowed sidewalk, passing several people who smiled and waved at them. "You know them?" Ashley asked.

Marc shook his head. "Nope."

They entered the store. It was surprisingly large, with about ten spacious aisles going back a good fifty feet and bare fluorescent lights hanging above. She figured that, next to the grocery store, this was probably the most-visited place in town, especially in the winter. It had to be a constant struggle against the elements out here.

Marc led her past piles of two-by-fours and what had to be fifty different types of drills, to multiple shelves filled with Christmas lights and decorations. "You said you wanted to decorate your cabin, right?"

"I did." She looked over the plethora of different items and considered what would look good on the roof and hanging from the walls. The good news was that, thanks to the enthusiasm of the other campers, there was no way she could overdo things. But she also wanted something that reflected her own personality and was not just some sort of generic mess of decorations.

Some electric lanterns caught her eye, as did some realistic holly. She grabbed a few of each, and then added a few more boxes of Christmas lights. She'd forgotten to grab a cart at the entrance and found herself carrying everything in her arms. "Think you could give me a hand?" she asked Marc, holding the top of the boxes down with her chin.

"I could," he said, "but watching you like this is pretty entertaining." She shot him a glare and he took a few of the boxes off of her hands.

The cashier, an older man with big bushy eyebrows and a mess of white hair, smiled as they approached and nodded to Marc. "How're things at Cedarwood?"

"Just great," Marc said. "That attachment you gave for the plow is phenomenal. Handled the dumping we got a few days ago like it was made of feathers."

"Oh good." The man entered each of Ashley's items on an old-school register. There were no barcode scanners here. "How will you be paying?"

She pulled her wallet from her purse. "Do you take credit card?"

Marc gave her a look while the man laughed. "Of course we do! Where do you think you are, the moon?"

She paid and he put all the items into large plastic bags. Ashley thanked him and Marc waved goodbye. They dropped the bags off in the trunk of his truck. "Where next?" Marc asked.

"I could use some winter clothes of my own." She gestured down to the expensive coat she was wearing. "The last thing I want to do is damage Janice's jacket. I still can't believe she let me borrow it."

He shrugged. "I can. She's like that. But I know where we can go. You okay to walk a few blocks?"

"Of course." After a few days of trudging across fields and through forests, a plowed sidewalk may as well have been a sandy beach.

They headed down the street, passing dozens of people as they went. Most of them carried large boxes or bags stuffed to the brim with presents, but Ashley spotted quite a few people going at a more leisurely pace, clearly just taking in the sights. Especially cute were the couples, from teenagers to the elderly, walking hand-in-hand or arm-in-arm, their heads raised and looking at the twinkling lights above.

At one point they passed by a couple, maybe a few years older than them, pushing a stroller, with a small boy running alongside them. The man reached down, picked the boy up and put him on his shoulders, allowing the tot to reach up for the Christmas lights overhead. Ashley sighed and felt a small pang in her heart. It sure looked nice.

Marc looked over at her. "You okay?"

"Oh, yeah, I'm great," she said. "By the way, Janice mentioned a Secret Santa thing that was going on. Should I get something for it?"

"No, no, it's fine. I was able to rearrange all the givers and receivers. It was mainly that Adam's giver wasn't able to make it, but his parents are just going to slap a 'From Secret Santa' tag on one of their gifts to him, so it's all good."

She furrowed her brow. "Is it? Sounds to me like Adam is going to be out a present."

"I've seen what his parents get him every year. I think he'll have more than enough." He stopped and pointed to the store on their right. In front of it was a snowperson wearing a thick parka. "Here's where you can get a coat."

They went in and were greeted by the shopkeeper, who also asked Marc how Cedarwood was going. While they talked, Ashley made her way through a bunch of coat racks, looking for something that fit and looked decent on her. She pulled out a few ski and winter jackets that seemed warm but were so bright and colorful they would likely stand out at a circus, as well as some darker jackets that looked good but were so thick and puffy she doubted she'd be able to move in them, let alone participate in the remaining Christmas Cup events. With only three left, and her team down a point, she had to be able to bring her A-game to whatever events she faced.

She caught her reflection in one of the mirrors and smiled to herself. "You're caring about a cheesy competition at a camp in the middle of nowhere," she murmured. "Like it's one of your biggest clients or something." She thought for a second, and then nodded. "Yeah, that seems right."

Ashley looked over and saw a light green coat hanging on its own. She took it off the rack and tried it on. It was warm, flexible and looked only slightly ridiculous. It was good enough for her. She carried it up to the cash register. The woman was in the middle of a conversation with Marc. "That's so sad," she said, putting a hand over her heart. "Do let him know I'm praying for him. He's such a nice boy."

"Everything okay?" Ashley asked. She put the jacket on the counter.

"Just telling her about Adam," Marc said.

"He was in here last year," the woman said. "He had ripped his jacket and needed it sewed up. Said he'd been running through a forest when it got caught on a branch. He was such a sweetheart! I patched it up in five minutes, didn't charge him for it, and he seemed so grateful! But you know, I could tell something was off with him. He was so skinny and frail, even for a young boy."

"Yeah..." Ashley said slowly. She briefly glared at Marc. This didn't feel like an appropriate conversation to be having. "Anyway, I'll take the jacket, please."

Again, an older register was used to ring the purchase up. Ashley didn't ask about a credit card this time and simply paid with it. The woman put the jacket in a large paper bag with handles and handed it to her. Marc said goodbye and they left the store. Ashley decided she'd wait until they were back at Cedarwood to start wearing her new jacket — the last thing she wanted was to take off Janice's expensive coat and then lose it.

"Why were you telling her about Adam?" she asked as they continued down the sidewalk.

"She asked," he said simply. "I didn't tell her everything, just that he's still sick. It wasn't like she didn't know it already."

"But it's private information," she said, her voice rising. She could feel her skin getting hot. "Do you even know who that woman is? What if she gossips about it to the rest of the town?" Her voice became even louder and her breath short. "Or what if he doesn't make it, and now everyone knows that it's because he couldn't beat cancer? What then, Marc?"

He stopped and looked at her, his eyes narrow in concern. He reached out and put a hand on her shoulder. "Are you okay?"

Her lower lip trembled as she spoke. "I just... I don't know. He's just such a good kid and I hate seeing him and knowing, you know, that... well, that he could die."

Marc squeezed his hand. "You're feeling protective of him."

She took a deep breath. Now tears were starting to form in her eyes. "Yeah."

He nodded knowingly. "I see it all the time in Cedarwood's counselors. They care so much about their campers that they want to shelter them and not let anyone else get close. Like the campers are their kids."

Ashley huffed out a laugh. "That's about it. I may have met this boy three days ago, but I would literally go to war for him if I could."

"That's a good thing. It means you have a heart." Marc withdrew his hand. "But as I tell the counselors at the start of every summer, you can't solve all these kids' problems, no matter how much they mean to you. All you can do is give them an experience they'll never forget and help them take their minds off whatever problems may be waiting for them at home."

He looked down. Ashley became aware that they were getting looks from passersby. Here they were, her on the verge of tears, him standing awkwardly. They must have looked like they were going through a breakup or something. The thought of it made her cough out a chuckle, which turned into giggling, and then full-on laughter.

Marc looked back up at her. "What? What on earth is so funny right now?"

She wiped her eyes. "Is there a toy store around here?"

"Yes, about a block further down."

"Great, then let's get going." She started walking.

Marc chased after her. "Why? What do you need to get?"

She looked back at him. "We're getting a gift for Adam," she said. "And it's going to be the best damned Secret Santa gift in Cedarwood's history."

Chapter 23

The toy store, located in a red brick building between a veterinarian's office and a law practice, was like something out of the distant past. Ashley was met with rows of puzzles and toys on the store's shelves, while stuffed animals, many wearing Santa hats or miniature bells, hung from the ceiling. Warm light came not from above, but from lamps scattered throughout the store, giving a more familiar feeling to the place. Ashley could smell cinnamon in the air. It felt more like she was in someone's home than in a place of business.

"What do you think he'd like?" she asked, peering at the boxes of puzzles and board games.

"Something brainy." Marc picked up a chess set and looked it over before putting it back. "He's a smart kid. I think ninety percent of all his gifts have involved building things."

"No video games?" She pulled out a puzzle of a rainbow over a city, then decided it probably wasn't the right thing for him.

"Not unless you want Paige to strangle you."

They moved on to the next aisle. It was full of dexterous games, like wooden mazes and plastic brain teasers. Marc fumbled with a set of metal rings that somehow had to be disconnected from each other. He wasn't able to figure out how.

"Hey, speaking of puzzles," Ashley said, "that last verse of the Camp Cedarwood anthem. You ever think about it?"

"Not really. What do you mean?"

"I'm not sure," she said. "There's just something strange about it. Like it's saying more than just the wonder of camp. Like there's a hidden message."

"Uh huh? What do you want to do, sing it backwards?"

She shrugged. "I mean, it's worth a try." He grinned at her and shook his head. "What? What's so funny?"

"Nothing, nothing." It clearly wasn't nothing, but she brought her focus back to finding a gift.

The final aisle had numerous electronics, though all of them were geared towards education. There were games with flashing lights and sounds for babies and toddlers, trivia and spelling games for kids and a whole section devoted to engineering and robotics. It was here that Ashley found a build-your-own-robot kit, one that included red paint to decorate it. "Perfect."

She held it up for Marc, who nodded approvingly. "He'll love it."

She checked the price tag. "Hoo boy. Is there a spending limit on these gifts?"

"Not really. Why? How much is it?"

She tucked the box under her arm and started towards the front of the store. "About what a kid like Adam deserves."

The front counter had a string of blue and white Christmas lights along its front edge, as well as two mini plastic Christmas trees with real candy canes hanging on them next to the register. The cashier was a young woman who seemed rather tired — Ashley could hardly blame her — but was nonetheless polite and grateful for the purchase. She asked if Ashley wanted it wrapped, but Ashley declined. If this was going to be a real Secret Santa gift, she had to wrap it herself.

She put the kit in the same bag as her new coat and left. "Thanks," she said to Marc. "This was a fun time."

"Who says it has to end?" Marc asked. "It's barely even eight. I think we can stay out a bit longer."

"I don't know, think of all the trouble we'll get into if we're not back at Cedarwood by curfew. You know the Director is a real stickler for the rules." She raised an eyebrow at him. "But really, I'm hungry and could go for some cookies or whatever Gunter's prepared."

"You want to go back to Camp to eat?" he asked incredulously.

"We're in town. How 'bout we get some real food? Patty's is just two blocks away."

Her eyes went wide. "It's still open?"

"You think the best diner in the region would have closed down?" He tilted his head down the street. "C'mon!"

It was hard to resist such an offer. Marc took off, nearly running down the sidewalk, and Ashley chased after him, her big bag swinging back and forth as she tried to keep up. They passed the church just as its bells sounded out the top of the hour, and crossed the street to the town hall, passing a large Christmas tree wrapped in a rainbow of lights.

"Can you… please… slow down?" Ashley panted. She was afraid the handles on her bag were going to break.

"C'mon Ash, this is worth running for!" Marc slowed from a run to a jog and Ashley was able to catch up to him. They continued on another block before making a left and heading down a darker road off of the Main Street. At the end of it, in front of the river, was Patty's.

It looked exactly the same: the brick exterior, with the orange lamps hanging from the roof to illuminate the painted name on a large white canvass. Large windows revealed the bright interior and Ashley could see quite a few patrons sitting at the booths and tables. Marc finally slowed down to a walk for the remaining fifty feet, allowing her to catch her breath. "Was that necessary?" she asked. "Is the place going to close in the next five minutes?"

He just grinned. "I wanted to work up more of an appetite for our second dinner."

He held the door open for her and she entered into a warm, welcoming dining room that was, rather surprisingly, only sparingly decorated for Christmas, with a few strings of lights and an obviously plastic tree next to the front counter. Given that the place was already decked out floor-to-ceiling with pictures of celebrities, funny cartoons and collages of past guests, it made some sense. There wasn't much room for Christmas things in the first place.

A teenage girl in an apron walked up. "Evening!" she said cheerfully. Her face lit up when she saw Marc. "Marc! How are you? Merry Christmas!"

"Hey Diane," Marc said. "Merry Christmas to you as well! Can we get a table for two?"

Diane nodded and led them to a table along the wall. Ashley looked around as they walked. Aside from adding a few more tables and cluttering up the walls even more, the place seemed almost exactly the same. Patty's had never been a traditional diner—there were no vinyl seats or an extended counter where coffee was poured and milkshakes were made—but the homestyle food was good, cheap and plentiful and it was run by genuinely nice people. Diane placed a menu in front of each of them and walked off.

Ashley opened the menu and scanned the items. "I don't think this has changed at all."

"Eh, maybe the prices," Marc quipped. His menu stayed closed on the table in front of him.

"At least we're both making money now."

Diane returned and asked what they wanted to order. Ashley found her eyes instinctively darting to the bottom right corner of the menu. It was still there. "I'll have the chicken club."

"Fries with it?" Diane asked.

Ashley passed her back the menu. "You know it."

Marc also handed back his menu. "The usual, please."

Their server left, leaving just the two of them at the table. Marc chuckled. "Just like old times, huh?"

"So much," Ashley said. "I remember we'd spend half the day here, talking about our lives outside of Cedarwood and what we wanted to do in the future."

Marc snorted. "I remember YOU talking about those things. I think I wanted to talk more about all the video game releases I was missing and how I was going to have them shipped up to camp when I started working there year-round."

"And look what happened. We both got what we wanted. I mean, I'm presuming you eventually got your video games."

"But did you really get what you want?" Marc leaned in. "Because I remember you saying you felt torn between two paths, and you settled for the one that paid better." There was a slightly accusatory tone in his voice.

"Two paths?" Ashley chuckled. "You mean going into policing? That was more of a silly wish than anything else."

"Not how I remember it." He raised an eyebrow at her and waved Diane over. "We're going to need some drinks. Do you have draft from that local guy?"

"You bet," Diane said. "I'll bring you two glasses."

She left and Marc looked back at Ashley. "I recall, very clearly at that, you saying you wanted to be a detective because you loved the puzzles and challenges that came with it, and you had a whole plan for how you were going to advance up the ranks, but you also knew that marketing would pay better and allow you a freer life."

Ashley brought a hand to her chin. "You're not wrong. Honestly, I completely forgot about the whole detective thing. I guess I took those skills and applied them to my current job. Marketing is all about understanding people and figuring out what makes them tick. It's really not that different from a police case, except instead of solving a crime I'm solving how to sell a product."

Marc briefly rolled his eyes. "Sure. If you say so."

Diane arrived back with two pints of a light amber beer. Marc thanked her and raised his glass. "To catching up, after far too long."

Ashley raised her own glass. "Here here." She took a sip. It was a surprisingly smooth beer. "Now that we've critiqued my career choices, how about yours? Do you enjoy being in the middle of nowhere year-round?"

"It's the best job in the world," he said, without missing a beat. "I get to meet so many people and see how Cedarwood changes their lives. I get to be there for special events and help families and friends bond together. There's nothing else I'd rather do."

She took another sip of the beer. "But doesn't it get lonely? Must be hard to be so far away from the rest of the world. I remember you wishing I could... you know..." She trailed off, realizing she'd said way too much.

"Um, yeah," he said, clearly trying to ignore her last few words, "it's hard at times. Dating around here is pretty sparse." He shrugged. "I guess you could say that I'm married to my work. At least it doesn't talk back to me!"

"A bit sexist, but okay." The beer went back in her mouth. The stuff was really, really good.

"How about you?" he asked. "You have a boyfriend?"

"Nope," she said, raising her hands and shoulders up. "Haven't been seeing anyone seriously for two years now." She caught herself too late. How strong was this beer?

"Two years? What happened before that?"

"I... uh..." There was no point in keeping it from him. It wasn't like everyone else in her life didn't already know. "I was engaged, actually."

He sat back up. "Really? I mean, I'm not surprised." Now Marc was stumbling on his words. "I mean... what happened?"

"We met at a conference—we actually worked for rival companies. We were together for like six years. He proposed after four, and then two years ago, just like a week before Christmas, he came into our condo and said he couldn't do it anymore, that he wasn't ready to marry me, and he ended things."

"Wow." Marc brought a hand to his chest. "I am so sorry. That must have been so painful."

She scoffed. "Yeah, it sucked. I thought we were going to spend the rest of our lives together and then suddenly I was single and living on my own."

"And for it happen so close to Christmas too. I can see why the season doesn't put you in a joyful mood."

"Ehh, I guess," Ashley said. "I'll be honest, Christmas hasn't been a big thing for me in like ten years. My parents retired to Spain, of all places, so getting out there to see them wasn't really possible, and Richard — that's my ex — and I would do a few gifts and maybe a mini tree, but Christmas is like the busiest time for us and celebrating wasn't much of a priority."

Marc's mouth twitched. "At least you've made a lot of money."

She laughed and took another drink. "I've gone on some nice vacations, I'll tell you that. We did a two-week safari after our engagement and it was amazing." She smiled at the memories before sighing. "Though I guess it doesn't mean a whole lot now."

"It does put your participation at camp in a new light though. It couldn't have been easy for you to do all these Christmas activities." He smiled. "I know Adam appreciates it."

"It's worth it for that kid. Anything to bring him a bit of Christmas magic."

Marc shook his hand a bit. "Well, it's not really Christmas magic if you're the one doing it."

"What do you mean? Who else would it be?"

"No one. That's the whole point of it. It's the unexplained parts of the season that make it sparkle with joy. Like a present that no one remembers buying. Or food that turns out to be delicious even when you thought you messed it up." He winked at her. "Or an old friend who shows up after fifteen years."

"I'm flattered." Ashley mimed fanning herself. "But it wasn't magic that brought me to Cedarwood. It was a massive blizzard, an empty tank of gas and a dead phone." She sat up straight. "Oh! My phone!"

She reached down into her purse, pulled it out of the side pocket and turned it on. As she waited for it to load, Diane brought their meals: a massive club sandwich with a mound of fries in front of her, and a double-patty burger with about seven different toppings for him. Ashley munched on a few fries—their fresh-cut taste so much better than the frozen and reheated fast-food junk she was used to at home—and watched as her notifications sprang up. A bunch of spam emails, a few messages for work, some general holiday well-wishes… but just a few texts directly to her, asking where she was. They were from Rebecca, a friend from her hot yoga class.

Girl, where are you? We're going out for drinks, u should come!
Hey u missed a great time last night! Tons of hotties there
Everything okay? Still busy with work?

With one hand, Ashley grabbed the sandwich and took a bite, while with the other she typed a response: *Got stranded and ended up at a camp where I used to work. Run by a guy I used to know. Crazy, right?*

She put the phone down and went back to the sandwich. It was a lot easier with two hands.

Her phone buzzed: *No way! Hope you're having fun! What's he like?*

She pulled up the camera and pointed it at Marc. "Smile."

Marc, mid-bite in his burger, looked at her. She snapped the photo and sent it to Rebecca.

"Missing much in the city?" he asked.

"Apparently I missed drinks at a club where there were, and I quote, hotties."

"Oh yeah? And you get to be here, in a tacky restaurant with limited cell reception. I bet all your friends are jealous."

"You joke, but I actually prefer this." The idea of being at a packed, noisy club, trying to flirt with strangers or order drinks at a crowded bar seemed like the most foreign thing in the world to her right now.

Marc grinned. "Me too."

Her phone buzzed again. *What a cutie! Better than the guys at the club!*

Ashley tried, but failed, to hide her wide smile. Marc asked what her friend had messaged her, but she told him it was nothing.

When they'd finished their meals, Diane cleared their plates, then returned a minute later and put a slice of chocolate cheesecake in front of each of them. Marc looked at her, confused. "Compliments of the chef," Diane said, pointing back to the kitchen. An older woman stood in the doorway, looking at them.

Ashley cocked her head to the side. "Is that...?"

"Yep," Marc said. "That's Patty."

Chapter 24

The woman—both tall and plump, with curly white hair and wearing a dark blue apron with her name on it—walked over. "Marc!" she exclaimed. Her Dutch accent hadn't diminished in the least. "It's so good to see you! It's been so long!" She turned and looked at Ashley. "And I remember you! Club sandwich with extra mayo, right?"

Ashley was impressed. She herself had forgotten about the extra mayo. "It's great to see you again, Patty. Still running this restaurant?"

"Of course! Why else would my name be on it?" She clasped her hands together. "Marc, why didn't you tell me she was coming up here?"

"Oh, this wasn't planned," Ashley said. "I was stranded... you know what? It's a long story. But I'm glad I was able to come back here again."

Patty grinned like she'd just won the lottery. "You're too kind! You know, I always thought you two were a cute couple. How long did it take for you to end up together?"

Ashley felt not just her face but her entire body go hot. She glanced over at Marc, who seemed frozen in place. "Oh, oh," she stammered out. "No, we're not—we're just—"

"We're just friends!" Marc said loudly. A few nearby patrons looked over.

Patty didn't show any embarrassment to her mistake. "Whatever you say. It's great to see you both again." She walked back into the kitchen.

Ashley's eyes met Marc's. She could see the pained expression on his face, probably matching her own. She quickly picked up her fork and took a bite of the cheesecake. Despite the creamy texture and intense flavors of cheese and chocolate, she could barely enjoy it. She kept her head down, not wanting to look up and make eye contact with Marc. In her peripheral vision, she could tell he was doing the same.

She stopped halfway through and pushed her plate back. She was already full and in no mood to eat anymore. Diane came by the table in seconds to grab it. "Sorry about that," she said. "My aunt can be a bit nosy."

"It's all good," Marc said, not sounding particularly convincing. He also handed his plate to Diane.

"So will that be one bill or—"

"Two bills," Ashley said quickly. Diane nodded and left. She looked at Marc and smirked. "I'm surprised you didn't have an issue with that."

"I learned long ago that you'd never let me pay for your dinner." His voice was flat and emotionless. He shrugged. "Why try?"

Diane brought the checks. Ashley paid hers, adding a sizeable tip, and they got up and left.

The bag felt even heavier in her hands as she and Marc walked back down the Main Street, neither of them saying anything. The sidewalk seemed emptier and the decorations less festive. The church bells, now signaling that it was nine o'clock, sounded duller.

Neither of them had said anything by the time they reached the truck. Ashley threw her bag in the trunk with her other purchases and got back in the passenger's seat. They drove five minutes before Marc pulled into a gas station. Ashley got out while he was filling up and grabbed a red plastic gas canister, then filled it up and paid for both inside. She carefully put it in the trunk.

"What's that for?" Marc asked as he climbed back into the driver's seat.

"For my car. Gotta be able to drive it away once camp is over."

Marc nodded but said nothing.

The truck drove away from the town's pretty lights and onto the dark, snowy road leading back to Cedarwood.

After a few more minutes, Ashley was unable to handle the silence. "This was fun," she said. "I'm glad I was able to see—"

"Why did we lose touch?" Marc asked suddenly.

Ashley was momentarily stunned by the question. "What do you mean?"

"After camp, fifteen years ago. Why did we lose touch? We had email and phones and a dozen other ways to talk to each other. So why is it that the first time we've talked is when you drove into Cedarwood in the middle of a blizzard?"

Ashley breathed out heavily and felt her heart start to race. "I... I don't know. I guess I never heard from you and—"

"No. I tried." His voice raised a bit. There was a hint of anger, or at least frustration. "I remember. The day after you left, while I was waiting to start working at the camp year-round, I emailed you and asked if you'd made it home safely. I never heard back."

"Oh." She didn't remember the email, but that didn't mean he hadn't sent it. "I guess I was really busy getting ready for school. I'm sorry."

"I sent you one more. That Christmas, I sent you a message wishing you a merry time and a happy new year. And again, never heard anything back. So I stopped trying." He shrugged.

A heavy silence filled the vehicle. Ashley tried to think of what to say. "Marc," she breathed, "I'm so sorry. I don't even remember what I would have been thinking back then."

"I mean, it's fine. You didn't owe me anything then and you don't owe me anything now." She smiled a tiny bit. Even when he was mad, he was still a gentleman. "It's just that we were friends. And the summer we had together meant a lot to me. And when you didn't show any interest in talking to me afterwards, I don't know, it really hurt."

Her heart sank. "I..." she started. What could she say? The truth, for one. "I wanted to stay in touch, I really did."

"So then why didn't you?" His voice was choked, like he was on the very of crying. He cleared his throat. "I couldn't have been that annoying, right?"

She snickered for a second. "No, you were great. And when I left camp, I missed you. But I guess I saw Cedarwood as a one-time thing, and it was like I was about to really start my life—to go off to school and begin my career and make a lot of money — so why would I look back on it?"

"Because you had a good time?" he asked, sounding rather accusatory. "Because you met people and made friends?"

"Sure, but, you know, Cedarwood wasn't my thing. It wasn't me. I came up because I didn't have anything else to do that summer and my neighbor knew the camp's director at the time. Going up there… it never meant anything to me."

He sighed. "And there it is."

She pinched the bridge of her nose. "No, I didn't mean it like that." She was renowned in her office for always having the right thing to say to clients. Why had she made so many gaffes these last few days?

"It's fine," Marc said. "Like I said, you've never owed me anything. I'm glad you're here and that we've been able to catch up."

"Yes, and I'm glad too."

"Just as I'm sure you'll be glad to be on your way." He gestured at the road, illuminated only by the truck's high beams. "You know, you can probably get to the highway in your car at this point. You don't have to stay for the rest of the camp."

She finally turned and looked at him. "Are you asking me to leave?"

"Of course not. It'd not my place to tell anyone to leave Cedarwood. But if you don't want to be here, if this camp doesn't mean anything to you —"

"Come on Marc, I didn't mean it —"

" — then I don't want you to feel like you have to stay. Either way, I'm glad we were able to catch up."

"Yeah," Ashley said softly. "Me too."

She went back to looking out the window. Marc turned the radio on — Top 40, with no Christmas music — and they spent the rest of the ride in silence. After going back down the large hill and Cedarwood's winding driveway, Marc parked the truck. "Do you need a hand with any of your bags?" he asked.

"I'm good," Ashley said. She climbed out into the thick snow and grabbed her stuff from the trunk. "Goodnight, Marc."

He closed the SUV's door and looked at her as though he had something to say, but merely said, "'night, Ash" and headed back to his cabin.

She went to her own cabin and dropped the bags on the floor. There was a lot for her to do with their contents, but she was exhausted, both physically and mentally, and her bed looked far too inviting. She quickly got ready and climbed under the warm blankets. Though she spent a few minutes lying in the dark, thinking about the conversation that had just transpired, she soon rolled over and fell asleep.

*   *   *

She awoke with a start in the pitch-black cabin, breathing heavily and covered in sweat. "What on earth..." she muttered. She took a few seconds to regain her senses and sat up, rubbing her forehead.

It had been a dream. But it was the kind that felt so real, so possible, that she briefly wondered if it had actually happened and she was dreaming now.

In her dream she was now a detective, working on a bank robbery. Somehow, she had determined that the missing money had been hidden in a warehouse with a giant rainbow over it. Ashley and her team of officers had stormed the warehouse and found it empty, save for a massive crate in the middle. When Ashley opened the crate she'd found a pile of gold bricks, which she somehow knew was worth ten million dollars.

While she was celebrating with her team, Marc had shown up, carrying a baby in his arms. "Look what Mommy did!" he exclaimed to the baby. "She saved the camp! Aren't you glad she stayed here?" He reached out to give the child to Ashley. At that moment Ashley felt a sense of peace, like all was right in the world, and then a brilliant white light hit her.

And then she'd woken up.

"What was in that beer?" she asked herself once again. She checked her phone. 5:15 in the morning. It was too early to go and see if Gunter needed any help, but she was feeling wide awake now and doubted she'd be able to fall back asleep. She flicked on the light and looked over the bags she'd dropped on the floor. She had a lot to do—it was Christmas Eve Day, after all—and with a few hours before anyone was going to be awake, she had time to do it.

Ashley got dressed and then pulled her new jacket out of the bag. She grabbed the bag of decorations and headed outside. It was unsurprisingly cold out, but her new jacket held up well. She slipped on her boots and started planning out how she was going to deck these halls.

Christmas Eve

Chapter 25

Marc's alarm woke him out of his slumber, something that hadn't happened in weeks, if not months. Normally he was up at the first light of dawn, or earlier in the winter months. For the first time in a while, he struggled to roll out from under his blankets and felt slow and lethargic as he got dressed and ready for the day.

It had been a rough night of tossing and turning, unable to fall asleep until well past one am. Did he feel bad for the way the conversation in the SUV had gone with Ash? Absolutely. Neither of them had left happy. But was it one that had to happen? No question. She had hurt him all those years ago, and telling her had taken a weight off of his shoulders. It also helped solidify a simple truth: nothing could, or would, happen between them. And now that it was out in the open, it would make the next two days a lot easier for him.

By the time he was showered and dressed it was past eight. He left the cabin and headed toward the Lodge. As he went by Ash's cabin, he saw that she had put the decorations from town to good use: a string of unlit lights went down each of porch's pillars, and bunches of holly hung from the awning. An electric lantern sat at each side of the doorway, while smaller lights were placed around the frame. Compared to the other cabins it was rather minimalist, but Marc had to admit it all looked pretty nice.

He walked up the steps to the Lodge and paused for a moment to collect himself. She would be in there and it could be difficult to see her now. But that was all part of the job. If he could sit opposite counselors who had told him they hated him and thought he was ruining the camp, he could be in the same room as the woman who had rebuffed him fifteen years earlier and then made it clear that he and his camp had meant nothing to her. He had to. He owed it to all the other guests to make this the best Christmas Eve and Christmas Day that Camp Cedarwood had ever seen. Especially since it could very well be the camp's last.

He took a deep breath and walked in. His eyes scanned for her and spotted her sitting on the left, next to Janice and Carol, eating and not saying much. He took a seat on the right-side table, with Adam, Paige and David. The two parents had large circles under their eyes but the boy was brimming with energy and nearly bouncing in his seat.

"Morning Marc!" Adam said.

"Hey buddy," Marc said. "You seem excited. And I bet I know why!"

"Why?" Adam asked, looking up at him with his big bright eyes.

"We're having waffles and hot chocolate for breakfast!" Marc used the tongs to put a few of the homemade waffles on his plate, then added maple syrup.

"No!" Adam said, shaking his head. "It's because today is Christmas Eve!"

Marc feigned surprise, bringing his hand up to his chest. "Is it really? I thought Christmas was next week!"

Adam grabbed his arm with both hands and shook it. "It's tomorrow! So you have to make sure Santa can find his way here tonight, okay?"

Marc smiled. "Don't worry, I know exactly what to do. Santa isn't going to miss this camp tonight, I promise."

Adam seemed to get even bouncier at that commitment and went back to his waffles. Marc cut up his own and ate them in minutes. His anxieties over last night's conversation with Ashley were fading and he was already feeling better.

When breakfast was over, David got up and joined Drew up on the stage. Drew still balanced an arm on David's shoulder. "Good morning everyone, and happy Christmas Eve Day!" David said. "I'm sure everyone is excited for Camp Cedarwood's Christmas Eve party tonight, and then for Santa to come. But in the meantime, we still have a Christmas Cup to compete for, and on that note, we have a big announcement."

Marc raised an eyebrow at Adam. "I wonder what that means." In truth, he had no idea. He had shared his plans for the Christmas Cup with David and Drew when they'd taken over two days earlier and given them free reign to make any adjustments or changes they wanted. Beyond that, he'd had zero input into the events.

"In past years, we have included a tree decorating competition as part of the Cup," Drew said. "This year we are doing it again, but it is now going to count for two events, instead of just one, and will be broken into two parts: first, instead of providing you with the trees, this morning you'll go out into the forest and find the perfect tree to cut down and bring back to the Lodge. Then, this afternoon, teams will decorate the trees for judging. The winning team will get the point."

"Because we're counting this as two events, there are now just nine points total up for grabs," David continued. "Which means if the Frost Bites win, they will have a two-point lead and are guaranteed to win the Christmas Cup!"

"Yes!" Marc shouted, clapping loudly. He nodded at a few of his teammates at the other tables.

"In addition, since this is an epic event, we have added a secondary prize," David said. "The winning team will also get to decorate the big Christmas tree in the middle of the cabins! And let's hope they do a good job so that Santa can see it as he flies over the camp tonight!"

Marc looked back at Adam. "See? When my team wins the competition, I'll make sure we cover the tree in lights! Santa will see it from a hundred miles away!"

Adam pouted and crossed his arms over his chest. "You're not going to win! We're going to have the best tree, right mom?"

Paige, resting her head on her hand, looked up. "Yeah, sure honey."

Drew gave the final instructions: "Teams, the Christmas Tree Competition starts right now! You have until noon to bring your tree into the Lodge. Captains, we have a few tools for you to help cut them down.

And as a reminder, please just cut down one tree. They help keep the air here so fresh!"

"Good luck everyone!" David said. The two left the stage.

Marc leaned back and faced Bill, sitting at the table behind him. "How about we meet in fifteen minutes and head out from there? I know some great places we can find trees."

Bill nodded. "Sounds good. I'll let the others know."

Marc sat back up and then stood up from his chair. David came back to the table. "Interesting twist on the competition," Marc said. "I wholeheartedly approve."

"I'm glad," David said. "We thought it'd give a real traditional feel to things. What's more traditional than cutting down your own Christmas tree?"

Adam got up and sneered at Marc. "See you when you guys lose!" He ran off to join Carol, Janice and Ash. Marc followed him with his gaze, but quickly turned away when Ash looked over at him.

"How're you guys doing?" he asked Paige and David.

The two shared an uneasy look. "Adam…" Paige said. She looked away and shook her head. "He was sick last night. Woke up in the middle of the night with stomach pains and a bit of a fever. We gave him some medicine and he seems fine now, but… well, we've been down this road before. This is how it starts. Fever, night sweats, aches and pains."

Marc again looked over at the kid, who was in deep conversation with the women. "I'm so sorry," he said. "If there's anything I can do, please let me know."

"Thank you." She smiled. "But there's only one thing we can do now, and that's to have the best Christmas ever, so we better get started." She walked over and joined her son.

Marc reached out and put his hand on David's shoulder. "You're a stronger man than I'll ever be," he said. "Should the Frost Bites just throw the competition now, or what?"

David snorted. "I've made it clear with them that even though I may be family, I am still an impartial judge. We didn't allow for any special treatment in past Christmas Cups and there won't be any this year."

Marc withdrew his hand. "Sounds good to me. I guess I need to go and win it, then."

He put his coat on and headed for the door. He took one last glance toward the group of Ice Dinosaurs. Adam and Paige were both laughing about something. He relaxed a bit. He couldn't change what was happening, nor could he pretend to understand it. But he could be there as a friend and provide the best Christmas possible—one that would stay in their memories for years to come. It was all he could do.

His gaze drifted and he locked eyes with Ash. He breathed in sharply and turned away, then left the Lodge. That was one other situation where there was nothing he could do to fix things. But in Ashley's case, he wasn't sure if he could even be there as a friend.

Chapter 26

Dressed in her new winter coat, Ashley left her cabin and walked all forty feet to Carol's, where she met the Southerner and Janice, both standing on the porch. "Is it as warm as it looks?" Carol asked, giving Ashley a quick look over.

"Even warmer," Ashley said. "You'd swear it was only fifteen degrees below freezing, not twenty."

"There you go," Janice said. "How was shopping with Marc? Did he help you find everything you need?"

"Um, y-yeah, sure." Ashley stumbled on her words. "It was nice. Felt good to shop again."

Harvey and his kids walked up, and they were soon joined by Emma and her daughter. The kids were all brimming with energy, the kind that could only come from it being the day before Christmas. Ashley couldn't help but smile. Seeing it again brought back her own memories of the day of Christmas Eve—finishing wrapping presents, helping with last-minute baking and food preparation, and getting all ready for a family party and then Santa's arrival. There was a manic joy to all of it, one that clearly still existed in front of her.

About five minutes later, Paige and Adam walked up, hand-in-hand. Paige had a scarf wrapped around her mouth and wore sunglasses, something Ashley hadn't seen on her before.

"Alright y'all," Carol announced, "this is do or die for the Ice Dinosaurs. We lose this and it's all over for us. So let's win! First things first, we need to find the perfect tree. Any ideas where we should start our search?"

"Ooh!" Adam shouted. He pointed to the east. "Let's go in the big forest! There are tons of trees there!"

"Or we can head back up to the archery range," Harvey said. "I remember seeing a few evergreens around that area, and ones that aren't too tall."

"What about behind the cabins?" Emma asked. "When we were there yesterday there were some nice firs. Maybe about my height? We could make a cute little tree!"

Carol looked out in thought for a minute. "As much as I love a cute little tree, we need a tree that's going to win us the event and keep us in the competition. And while we could probably find a heckuva tree out in the eastern forest, they're all twenty feet tall and would be a real pain to carry out through all the brush. No, let's head up to the archery range and see what we can find."

She reached down and picked up an axe and a hacksaw. Both Adam and Ian rushed forward to try to carry them, but Carol passed the axe off to Harvey and carried the saw herself.

The group headed up the driveway, back towards the archery range. Ashley scanned the camp's large field, looking for any sign of the Frost Bites. There weren't any. She had no idea where they were.

"Bringing up bad memories?" Janice asked, coming up next to her. "You know, of bows and arrows?"

Ashley scoffed. "Please, I wish we'd do it again. All I have to do is aim as far away from the target as possible and I'm bound to hit it!"

Janice laughed and rubbed her arm. "If it's not archery that's bothering you, then what is?" Ashley looked over at her. "Come on. I may not be a brilliant detective like you, but I can tell something is up. You were quiet at breakfast and you seem anxious now. Is everything okay?"

Ashley sighed and checked to see if anyone else was listening. Seeing no one, she said, "Marc and I had a bit of a fight last night."

"A fight? About what?"

"About us. It's complicated. I may have been a bit blunt with him about what Cedarwood had meant to me when I was younger. And he was pretty blunt with me about some things too. I don't know. There was a lot of bluntness."

"I'm sorry," Janice said. "This can't be easy for either of you. To see each other after being apart for so long. Could I hazard a guess that you're feeling pretty confused about all this?"

"Among many other things, yes."

"Then if you don't mind me asking—" Janice lowered her voice. "—what's the history between the two of you? Did something happen back when you were kids or what?"

Ashley shrugged. "It's hard to say. We were good friends during the one summer I worked here. The final night, he tried to kiss me and I told him no, even though, honestly, I wanted to. But I was scared to do it at the time because I knew it'd be our last night together. Why start something that was about to end, you know?"

"You couldn't see it going past the summer?"

"Back then I couldn't see anything going past the summer. I was so much more excited to start school and internships and all that." She rolled her eyes. "And to make money. There was nothing more in the world that mattered to me than that."

"Look, I'm not judging. You've seen my clothes."

"Of course. And don't get me wrong, I'm proud of myself for what I've done. I just… looking back on it, I wish I hadn't been so quick to cast away everything about Cedarwood as soon as I'd left. Last night Marc told me that I'd hurt him, and I'd never even thought of that. And now I just feel awful for it."

"Yep, that's called empathy. It's a good thing to have, though a bit surprising for someone who works in marketing."

Ashley nudged at Janice with her elbow. "Says the lawyer."

"What are you going to do? No offense, but if there's going to be weird tension between you two for the rest of the camp, I'm just going to check out early. I came here specifically to get away from relationship drama."

"I'm not sure," Ashley said. "I need to patch things up with him, or at least show him I'm sorry for how I treated him. I'll have to think of something."

The group made its way up the winding driveway and reached the archery range. There were a few pine trees nearby, but they were all fifty feet tall and had trunks as wide as the inner tube Ashley had taken her terrifying ride on the day before. "Let's head in deeper," Carol said, pointing to a path leading into the forest.

They started in, and Ashley sidled up next to Paige. "Hey, everything okay?"

"Of course. It's Christmas Eve," Paige said, her voice muffled by her scarf. "Why wouldn't it be?"

"Well, you're wearing sunglasses for the first time and a scarf despite the lack of wind. Just wanted to check in on you." Also, thinking about Paige meant she'd think less about Marc.

Paige's shoulders slumped forward. "There's just a different set of rules when you're a parent to a special kid. I don't know how else to put it."

Ashley put her arm around her friend. "I'm sorry," she said. Up ahead of them, Adam was jumping up and knocking snow off of branches and onto his head. "If it helps, he's sure looking pretty good."

"I know, and that's the problem. He'll be like this until he's physically unable to move. It's hard to know if your son is doing okay when he's always so upbeat and energetic."

Ashley nodded. She hadn't thought of that. Then again, there were a million things she hadn't thought about before she'd met Adam.

They continued on, going deeper into the woods behind the archery range. After about ten minutes of walking, the trees began to clear and the team reached the road that led to the other cottages on the lake. They hadn't seen any trees worth cutting down — all the evergreens were too big to fell, carry and decorate.

"If this was easy, it wouldn't be a challenge, would it?" Carol said. "I suggest we all head back in and see if we can find anything better. But if we can't, one of those pines at the archery range may just have to do. A bit big, but we can trim it down."

There weren't any objections. They turned around and went back into the woods. Ashley found herself next to Harvey, the axe slung across his shoulder. "How are you holding up?" she asked.

"You know, there's just something about this place," he said, taking in a deep breath and then exhaling loudly. "I was scared about bringing the kids back here when they had so many memories of doing Christmas with their mom, but, honestly, this has been so healing for us. Last night they were saying that their mom would be so happy to see all of us back here. What more could I ask for?"

"That's a really inspiring way of looking at things."

"Well, I'm not trying to be inspirational. I'm just trying to live my life as best as I can for me and my kids. And for me, that means recognizing the areas where I can change the things around me and the areas where I just have to change myself." He shifted the axe to his other shoulder. "Though right now, I hope I don't have to change myself too much to cut down our tree. More than a few swings and I'm afraid I'm going to throw my back right out."

Ashley took another look around the forest. For all the majestic pines and cedars that surrounded them, there just weren't any that could reasonably be taken down by an axe. "A shame they didn't offer us a chainsaw," she said.

"If they did I think we'd end up with a very different set of problems." He tugged at his beard. "I hope we can find something soon, though. Still would be nice to have a shot at the Cup tomorrow."

"Is that when we have the final event?"

"Yep. And it's always something wild. Last time we were here it was a relay race around the entire camp. Took like two hours to do. I think they'll tone things down for tomorrow."

Up ahead, Adam cut away from the group and started walking deeper into the forest. "Hey Adam?" Paige asked. "What are you doing?"

Adam raised his mitt and pointed. "Look!" he said. Ashley followed his gesture and saw, about fifty feet away, a deer with a large set of antlers.

It looked so similar to the one she'd seen with him two days earlier that she was almost certain it was the same one.

The deer faced Adam for a few seconds, and then took off running deeper into the woods. Without hesitation, Adam chased after it. "Adam!" Paige shouted. She ran after him.

Ashley joined in the pursuit, running through the branches as fast as she could. Now that she was in her own, non-luxury jacket she had no concerns with a few scratches or tears. Snow fell on her as she knocked through leaves and limbs, but she hardly noticed.

The deer vanished among the trees, and a half minute later Ashley caught up with Adam. Paige was right behind her. She fell to her knees and grabbed her son in a tight hug. "Sweety," she said, pulling her scarf down from her mouth, "you can't run off like that! You could have tripped on a stump or run into a branch. You have to be careful."

"Sorry," Adam said. "But the deer wanted me to follow him!"

Paige brushed his cheek. "Honey, what would make you think that?"

"He was looking right at me! And we'd seen him before, remember Ashley?"

"We did, or at least a deer that looks similar to him."

Adam shook his head. "No, it was definitely him! He's my friend. I think he was trying to show me something."

"Show you what?" Paige asked.

Ashley took a few steps back and looked around. The deer's tracks were clear in the unblemished snow. She followed them about twenty feet, which took her behind a large oak tree. "Oh wow," she said. "Hey guys? You might want to check this out."

Hidden behind the oak's trunk was a pine tree, about ten feet tall and with a perfect triangular shape from its base to its top. Its needles were a rich green and were spread out evenly across every branch. It was an almost stereotypical Christmas tree. Had it not been in the middle of the woods, Ashley would have taken it as a fake.

"Holy moly," Adam said, coming around the oak tree with his mom. "That's it! That's our tree!"

"It's beautiful," Paige said. She twisted around and put her hand to her mouth. "Over here, everyone! We've found it!"

Ashley looked back at the snow. The deer's tracks led to the tree, but she couldn't see any going past it — just white, untouched snow. She looked back at Adam. He held his hands up in a big shrug, but the massive grin on his face made it clear that he didn't care. Paige was right: he was a really special kid.

Chapter 27

The rest of the Ice Dinosaurs arrived and had the same reaction to finding the ideal tree. Harvey's kids crawled under the pine needles and brushed away the snow around the trunk, then held back the branches as their dad wound up and drove the axe head into the wood. After a few chops he was able to take a large chunk out. Carol squatted down and used the handsaw to cut deeper into the gap. The tree started to lean after a few minutes of sawing. "All right y'all, time to push."

Ashley joined the other adults around Carol. She reached out and pushed against the closest branch, as Carol continued to drag the saw across the trunk. The wood began to creak and then crack. "Here we go!" Carol shouted. The tree fell away from Ashley's hands. "Timber!"

It hit the ground, sending powdery snow into the air. Carol cut through a few remaining tendrils of wood. Harvey grabbed the base of the tree and lifted it. "It's not too heavy. If we all help out, it should be easy to get it back to the Lodge."

Ashley stepped a few feet behind Harvey and reached through a few branches to grab onto the trunk. The others did the same, with the kids picking up the tree at its very tip. "Let's go!" Harvey yelled. They all started back through the forest.

It wasn't a particularly difficult path, due to the smaller size of the tree, and there were only a few times they had to stop when a branch got snagged. They made it to the forest trail in minutes and then were able to navigate to its exit next to the archery range. Harvey stopped the group to give them a quick breather.

"This tree is perfect," Janice said. "How on earth did you find it?"

"The deer led me to it!" Adam exclaimed. "I saw it in the forest and it ran off, and then when we followed it we found the tree!"

"Well there you go," Emma said. "It's a Christmas miracle!"

Ashley thought back to what Marc had said about Christmas magic. Was this what he was referring to?

Before she had a chance to consider it further, Harvey called them all to pick up the tree and carry on. The wide driveway was even easier to move down. The team made it to the cabins in ten minutes.

David was waiting at the Lodge's doors. He opened them wide to let the group in and guided them to one of the tree stands that had been sitting at the stage. Once the tree was firmly in the stand, Drew and David set up a cloth barrier between the two stands, so that neither team would be able to see what the other was doing.

"And now your decorations," Drew announced with flair. He placed a large plastic container at the front of the tree. "It's just before 11:30 now. Judging will be at three. Good luck!"

Carol pulled the lid off the box and began taking out all the items inside. There were, to Ashley's complete lack of surprise, a ton of things. Multiple boxes of ornaments, a half-dozen strings of Christmas lights, several bags of Christmas candies, candy canes and popcorn kernels, as well as a hundred pages of colourful construction paper, pipe cleaners, stickers and scissors and glue. "Well then," Carol said, "I certainly have an idea in mind."

"We're all ears, Carol," said Janice.

Carol briefly explained her plan: multiple strings of lights, popcorn, and construction paper links, all wrapping around the tree from top to bottom, like a spiral. The others liked it and Carol delegated each of them assignment. She gave herself and Ashley the responsibility of making the popcorn.

"You ever done this before?" she asked. She took the bag of kernels and led Ashley into the kitchen.

"I've made microwave popcorn. Does that count?"

Gunter was in the kitchen, standing beside the industrial oven. He only nodded at Carol as she pulled a large pot out and put it on the stove. She grabbed a jug of canola oil from a nearby shelf and poured it into the pot, then added all of the kernels. She put the lid on and turned on the range.

"This'll take a few minutes to warm up, and then you just gotta keep shakin' it," Carol said. She grabbed the handle and quickly moved the pot back and forth to show what she meant.

Ashley nodded. "Looks simple enough."

"I hope so. We need this popcorn to be perfect if we're going to win this one! I'm not going to let Bill gloat about beating me for all of today and tomorrow. Just as I'm sure y'all don't want Marc to do the same. You two seem to have quite the rivalry going."

"Oh, uh, you know, it might be a bit overblown."

"Really?" Carol looked up at her. "Wasn't he the reason you joined in with the Christmas Cup in the first place?"

A hissing noise began to emanate from the pot. "Not really," Ashley said. "It was more that I was here and once I was on your team I wanted to see you all win. Though I guess beating Marc would be a bonus for that."

A pop sounded from inside the pot. Ashley grabbed the handle and began to move it back and forth over the burner. "There you go!" Carol said. "Keep it up. Should take just a few minutes."

As she slid the pot around, quickly working up a sweat, Ashley, for the first time, considered just why she was doing such a thing. It hadn't been to compete with Marc—heck, he hadn't even entered the Christmas Cup until after the second event. No, it was because she wanted to see her team win. Her team, which consisted of total strangers at the time, all of whom she would never see once camp was over. For this group, she had braved the cold, humiliated herself at an archery range, flung herself down an icy track on an inner tube, and embraced Christmas traditions that didn't exactly fill her with tidings of comfort and joy.

The kitchen suddenly felt hot. Too hot. She kept moving the pot back and forth, now at a more frantic pace. Why was she doing this? She could have borrowed a few books and stayed in her cabin until the snow cleared. She could have gone on long walks through the woods and around the lake. She could have seen if there were people in the cottages that she could befriend. Or she could have stayed on the phone, on hold for seven hours, and waited until the tow truck came and took her back to the city (the idea of going back to the city before the end of camp now seemed patently absurd to her).

An explosion of little pops sounded from inside the pot. The lid rattled in place. "That's it!" Carol shouted. "Keep going!"

Ashley brought her focus back to the popcorn. She shook the pot as hard as she could for a good minute, until the popping subsided. Once it had, Carol grabbed it and dumped the contents into a large plastic bowl. It filled to the brim with large, fluffy pieces of popcorn. Ashley admired it while leaning on the counter, catching her breath. It was as winding as one of her exercise classes.

"Great work!" Carol gushed. She grabbed one of the pieces and put it in her mouth. "Perfect. This will make for a great string."

She carried the bowl back out to the meal hall. Ashley pushed herself off of the counter and followed.

There was a lot of noise and activity coming from the other side of the divider. The Frost Bites had returned and were working on their own decorating. Ashley briefly wondered what Marc was doing to help before pushing the thought away and focusing on her own team. Things were starting to take shape: Harvey and Janice had untangled the Christmas lights and were testing each one in a socket, while the parents and kids were cutting and pasting the construction paper to make a chain.

Carol placed the bowl down and pulled out a roll of red-colored thread. She held up a needle and put the thread through the eye, then showed Ashley how to put it through each popcorn piece. It took Ashley just a few tries to get the hang of it and not break any pieces. Carol left her to it while she started going through the ornaments.

Gunter walked out of the kitchen carrying a long tray with two large pizzas. He placed them on a nearby table, along with a wad of napkins, then added a pitcher of water and a stack of cups. The kids jumped up and grabbed a slice. A few minutes later, Gunter carried out the same things, now to the Frost Bites' side. "Thank you," Ashley said as he walked back. "You really don't have to do any of this."

"I know I don't!" he said. "But this is always the best part of Christmas Camp. I don't want to miss it!"

Ashley waited until the kids had cleared before grabbing herself a slice. It was surprisingly crispy on the bottom, but with plenty of dough and sauce. It felt like something from a real pizzeria. Was there anything Gunter couldn't cook?

When she was done, she wiped her hands off and went back to stringing the popcorn. Christmas music once again started playing through the speakers, but she didn't mind. If anything, it gave her a good rhythm to add each piece. After a few songs, she had accumulated about ten feet of popcorn along the thread, with more than half the bowl still left.

An instrumental version of "Blue Christmas" began to play. She stopped stringing the popcorn and looked up at the barrier. Marc was behind it, probably putting ornaments up or unraveling Christmas lights. She sighed and dropped her head. The guilt she had felt since the previous night hadn't gone away — if anything, it was now even stronger. It wasn't just telling Marc that her time as a counselor at Cedarwood hadn't meant anything to her, though she really wished she could take those words back. No, it was feeling that way in the first place. That she was better than this camp, that it was just a way for her to pass the summer, that the person she was about to become — successful, powerful, wealthy — was more important than who she had been at that moment.

She remembered that feeling well, because it was still with her. It was what drove her to work her butt off for clients, to spend late nights brainstorming new ideas and drafting up new proposals, to drive to a different city to pitch to a new client just a few days before Christmas and then drive back in the middle of a blizzard. It was a feeling she was always chasing. She wanted the bigger clients, the fatter bonuses, the more-powerful promotions. Especially these last two years, after she'd been so unceremoniously dumped by her fiancé. She'd made it her goal and her source of pride to keep on doing more and making more and climbing and climbing and climbing.

"And for what?" she muttered to herself. Where had that pursuit of success and wealth led her? After she'd come far too close to getting stranded in a snowstorm, it had led her here, to the camp where the cycle had started. Where she had first decided that the money and status that came with her work meant more than anything else. Including a relationship she now truly regretted abandoning.

She sighed again. Her head was a blur of thoughts and feelings. She needed to sort them out.

"Ash!" Carol walked back up to her. "How's the popcorn coming along?"

"Pretty well," Ashley said, snapping out of her thoughts. "Should be done in twenty minutes or so."

"See if you can pick things up a bit. It's a big tree and it's going to take some time to put everything in place. I don't want to rush the decorating."

Ashley gave her a thumbs up. "I'll do what I can."

Carol nodded and walked over to where the kids were assembling their construction paper chain. "Blue Christmas" finally ended and a cheery version of "I Saw Mommy Kissing Santa Claus" came on. Ashley picked up the needle and continued adding more popcorn to the thread. She pushed all her confusion away, telling herself that she was overreacting, that her job was good and fun and rewarding, and that she couldn't get down on herself for doing something that allowed her to live well and never have to worry about money.

It was something she'd been telling herself for years.

Chapter 28

She added the final piece of popcorn to the string about fifteen minutes later. All in all, the thread was about thirty feet long, which would hopefully be enough to cover the entire tree. Ashley tied the ends with a large knot, to ensure that none of the pieces would fall back off, and walked around the tree to where the others were doing their work.

The kids had created a massive chain of red, green, white and yellow loops, along with paper stars the size of her hand and candy canes with pipe cleaner antlers. Harvey and Janice were just finishing laying out their lights. Carol looked at each of them approvingly. "Y'all, let's decorate that tree!"

They started with the Christmas lights. Harvey stood up on a chair and tied the end of the lights around the top of the tree, and then Janice walked around it, wrapping the strands along the pine like a ribbon. After five circles, the lights reached the bottom, with a few feet to spare.

Next was the popcorn. Ashley grabbed one end and handed it up to Harvey. There were a few "oohs" and "ahhs" from her teammates as they saw what she had made. Ashley smiled to herself and began to move around the tree, trying to keep the popcorn in line with the Christmas lights. There were a few snags, but five minutes later she reached the bottom of the tree and the end of her string. It had been the perfect length.

Finally came the construction paper chain. The kids all held onto it and ran around the tree, in a manner that reminded Ashley of a maypole dance, albeit a bit more chaotic. Emma and Paige helped them keep it in line with the popcorn and Christmas lights. There was still a good ten feet of chain remaining as they reached the bottom.

"Wow," Carol said, "this is… really, really good."

Ashley couldn't help but agree. The spiral around the tree made it look a bit like wrapping around a gift. It looked professional, which was certainly something she could never say about any trees she had decorated before.

Carol held up the boxes of ornaments. "Now let's finish this baby off, y'all!" She passed them out and the group began putting ornaments up on the free branches.

"Don't forget the reindeer!" Adam said, holding up the candy canes with pipe cleaner antlers. He took a step towards the tree, then stopped suddenly and grabbed his stomach. One of the reindeer fell to the floor.

"Adam!" Paige ran over and put her hands on her son. "Are you okay?"

He shook his head. "My tummy hurts," he groaned.

"Let's go back to the cabin. I've got some medicine you can take." She helped him stand back up and led him to the front of the Lodge and out the door.

The rest of the Ice Dinosaurs watched him leave in silence. Ashley could feel the awkward tension among the other adults. Paige's words came back to her: it was a different set of rules with Adam. Maybe it was just a stomach-ache. Or maybe it was a sign of something much, much worse. She just couldn't know.

Carol clapped her hands together. "We better make sure this tree is ready for when they get back. Let's keep at it!"

That broke them all out of their trance. They went back to hanging up ornaments, while Ashley picked up the candy cane reindeer that Adam had dropped. It hadn't broken. She hung it on one of the branches, then grabbed a box of four plump plastic Santa ornaments and went around the tree, looking for the perfect place to put them.

"Fifteen minutes!" Drew announced. Ashley placed another Santa on a branch. Where had the time gone?

She continued adding ornaments until the tree was covered from top to bottom. Every few minutes Ashley turned and looked at the door, hoping that Adam and Paige would be coming back in. She hoped it was just a minor stomach-ache, caused by eating too much pizza. She felt terrible for Paige and David. It was Christmas Eve — the last day that any parents should have to worry about their child's health.

"One minute!" Drew shouted. The Ice Dinosaurs gathered in front of the tree to admire it. Janice grabbed the end of the lights and plugged them in. The tree lit up in all the colors of the rainbow. Combined with the paper chains, popcorn string and dozens of ornaments, it was the best tree Ashley had seen in years.

"Harv, the star!" Carol held up a cardboard tree topper. "Hurry!"

Harvey grabbed the star, jumped up on the chair and placed it on top, just as David and Drew called out that time was up.

"Okay teams," David said. "It's time to see each other's trees. As a reminder, if the Frost Bites win this event, they will have won the Christmas Cup! In three… two… one…"

Ashley clenched her hands together. What the Ice Dinosaurs had was perfect. But what if Marc and his team had managed to do even better? What if they had a bigger tree, or a more creative use of the decorations, or…

The barrier dividing the two teams fell away, revealing her opponent's tree. "Huh?" Ashley asked aloud. It was echoed by a few of her teammates.

The Frost Bites didn't have a bigger tree. Instead, they had a sapling, barely three feet tall and with pencil-thin branches, which drooped under the ornaments hanging off of them, and sparse needles that were barely visible under the Christmas lights wrapped around them.

Ashley struggled to take it in. What were they doing? Was it some kind of joke? Was there another tree hiding somewhere? She stared in open-mouthed silence, until Harvey smacked his forehead. "It's a Charlie Brown tree!"

"Of course!" Janice said. "Like in the movie!"

"The movie?" Ashley asked. She vaguely remembered it from her childhood, but couldn't recall what happened with a tree.

"Yeah, they find a cute little tree and decorate it to show that even something small and unimportant can be special at Christmas," Harvey said. "It's clever. I'll give you that."

"Thank you," Marc said. It was crystal clear that it was his idea. "Yours looks amazing too. Where did you find it? We searched all morning for one that was a good size to cut down."

Again, Ashley looked back to the door. No Adam or Paige. "A bit of Christmas magic," Carol replied.

David and Drew walked around each tree, each of them stroking their chins and occasionally whispering to each other. When they were done, they huddled off to the side for a minute before facing the two teams. "First off," David said, "congratulations to both teams for not knocking down your creations this time. It made our judging jobs a lot harder."

"Oh har har," Marc said, glaring at them.

"We had two very different interpretations of this competition," David continued, "and we both liked what we saw. But after discussing, we both agree that the superior tree, the one that really amazed us, is from the… Ice Dinosaurs!"

Ashley jumped in the air and pumped her fist, while the rest of her team cheered and hugged each other. "That means that tomorrow's event will decide the winner of the Camp Cedarwood Christmas Cup!" David said. "It also means that the Ice Dinosaurs have won the opportunity to decorate the camp's tree outside. We'll go get your decorations for that one and meet you out there in a few minutes."

Marc raised his hands. "And while they're doing that, a reminder that the Cedarwood Christmas Eve party will begin tonight at 6:30 and go until we're all ready to sleep. I don't know about you, but for me that's going to be pretty early." All of the parents nodded in agreement.

Janice came up to Ashley and rubbed her shoulders. "Great work! I have to admit, I was more nervous about that than I wanted to be."

"I never doubted," Ashley said. "Once we had our tree, I knew it was in the bag."

"Still, that was fun." Janice chuckled to herself. "Just think, right now there are probably millions of people rushing around, trying to buy a last-minute gift or get ready for their guests. And here we are, cutting down and decorating trees and just having a blast. It's a shame more people don't know about this."

"No kidding. They'd definitely…" Ashley's hands dropped to her side as her eyes went wide. "Oh my gosh, that's it!"

"What's it?" Janice asked.

"I know what to do for Marc, to make things up to him." She ran over to the table and grabbed a few of the remaining sheets of construction paper.

"Okay… and what about decorating the big tree?"

Ashley waved her hand dismissively. "I'm all decorated out. This is more important anyway. I'll see you in a bit." Holding the paper against her body, she ran to the door and out into the cold.

"Ash!" Adam and Paige were coming down the path, both looking much happier than when they'd left. "Did we win?" Adam asked.

Ashley grinned. "Why don't you head inside and find out? Are you feeling better?"

Adam nodded several times. "Oh yeah! Just needed to lie down for a few minutes."

"That's great." Ashley looked at Paige, who gave a bit of a shrug. "Look, I need to do some work, but I'll see you tonight, okay?"

"Sounds good!" Adam ran into the Lodge, with his mom right behind him.

Feeling even better now that the kid was back in action, Ashley went to her cabin and hopped onto her bed. She put the construction paper on the blanket and pulled a pen out from her purse. This would be exactly what Marc, and the camp, needed, even if it wouldn't be enough to make up for the way she had treated him.

She clicked the pen, held it to the paper, and started to write.

Chapter 29

The bell woke Ashley out of her sleep. She groggily rolled over and wondered if it was time for breakfast. Then she remembered that it had been mid-afternoon when she'd finished writing and laid down to rest her eyes.

She got off the bed and changed into one of her own blouses, a sleek dark-green professional-looking one that she got a lot of mileage out of when giving presentations. She put her heels back on, and then went into the washroom, threw some water on her face and put her hair in a ponytail. Even though it was camp, it was still Christmas Eve and she figured she should dress up a little.

Before going to the Lodge, she plugged in her Christmas lights, then took a moment to admire her work. The porch columns lit up, illuminating the holly she'd hung from the eaves. Was it as impressive as the other cabins? Hardly. But it was the first time she'd ever decorated an exterior and she felt pretty proud of herself for it.

She walked past the large tree in the middle of the cabins and was surprised to find it unlit. Two ladders lay in the snow next to it. She could make out a few ornaments on it, but otherwise it remained shrouded in darkness.

The Lodge was loud and lively as she walked in. Marc hadn't been kidding when he'd called it a Christmas Eve party — instead of the typical sit-down dinner, the tables had all been pushed to the side and were covered in different foods and drinks. Several cocktail tables had been set up in the middle and served as the congregating spot for most of the adults. In the corner to her right the kids had gathered in a makeshift play area with games, puzzles and coloring books. She saw Adam staring down at a half-completed Christmas puzzle, his eyes narrow in focus.

Jaunty jazz music played, but there was something different about it. At the back of the room, on the small stage, was a jazz quartet consisting of a pianist, drummer, trumpeter and upright bassist. They were all older men, dressed in dark dress shirts with Christmas-themed ties and miniature top hats. She had no idea where Marc could have found them, but had to admit they certainly added a degree of fanciness to the event.

Carol, Emma and Janice stood around one of the cocktail tables, a few glasses of wine and juice in front of them. Ashley walked up, and then nearly fell back when she saw Janice's dress. "Holy cow," she said. "Since when did this become the Met?"

Her friend wore a black sleeveless piece that hugged her every curve and came down to just past her knees. Two wide straps led from her navel up to each shoulder, creating a wide V below her neck. It was complemented by a stunning diamond necklace as well as several gold bracelets on her right wrist. Ashley felt severely underdressed compared to it. Heck, she would have felt severely underdressed if she'd arrived in her own evening gown.

"I know, right?" said Carol, wearing a knitted sweater with a reindeer (including a pompom red nose). "Are you tryin' to outclass us all here?"

Janice laughed. "C'mon, it's Christmas! I figure if there's ever a time to dress up, it's for Santa, right?" She gestured over to another table. "Also, I'm not going to let my husband be the only one wearing something ridiculous tonight."

Roger, standing at another table, was decked out in clothes bearing his school's logo, from the pants to the sweater to the baseball cap on his head. "You two have the weirdest relationship," Ashley said.

"Weird beats boring."

Emma put her wine glass on the table. "At this point I would kill for boring. I still have about twenty gifts to wrap once the girls are asleep tonight. I always forget how much there is to do here and how fast the time goes by."

"You're tellin' me," Carol said. "Feels like just a few hours ago we all arrived here. Hard to believe we'll all be headin' home tomorrow."

"Eh, I'm ready," Emma said. "I don't know about you, but Christmas Day is just the start of the holidays for our clan. We've got my family, Jack's family, probably a neighborhood gathering, and then it's New Years and we somehow still have to keep the party going."

"See, that's why we come here," Carol said. "To avoid all that!"

They all laughed. The jazz band kicked up the tempo with a snappy rendition of "Have Yourself a Merry Little Christmas." Bill walked over and held out his hand to Carol. "May I have this dance?"

"Well, I do say!" Carol said, putting on an even thicker Southern accent. "What a charming gentleman! How can I say no?"

Bill took her hand and led her to the middle of the Lodge, where they started dancing, a bit awkwardly, to the music. Drew and Sally joined them, and then Janice and Emma left to meet up with their husbands on the dance floor.

Ashley rolled her eyes and walked over to the tables against the wall. It was a real selection of party food: nachos (with red and green peppers), wings, chicken bites, fries, veggies and dip, and an assortment of cookies and brownies for dessert. Ashley put a little bit of everything on her plate and munched on them while watching the others dance.

As silly as they all looked, she felt an ache in her chest while she watched them, couples and friends, clearly having a blast with people who were so close to them.. When was the last time she'd felt a connection like that? Not since the engagement had been called off. Not since she'd been left with such a heartbreak, one she'd since associated with the Christmas season.

She grimaced slightly and looked around the room. She spotted Marc next to the kitchen, with great big oven mitts on his hands. He was also watching the dancers, though clearly looking a lot more amused than her. He looked over at her, their eyes briefly making contact, and she quickly looked down at her food and kept eating.

When she was finishing the last wing on her plate, Harvey came up. He was dressed in his typical plaid button-up, though his hair and beard looked neater. "Hey," he said, "you want to dance? Seems unfair that we're the only two without a partner."

She smiled and shuffled her shoulders a bit. "Of course!" It was a nice gesture, and hardly a surprising one. This was camp, after all.

The two walked onto the floor as the band shifted to a lively version of "Santa Claus is Coming to Town." Ashley had never been much of a dancer, but was able to find a rhythm in her body as she danced opposite Harvey. Soon all the couples had merged into one large group, as the band played song after song. Marc joined in as well, but seemed to keep his distance from her.

At one point the kids all came onto the floor, then the musicians shifted into country music and Carol attempted to show everyone how to square dance to "Deck the Halls." She was somewhat successful.

After a raucous finish to the tune, the band cut out and Marc walked up to the stage. "Ladies and gentlemen, let's give a big hand to our neighborhood jazz quartet!" Ashley joined in clapping as the four musicians took a bow. Marc continued, "And now, it is time. Let's head outside for the lighting of tree!"

The guests all made for the exit. Ashley, sweating from all the dancing, grabbed her coat but didn't bother putting it on. She needed some winter air to cool herself down.

They all gathered around the tree, with most of the guests struggling through the snow in their dress shoes and heels. Ashley was no different and kept to the plowed pathway. Once they were all outside, Marc began a countdown. "Ten, nine, eight..."

They all joined in. At zero, Marc hit a switch on the Lodge and the tree lit up with hundreds of large, bright lights, going all the way up its thirty-foot frame and showing off the numerous ornaments hanging from its branches. She clapped and cheered loudly. It was something else.

"But," Marc said, his loud voice echoing off the trees, "I understand that some of you are still concerned that Santa might not see the tree tonight. So, to ensure he does..."

He hit another switch, and four spotlights, each positioned in the snow about twenty feet from the tree, came on, shooting a bright beam of light into the sky. The kids screamed and squealed. Adam jumped up and down, nearly beside himself with excitement.

"Speaking of Santa, I think it's time we all got ready for his arrival," Marc said. "Thank you all so much for making this Christmas Eve party so much fun. A reminder that tomorrow morning is all yours and breakfast will be at your leisure, and then we'll be doing Secret Santa gifts at lunchtime, so be sure to drop your present off before then. Then in the afternoon we will have our final event in the Christmas Cup, followed by our Christmas dinner!"

The group started heading back to their cabins. Ashley caught up with Emma. "Hey, would you happen to have some extra gift paper?" she asked. "I have a gift of my own that I need to wrap."

Emma smiled. "Of course!" She led Ashley to her cabin and went inside. A few seconds later she emerged with a full roll of giftwrap, as well as a pair of scissors and some tape.

"Oh wow, thank you!" Ashley said. "I'll get these back to you as soon as I can."

"Don't worry about it. I only brought five of each." Emma's girls ran up onto the porch and started babbling about how Santa was on his way. Emma winked at Ashley. "I better get these two into bed. See you tomorrow! Girls, what do you say to Ashley?"

"Goodnight Ashley!" the girls said in unison. They removed their boots and ran inside.

Ashley carried the wrapping items back to her cabin and pulled Adam's robot gift out of its bag. It took a few tries, but she was able to cover it in the blue-and-silver paper, in a way that looked at least somewhat professional. When she was finished she placed it on top of her dresser.

Movement outside her window caught her eye. Thanks to the bright lights by the tree, she could see Marc walking down the path, towards his cabin. She watched him go until he was out of sight, then she sat down on her bed.

She shook her head. This wasn't right. It was nearly Christmas — this was the worst time to have this sort of cloud hanging over them. She owed him an apology, and the longer she waited to do it the worse she would feel.

She grabbed the construction paper off her bed and gave it a quick read-over. Satisfied with what she'd written, she put her winter clothes back on, left her cabin, and headed for Marc's.

Chapter 30

Ashley was the only one outside, but she could hear plenty of talking and laughter from the other cabins as she moved down the path. From Emma's she could hear the mom reading "Twas the Night Before Christmas," while Carol's and Bill's had the sounds of glasses clinking and Elvis singing "Here Comes Santa Claus."

Holding her papers firmly, she walked behind the camp's office and up to Marc's cabin. She stopped at the door and held her hand up, but then paused and asked herself if she really wanted to do this. Maybe it would be better to avoid the conversation, to hand him her work tomorrow and then be on her way. Then they would both avoid another potentially awkward talk.

"No. Don't be a coward," she muttered to herself. She had to. She owed him an apology. That's what friends did when they wronged each other.

So why was it so hard for her to knock on the door? Her shaking fist hovered inches away. She just couldn't bring herself to move it.

"Hello?" Marc's said from inside the cabin. "Is someone there?"

There were creaky footsteps and then the door opened. "Oh," Ashley said, still holding up her hand. "Hey."

Marc cocked his head to the side. He was still wearing his grey button-up and dark jeans from the party. "Hey. Everything alright?"

"Yeah. It's great." She stood in place for a second. "Can I come in?"

"Of course." He opened the door all the way and gestured for her to enter.

Marc's cabin was like something out of an old-fashioned story. It was a single room, save for a small bathroom to her left. Along the right wall was the bed, same size as hers but with a wooden frame with shelves underneath. A dresser sat next to it, also made out of wood but clearly hand-carved, with ornate designs running up and down the sides and along the edges. In the middle was a wood stove, with bright orange flames burning inside. Two large easy chairs with thick cushions sat on either side of the stove, about five feet apart, and a small kitchen with a sink, toaster oven and miniature fridge were to the left of that.

Hanging from the log walls were picture frames with various photos of the camp, some old and in black-and-white and some new and showing Cedarwood in different seasons. The ones in fall—with trees showing leaves in brilliant reds, yellows and oranges—were particularly gorgeous.

"This is cozy," she said, taking it all in.

He chuckled. "When you live here year-round, it pretty much has to be." He offered her a seat in the easy chair. She took it and he sat down opposite of her. "What's up?"

"I wanted to talk to you. About two things, actually. And I'm going to start with the easy one." She handed him the papers. "This is for you. Sorry that it's on construction paper. Normally I'd type it up and put it in a nice template."

He took the pages and read the first one. "'Camp Cedarwood Marketing Plan.' What is this?"

"It's a guide to getting more people here, both for the summer camps and your year-round programs. What you have here is really special and I know that you could pack the place every week if more people knew about it."

He flipped through the pages. "Target markets… earned media… key messages… wow." He looked back up at her. "Thank you. If we're able to keep the camp running next year, I will do everything you've put down here." He smiled. "I really appreciate this."

"It's the least I could do," she said. Her heartrate began to pick up. It was time to get to the harder conversation. "And I mean that, Marc. I feel awful about how things went last night and what I said to you. I'm sorry. I really am."

He nodded. "We both said things last night that we regret. I shouldn't be judging you by things you did fifteen years ago. You're a good person, Ash, and clearly an excellent marketer." He held up her plan. "I'm sorry as well. It just… I don't know. Even though it was so long ago, it hurt to feel like what we had meant nothing to you. Because it meant so much to me. I remember the next year, I kept hoping you'd show up and we'd get to spend another summer together. And then you didn't, obviously, and that whole summer felt so empty." He shook his head. "This is silly. I'm sorry. I shouldn't be ruminating on something that happened so long ago."

"No," Ashley said. "It's okay." She looked down and sighed. "You want to know the truth? This place didn't mean a lot to me when I was younger. That's just a fact. But you… Marc, you did. You made my time here bearable. Heck, you made it more than bearable. You made it great. I still remember waking up each day and having to get my campers ready and wishing I could just go back to bed. And then I'd think of seeing you at breakfast and that would be enough for me to keep going." She looked back up at him. His blue eyes shimmered in the firelight. "I loved the days off that we spent together, or how we'd sneak off and explore the forests while the campers were doing their activities, or just hanging out on the dock and watching the sunset. All of it. And you know, even when I was engaged, it wasn't the same. There was never that sense of fun and adventure that I had with you. I guess I told myself that I was an adult now and I shouldn't expect my relationships to be all fun and laughter." She shrugged. "Maybe I sold myself short."

For a minute, the only sound was the crackling of the fire. Then Marc spoke, his voice barely above a whisper. "You were my first love." He sighed and laughed to himself. "There, I've said it. I loved you, Ash. You were the first girl to really make me understand what it meant to fall in love with someone. And I guess, in a sense, you were also the first one to really break my heart."

She leaned forward. Her senses suddenly went into overdrive: she could hear every crack and crackle from the fire, feel the soft, worn-out cushion underneath her, smell the strong scent of cedar in the cabin. "When I left camp," she said slowly, trying to choose the right words, "I knew I couldn't stay in touch with you. So when you sent me that email, asking if I'd made it home, I must have deleted it. I honestly don't remember, but I had to have done it. Because I do remember feeling like you could convince me to come back to Cedarwood. And I was afraid that if we stayed in touch, and I thought about all the things we'd done together, and all the things we could do together in the future… I was afraid I'd lose sight of my goal."

Marc brought a hand up to his chin. "I get it," he said. "If it had been the other way around, and you'd asked me to leave Cedarwood to be with you, I probably would have said no as well."

"Doesn't change that it was unfair to you. You're right, we were friends. We had something special. I shouldn't have cut you out all these years. Again, I'm really sorry."

He smiled, this time wider. "I know you are. We both were foolish about this. But that's what happens. Sometimes friends fight."

She grinned. "And sometimes good friends have good fights."

"Good friends. I like that."

"Me too." She stood up. "When I go home tomorrow, I promise I'll keep in touch. Who knows, maybe I'll even find my way back here in the new year. When there's not three feet of snow on the ground, it's only, what, a two-hour drive from the city?"

"If that." He stood up and walked over to the mini fridge. "Before you go, I think this deserves a drink." He pulled out two glass bottles. "I noticed you enjoyed the beer we had last night. Fortunately, I happen to buy a case every month or so." He walked back and handed her one.

She twisted the cap off and raised it. "To our friendship."

He clinked it. She took a few gulps and looked back at him. She couldn't help but wonder, at that moment, what would have happened if she'd stayed with him. What if she'd dropped the Marketing program said yes to Police College, and kept coming back to Cedarwood for the summer? Would it have worked out between them? Or would it have been a summer romance that fizzled away?

"What are you thinking about?" Marc seemed closer now, just inches from her face.

She shrugged. "Nothing." There was no point in having regrets. Not after all the time that had passed. "How about you?"

He took another drink. "You know."

"I don't know." She found herself leaning closer to him. She could hear his soft, deep breaths, smell the smoke on his shirt.

"Yeah," he said. "Me either." He leaned in.

Ashley felt the hair on her skin stand on-end. She wasn't going to allow herself to regret something she did fifteen years ago.

But she also wasn't going to regret not doing something now.

She brought her mouth up to his. The bottle in her hand was trembling. She wanted this. She wanted to feel his lips, to taste his breath. It was only clear to her at this very second.

They were just inches away. With his free hand, Marc grabbed hers. She breathed out blissfully and closed her eyes. She could feel his breath against her face. She moved forward, ready for impact.

They were interrupted by a piercing scream.

"ADAM!"

Chapter 31

The two pulled away and looked at each other in surprise. Marc let go of Ashley's hand, ran to the door and yanked it open.

Paige was on her porch. Even from the distance, Ashley could see that she was distraught, with tears streaking down her face. "Adam!" she shouted again. "Please! Where are you?"

Ashley threw her coat on and ran outside with Marc. "What happened?" Marc asked. Around them, the other guests had opened their doors and were looking out at the commotion.

Paige wiped her eyes. "H-he had gone off to the Lodge to grab his hat. And while he was out I was talking with David about his health and how scared I was that the cancer would come back. I... I..." She let out a sob. "I said I was afraid that this would be our last Christmas together. And then next thing I knew he was in the doorway, saying he'd heard what I said and asking if he was going to die."

"Oh no," Ashley breathed. She put a hand to her mouth.

"And then he ran off," Paige said. "I thought maybe he just needed a second to cool down, but when I looked out he was gone. I have no idea where he went."

"We'll find him," Marc said. There was a strength and determination in his voice. He turned around and called out. "I need everyone to grab a flashlight and meet me at the Lodge right now! We're doing a ground search!"

He headed towards the Lodge. Ashley stayed still, looking from Marc to Paige, and then to the forest behind Marc's cabin. "I know where he is," she said.

"Really?" Paige asked. "Where?"

"In the woods. Follow me."

She took off running down the path, through the parking lot and into the forest. Ashley slowed down as she moved through the trees, trying to remember the way they had walked two days prior. The moon — bright and round in the sky — provided enough light for her to spot and follow their footprints. She tried to keep as quiet as possible, out of fear that Adam would run if he heard her coming. She couldn't even imagine what he had to be feeling at that moment. To be ten years old and have that sort of weight put on you... it was unthinkable.

She passed through two large trees and heard a loud sniffle from behind a pine just up ahead. Tiptoeing as much as she could in large, thick boots, she came around the branches and saw the shelter. A whimpering sounded within it.

"Hey Adam?" she called out.

"Go away," came a choked voice from inside.

Ashley walked up to the entrance and crouched down. Adam was sitting against the wall, knees pulled up to his head and arms wrapped around his legs. "I can't do that," Ashley said softly. "Everyone's looking for you. They're all worried."

"I don't care," Adam said into his knees. "I heard my mom. She thinks I'm going to die. It doesn't matter what I do." He pulled his head back and looked at her with big, watery eyes. "Do you think I'm going to die?"

Ashley got on her hands and knees and crawled into the shelter. Unlike the first time, she could not have cared less about getting her clothes muddy. "I don't know," she said, sitting opposite of Adam. "From what I hear you're a really strong boy who's been able to handle everything that's been thrown at you so far. So I'd bet on you, that's for sure."

"My mom doesn't." He put his head back in his knees.

"Yes she does. Believe me, I've talked to her a lot. She thinks you're the toughest kid in the world. But she's scared. She loves you so much and that love means she is going to worry about you."

Adam took a deep, raspy breath. "But what if I die? What if the cancer comes back and I can't beat it this time?" His voice rose. "I don't want to fight it again! It's so hard and it hurts so much. I just... what if I die?"

Ashley struggled to think of what to say. Her whole job was telling people things to make them feel good. But at that moment, she had no idea what could possibly make Adam feel better. "Then..." she started. "Then you just have to enjoy life as much as you can."

Again, his head rose from his knees. "What? So you really do think I could die then?"

It felt like a bit of a trap he'd led her into, but she moved past it. "I really think you're going to beat this, and that the next time I see you you'll be cancer-free." She scooted closer to him. "But if you don't, that just means your life was all the more precious. Let me ask you this: do you love Christmas?"

"Y-yeah," came the timid response. "Of course I do."

"But Christmas ends, doesn't it? Every year it comes and then it goes. Does that make you love Christmas any less?"

He shook his head. "No."

"And if Christmas was every single day of the year, would you like that?"

Another head shake. "No. Then it wouldn't be special."

"Exactly. Christmas is special because it's just one day a year. You wait for it, it happens and it's the best thing in the world, and then it's gone. It's kind of like life. We all go through it but at some point it ends for all of us. No one's life lasts forever, but that doesn't mean that our lives aren't special. What matters is that we make the most of the time we have, especially with our family and friends."

Adam wiped his eyes with his glove. "Just like Christmas."

"Now you've got it."

Adam was quiet for a minute, except for taking deep, heavy breaths. Then he lunged forward and wrapped his arms around Ashley. She grabbed him and hugged him tightly. "Thank you," he whispered.

"Anytime."

From outside came voices. "Adam? Where are you?"

Adam released himself from the hug and crawled to the shelter's entrance. "I'm here, mom!"

There were heavy footsteps outside, followed by a cry of relief. "Oh thank God." Paige knelt down and looked inside. "We were so worried about you! Are you okay?"

Adam crawled out and hugged his mom. Ashley followed him. "I'm fine," Adam said. "Ashley and I had a good talk about Christmas."

Ashley laughed as she stood up and brushed herself off. Adam let go of his mom and ran to his dad. "Thank you so much," Paige said. In the moonlight, Ashley could see her trembling. "What did he say?"

"Just that he was scared," Ashley said. "He's afraid that if he has to fight the disease again, he might lose."

Paige nodded and looked over at her son, as David picked Adam up, swung him around and placed him back on the ground. "He's not the only one," she said. She sighed. "But that's neither here nor there. Thank you again. I take it this is the place Adam wouldn't let you tell us about?"

"Yes it is."

David walked over. "I think we have some difficult conversations ahead of us," he said, keeping his voice low. "He's getting older now. He's going to be asking questions."

"Then we'll just have to answer them," Paige said.

"He's smart," Ashley said. "Which I suppose has its pros and cons."

"He gets that from me," Paige said. In a louder voice she said, "Adam, come show us what you've made here. Adam?"

Adam stood still, about twenty feet away from them, facing off deeper into the woods. "Hey Adam," David said. "What did you — oh."

Ashley followed Adam's gaze and saw, illuminated by a beam of moonlight coming through the trees, the deer that they'd seen earlier. Its antlers seemed to gleam in the light as it stared right at the boy. Then it turned and walked further into the trees.

Adam started walking after it. "Honey," Paige said. She chased after him and put her hands on his shoulders. "We should get going."

Ashley and David moved up to them. "It's late," David added. "We need to get back to the cabin for when Santa comes."

Adam looked down with his shoulders slumped. "Fine," he said. "But I better... wait. What is that?"

He took a few more steps and pushed away a thick branch, sending a pile of snow onto the ground. "Adam," Paige pleaded. "Please, it's cold and dark and we all want to go to bed."

Adam pointed further into the forest. "Look."

The three adults crouched down and gazed out. Deeper in the forest, behind a cluster of pine trees, was a light. Ashley narrowed her eyes, trying to make out the source. This forest went on for miles — there was no way it could be from a cottage.

The deer suddenly ran out in front of them. It bolted through the snow and disappeared behind the trees. Adam took off after it, causing the branch to snap back and nearly hit his parents. They pushed through the limbs and went after him. Ashley, not knowing what else to do, followed.

Adam was able to move through the trees more quickly and outran his parents to the pines. He stopped in front of them and waited for the others to join him. David and Paige reached him, with Ashley close behind. In the golden light coming from the other side of the trees, she could see a mixture of confusion and curiosity on their faces.

When they were all together, Adam led them all through the branches. Ashley was briefly blinded as the bright light hit her. When her vision cleared, she found herself looking at dozens, if not hundreds, of towering pine trees, each easily thirty feet tall. Every single one of them was decorated with gold and silver bulbs and illuminated by red candles in holders and lanterns that hung from the limbs. The bulbs shimmered in the candlelight so authentically that Ashley wondered if she was looking at the real material, not some sort of replica.

The trees parted right in front of the four to form a wide path. Adam reached his hands out towards his parents. Paige grabbed his right and David his left. The three of them started down the path. Ashley walked behind them, staring up and around at the trees. She caught her reflection in the ornate bulbs and became convinced that this was really silver and gold that surrounded her. She made no effort to reach out and find for sure.

They continued down the path in silence, the only sound the crunching of the untouched snow beneath their boots. The pines seemed to go on forever, each one decorated just as beautifully as the last. There were no other types of tree, nor anything to block the bright moon from above. While still aware of the cold, Ashley found that it didn't bother her. If anything, the air smelled fresher, with the frosty scents of pine filling her lungs with every breath.

She looked to the family in front of her. Adam still held onto his parents' hands as the three of them walked slowly, taking in the sight with awe and wonder. Their shadows stretched out in front of them in the moonlight, the son's as long as the parents'.

After walking for what could have been five minutes or fifty, the trees in front of the group began to widen, leading to a clearing, about fifty feet long. It too was surrounded by decorated pines, but these ones had bulbs of red, green and white, as well as ornaments that resembled classic toys: rocking horses, drums, jack-in-the-boxes and teddy bears.

In the middle of the clearing was a large stump, about three feet high. As the four of them walked closer, Ashley could see a small chest sitting on it. It was made of wood and had red and gold spirals painted along its sides, with a small metal latch at the front. Adam and his parents stopped in front of it. Adam let go of their hands and pulled his gloves off.

A noise to her left caught Ashley's attention. The deer stood at the edge of the clearing, looking at them. The other three didn't notice. The animal was still for a few seconds before retreating into the trees. Ashley watched it leave and kept her eyes on the spot for a few seconds before moving back to Adam.

He reached out with his bare hands and grasped the latch. It slid off with a click. He opened the chest and slowly reached in. His parents stood on either side of him, his father's eyes wide in awe and his mother beaming with pride.

Adam pulled his hand back out of the chest and held up a star ornament, the kind used to top a Christmas tree. Initially Ashley thought that it was silver, but as the candle and moonlight shimmered off of it it seemed to change colors, going to red and purple and gold.

Adam turned around and held it up, a large smile on his face. Around them, the candles seemed to glow brighter, until it was light as day, and the reflections of the different ornaments created a rainbow of colors on the snow and in the air. Adam's parents opened their arms and grabbed their son in a tight hug, and then Paige reached out and pulled Ashley into it as well. She wrapped her arms around the three of them as best as she could. For a minute, their soft breaths were the only sound she heard.

"Hey!" Marc's voice rang through the trees. "Where are you guys?"

The forest was suddenly dark again. Ashley broke away from the hug and saw that the Christmas trees were gone. Tall, dark trees now surrounded them. The air felt colder and the strong scents of pine had vanished. Ashley looked over at Adam's hands. They were empty.

Marc came crashing through the trees, skidding to a stop in the snow when he saw them. "There you are!" he exclaimed. "Are you okay?"

Ashley, Paige and David looked at it each. "Yes," Paige said, after a second. "We are. We just went on a little walk."

Marc's face twisted in confusion, but he didn't question anything. "Let's get you back to camp. We were all worried about you!"

He started back the way he'd come. The group followed him.

After walking through a few trees, they reached Adam's shelter. Marc gave it a quick lookover, seemingly impressed, but didn't say anything.

As they moved toward the camp, Ashley whispered to Paige, "What just happened?"

Paige shook her head and laughed. "I have no idea. Pretty amazing, huh?"

Chapter 32

The five of them reached the camp and found the other guests waiting for them. Cheers and sighs of relief erupted as Adam emerged from the woods, though they all seemed to understand that now was not the time for questions and instead wished each other goodnight and went back to their cabins. Marc told Paige and David to let him know if they needed anything, and then headed back towards his cabin, but not before giving Ashley a quick glance.

When just the four of them were left standing in the parking lot, Paige said to Ashley, "Thank you again. Adam is lucky to have a friend like you, aren't you Adam?"

Her son nodded. "Thanks Ash. See you tomorrow!"

"You bet," Ashley said. "And speaking of tomorrow, we should get to bed. I swear I hear sleigh bells in the distance."

That was enough to get Adam to start back towards his cabin, dragging his parents in tow. Ashley followed and split off towards her own cabin. She passed the other ones, marveling in their decorated glory one last time. Were the abundance of lights and trinkets over-the-top, to the point of being gaudy? For sure. Did she love them nonetheless? Ditto.

At her cabin, she stopped and looked at the massive tree in the middle of the area. Words could not describe what she had just seen—what she had just experienced—and she didn't even try to come up with them. She simply stared at the Christmas tree and remembered all the other ones that she'd been walking through just minutes before.

A light at the top of the tree caught her eye. There was a star on it now, glowing blue in the moonlight. As Ashley watched, it changed colors to a burning red. She squinted up at it and muttered, "What on earth…"

It was the star Adam had found in the chest. There was no doubt in her mind.

Marc's words about Christmas magic came back to her. She shrugged—because how else could she react to something so incredible?—walked into her cabin and went to bed.

Christmas Day

Chapter 33

The bright sun coming through the windows stirred Ashley out of her sleep. She rolled over, looked up at the ceiling and asked herself what had happened last night. The whole experience had been so surreal that she considered for a few minutes that it had all been a dream. But then she remembered that it had been real, even if it was completely inexplicable.

Her phone told her it was 9:30. She'd slept for over nine hours. Since the other guests were all celebrating Christmas morning in their cabins and there was no structured breakfast time, Ashley meandered through getting ready, enjoying a nice hot shower and then laying back in bed to take in the soft mattress and heavy covers one more time before heading to the Lodge.

She was the only one in the Meal Hall, not that it bothered her. A small buffet of breakfast foods had been laid out on the tables. Ashley grabbed a paper plate and added a large cinnamon roll (smothered in thick icing), a warm croissant, a bowl of strawberry yogurt and a handful of fruit. All the chairs had been set up in front of the stage, which didn't make for a very comfortable eating experience, so Ashley left the Lodge and headed back to her cabin.

As she was passing the cabin with purple-and-gold lights and school paraphernalia, the door swung open and Janice stuck her head out. "Ash! Merry Christmas!"

"Same to you!" Ashley said.

Janice beckoned with her hand. "Where are you going? Come join us for breakfast!"

Ashley gestured down the path. "Oh, that's okay, I was just going to —
"

"C'mon. It's Christmas morning! No one should be celebrating alone!"

Ashley knew there was no way she'd be able to get out of the invitation. Still holding her plate, she went in, removing her boots at the door.

The cabin's floor was littered in thick metallic wrapping paper and a bunch of boxes lay at the foot of the bed. Roger, dressed in pyjama pants and a long-sleeved shirt, sat in one of the two chairs, eating a plain bagel with cream cheese, while Janice invited Ashley to take the other chair while she sat down on the bed. "Merry Christmas!" Roger said, his mouth full.

"Merry Christmas to you," Ashley said. "I take it Santa was good to you guys?"

Janice looked over at her husband and grinned. "Maybe not Santa, but a different big, jolly guy sure was." She held up her left hand, revealing a stunning diamond ring on her finger. It glistened in the light.

Ashley's jaw dropped. "Oh my goodness." She looked at Roger. "Did you get her that?" He only smirked and took another bite. "Husband of the year right here. Maybe the decade."

"It is beautiful, isn't it?" Janice brought her hand to her face to admire it. "But I still think I won Christmas this year, right honey?"

Roger swallowed the bagel and nodded. "She booked us a week-long trip to my alma mater for Homecoming. Royal suite at the hotel, a day at the spa and —" He danced a bit in his seat. " — motorcycle rental!"

"Sounds like quite the trip."

Janice rolled her eyes good-naturedly. "And there's one other present, but it's going to have to wait a little bit." She turned to Ashley. "How are you doing?"

"I'm great. I slept in, my breakfast was made for me and I don't have anywhere to be for a few hours. This is the best Christmas ever."

"See, that's the right attitude to have," Roger joked. "I made the mistake of setting high expectations with my wife and now I have to exceed them every year. It's exhausting."

Janice looked at her new ring again. "It's good from my side of things." Her tone dropped lower. "So what happened last night? Did you find Adam in the woods? Was he okay?"

"He was fine," Ashley said. "He was in a fort he and his friends had built during the summer. He... he needed some reassurance." And he sure got that, she thought.

Janice nodded. "He seemed pretty happy when he came out. Whatever you said to him, it must have worked."

Ashley scratched at her neck. "It, uh, was more of the experience, I guess. He seemed to find some comfort in the woods." She briefly considered telling them what she had seen, but decided against it, not only because she was concerned they would think she was crazy, but also because what had happened had clearly been a special experience for Adam and his family. She didn't think it was right to share it with others. Instead, she said, "Anyway, what can I expect for today?"

She ate her breakfast as they explained how the rest of the day would go: the Secret Santa, which always had a few hilarious surprises; the final event of the Christmas Cup ("I'm looking forward to taking both of you down," Roger boasted); and then a full Christmas dinner in the early evening. After dinner would be goodbyes and then the guests would be on their way. "Marc used to close camp on the 26th, but most people prefer to go home after the dinner, and we know he needs a break anyway, so no one complained when he moved it to Christmas night," Janice said. "Though if it's an issue I'm sure he'll be fine with you staying one more night."

"No, I need to get home," Ashley said. The roads had to be cleared by now, but she remembered she still needed to fill her car with the gas canister in Marc's trunk.

They spent the next few minutes talking about their plans for the rest of the holidays—for all three of them, it involved some sort of work for their jobs—and what they wanted to do for New Years. They were interrupted by laughter outside the window.

Harvey and his kids ran by, each carrying a new sled. "To the tubing hill!" Ian called out. His sister dove forward onto the snow.

Janice grinned. "No better place to be, huh?"

"Hard to think of a better one," Ashley said.

After some more light chatter, Ashley grabbed her plate and stood up. "Thanks for your hospitality. I'll see you two in a bit." She put her boots on and walked back outside.

More laughter and shouts came from the field as she went back to her cabin. Emma, Jack and their daughters were playing in the snow, with the two girls chasing their dad around. She looked right, to the other side of the section. Drew and Sally sat on Drew's deck, each nursing a mug in their hands. They waved at Ashley.

Ashley went back into her cabin and grabbed the wrapped present for Secret Santa. She headed back to the Lodge and placed it with the other presents under her team's tree. Then she took a seat and waited for the other guests.

They trickled in, each wishing a Merry Christmas as they entered. Just before noon, Harvey and his kids came in, their faces and hair covered in snow, followed soon after by Paige, David and Adam, who carried a sizeable Lego spaceship in his hand. They sat down next to Ashley.

"Merry Christmas!" Adam exclaimed. "I got this ship this morning and I already built it! But it came with extra pieces to give it bigger wings and an extra cabin!"

"That's awesome," Ashley said. She glanced over at his parents. They both seemed upbeat and cheerful. If the strange events from the previous night were weighing on them, they sure didn't show it.

A sudden stomp came from the door. "Ho ho ho!"

Marc, dressed in a Santa hat and beard, walked in and went up on the stage. "Merry Christmas everyone! I hope you've all had a wonderful morning and are ready for the best day of the year! Since time is precious, let's get to the gifts!" Ashley smiled and rolled her eyes. What a ham.

Marc reached down and grabbed a small box. "This one is for... ooh, Carol! Why don't we see what's inside?" He handed it to her.

She carefully unwrapped it and pulled out a snow globe. "Oh my," she said, holding it up for the others to see. Inside the glass dome was an old-fashioned covered wagon and a cactus. "Now there's something you don't see every day." She held it close to her chest. "Thank you Santa, I love it!"

"You're welcome!" Drew said. "You would not believe how many websites I had to look through to find it."

Marc — or Santa — continued with the gifts for each of the guests. Some seemed elated (a set of beard oil and a comb had Harvey promising he'd use it as soon as he was back in his cabin), while others were clearly trying to put on a brave face (Jack's gift of a tire wrench and car jack weren't well-received). There were also a few gag gifts, including a pair of bright-colored, four-foot long knitted socks for Bill that had to be some sort of inside joke, based on how hard the other adults laughed when he opened them. The platinum-blonde hair dye for Marc needed no explanation, though, and Ashley was nearly crying with laughter as he opened it.

There were just a few gifts left when Marc picked up another and said, "And this is for Ashley!"

"What?" Ashley said. "I mean... okay!" He handed her a rectangular box with a separate lid and a ribbon tied around it. She undid the ribbon and pulled out a small crystal vase. "Oh my gosh..." She held it up and examined it. There were carvings along it in the shapes of trees, small buildings and a fire pit. It took her a second to realize they all represented Camp Cedarwood. "This is amazing. Thank you so much Santa. I was not expecting this."

Carol said, "I guess Santa always comes prepared with an extra gift." Ashley leaned over and gave her a hug.

Marc reached down. "Now what do we have here?" He grabbed Ashley's gift. "To Adam. Is there an Adam here?"

The giftee jumped up in his seat. "Yes! I'm here!" He took the present and ripped the paper off. "No way! Look! It's a robot you can build!" He put the spaceship on the ground and started opening the box, only to be stopped by his parents, who suggested he wait until they were back home and he had the space to build it. "Who gave this to me? Who's my Santa?"

Ashley raised her eyebrows at him. "Who do you think, you little squirt?"

Adam dropped the box and lunged at Ashley with his arms wide. "You're the best! This is the best gift ever!"

She felt her heart warm in a way she wasn't sure had been possible. Marc chuckled and grabbed the final present under the tree. "And last, but not least, Roger!"

Roger opened the gift, a bottle of Jamaican rum. "Mmm, I can't wait to try this," he said. "I know what I'll be having for New Years!"

Emma waved. "I'm glad you like it."

Adam finally let go of Ashley and sat back down. "Hmm," Marc said, still in his deeper Santa Claus voice. "That's odd. There's still one gift left here." He held up a small box, just a few inches long and wide. "And it's also for Roger. I wonder what it could be."

He handed it to the man, who pulled off the ribbons and wrapping paper, and then opened the top. He reached in and pulled out a blue pacifier with a pink handle. "Huh?" he said. "What's this about?"

He looked over at his wife. Janice bore a massive smile and large, watery eyes.

Emma was the first to gasp and cover her mouth, and then Harvey and Paige both seemed to be trying to contain themselves. Roger opened his mouth slightly in confusion. Then it went wider, and wider, along with his eyes. He held his hands in front of him. "No! No way!" He jumped up and grabbed his wife. "NO WAY!"

"Merry Christmas, honey," Janice said. She wiped her eyes. "Next year, there'll be another person to buy presents for."

A river of exclamations, and a few obscenities, flowed from Roger's mouth. He wrapped his arms around his wife and lifted her up. Everyone else rose to their feet, cheering louder than they had for anything else at camp that week. Ashley found herself wiping away a few tears. She looked over at Marc. Under his beard, he was clearly beaming.

Once the noise had died down, and it took a few minutes to do so, Marc said, "Well if this hasn't made your Christmas, I don't know what will. Though the fun still isn't over. I've been asked by David and Drew to inform you that the final event of the Christmas Cup will be taking place in half an hour. Meet in the middle of the field, and be ready to fight to the finish!" He coughed a few times and took the beard off. "Gah, this thing is nearly impossible to talk in. As a reminder, there's still plenty of brunch food if you need extra energy for the event. Frost Bites, I suggest you load up. We have a Cup to win!"

Ashley, Paige and Janice booed him good-naturedly. Marc got off the stage and was the first to go up to Janice and congratulate her. An informal line formed as everyone else wanted to do the same. When it was Ashley's turn, she gave her new friend a tight hug. "When did you find out?"

"Since yesterday," she said. "I brought the little gift with me because, you know, I suspected, but I only found out for sure last night." She squeezed Ashley's shoulder. "I guess there was a lot of Christmas magic in the air, huh?"

Ashley nodded. "There sure was," she said, stealing a look over at Adam and his family. "There sure was."

Chapter 34

Ashley grabbed a blueberry muffin and ate it on the way back to her cabin. When she was back inside she took off her outerwear and spent the next twenty minutes stretching her body, from her legs up to her head, using a routine from her fitness club that she was more or less able to recall. When she was done, she felt energized and ready to go.

She put her jacket and boots back on and pulled her hat and gloves on tightly. Then she walked back outside and headed onto the field. The final event of the Christmas Cup was just minutes away. A chill went down her spine just thinking about it. She couldn't remember the last time she'd actually felt excited for something that wasn't work-related, especially a physical activity in the snow.

A crowd had already gathered in the middle, with the Ice Dinosaurs in one group and the Frost Bites in the other. Paige was among them. "I don't think I've ever seen Adam react to a gift like that," she said. "So while I am a bit jealous as his mother, all I can say is thank you. You didn't need to do that, at all."

"I know, but it's Adam. Like you said, he's a special kid." Ashley looked around to check if anyone was listening and leaned in closer. "About last night…"

Paige held her hand up. "Let's not dissect it. Whatever it was, it was something special, especially to Adam. I don't need to know anything beyond that."

Ashley nodded. "That works for me. Though I wonder —"

Paige held her hand up again. "Not a word," she said, with a bit of a smirk.

The other competitors arrived, including David and Adam, who couldn't stop gushing about the robot and all the cool things he was going to do with it. Ashley was sure her heart was about to break out in song.

When they had all gathered, David and Drew stood between the two teams. "Ladies and gentlemen," Drew said. "Welcome to the final event of the Christmas Cup. You have both fought hard to get here. You've braved the elements, gotten messy and endured a few embarrassing incidents." Ashley glanced over at Marc. He rolled his eyes. "But now, all that comes down to this last competition. The winner of this year's Christmas Cup will be determined by an all-out, no-holds-barred, winner-take-all… SNOWBALL FIGHT!"

"Hoo boy," Carol said.

"Here is how it will work," David continued. "Both teams will have thirty minutes to build their forts and assemble their snowballs. After that time has passed, the battle will begin. The rules are simple: if you are hit with a snowball, you are out. The last team standing will win the event, the point and the Christmas Cup!"

Ashley jumped in place, her nerves radiating through her body. It had been decades since she'd last been in a snowball fight, but she didn't care. She was going to win this one. "Teams, when we start, please walk twenty feet back and then begin constructing your forts," David instructed. "In three, two, one, go!"

Ashley and her teammates ran back a dozen paces and gathered together. Harvey immediately took charge. "We should build a curved wall," he said. "It will give us better protection and force them to go around." He pointed at all the kids. "Your job is to make as many snowballs as you can. We're going to need hundreds if we want to win this. Sound good?"

Adam, Ian and the girls all nodded and dropped to the ground. The first few snowballs were formed in seconds. Harvey looked at the adults. "Let's get started on the fort." He stomped at the snow. "It's warmed up a bit, so this is good packing snow. As long as you're all willing to get a little damp, we should be good."

"Let's go!" Janice shouted. Even though she was no more than a few days pregnant, she was already glowing. She got on her hands and knees and began digging up snow.

Ashley knelt down as well. The snow was a bit wet, but she got used to it quickly as she dug and started forming the wall. With everyone else pitching it, it quickly grew in size, first to one foot and then two.

She looked over at the Frost Bites. They were making about the same progress, though with fewer kids on their team she wondered how many snowballs they'd be able to make.

As she watched, Marc grabbed a big pile of snow in his arms and added it to the wall. She sighed. In all the magic that had taken place with Adam and his family in the forest, she'd almost forgotten that she and Marc had been milliseconds away from kissing. What was she supposed to make of that? They obviously liked each other. But it wasn't a lack of attraction that was keeping them apart. It never had been.

She added more snow to her part of the wall and sunk deeper into thought. Fifteen years ago she had found Marc cute. Now he was tall and handsome. And he still had the same personality—outgoing, funny, caring, and not afraid to look ridiculous if it made someone else laugh. In the four days they'd spent together she felt closer to him than any man she'd been with in the last two years. "Maybe even more than the man you were engaged to," she muttered to herself as she patted down the snow.

But she lived in the city and he lived at camp. Even if Cedarwood somehow shut down, Marc would never want to move to an urban dwelling. He'd probably just find another camp to run, or he'd work for a children's charity. Because that's just who he was. It was such a shame that the thing keeping them apart was his best attribute.

She picked up more snow and put it on the top of the wall. What could she do, she wondered. Was there a way to make it work? Or to even give it a try? If there was, it wasn't coming to mind. And now she was facing a deadline: in a few short hours, she'd be heading home.

"Looking great, Ash," Harvey said. Ashley broke out of her thoughts and realized she was outpacing everyone else in her section of the fort. She smiled to herself and kept going, letting her body go on autopilot as her mind went back to how she could possibly make things work with Marc.

By the time the fort was ready, Ashley was no closer to a solution. She focused her attention back to the event. The fort's wall was just about done, going four feet up and ten feet wide. Behind it, the kids had made a sizeable pile of snowballs. She surveyed the wall opposite theirs. This one was a perfect line, maybe a bit longer, but also a bit shorter.

"Okay teams," Drew announced, "the time has come! Can I get everyone to come back to the center, please?"

Both teams left their forts and met in the middle of the battle area. Ashley narrowed her eyes and tried to look as intimidating as possible as she sized up her opponents. Her heart was racing. After all this back and forth, they were finally here.

"On my go, the game will begin," Drew said. "You are free to go wherever you want on the field. If you get hit, you are out. Is everyone good?" There were a whole bunch of head nods. "Then, in that case, to claim the Camp Cedarwood Christmas Cup, ready… set… GO!"

Ashley turned and ran back towards the fort. Most of her teammates joined her, but Emma crouched down, formed a snowball and threw it at her husband. It missed, but he returned fire and got her in the stomach. "Already Emma has been eliminated!" Drew said. She scowled and walked over to him and David.

Harvey was the first one to the fort. He went around the wall and then slid behind it. Janice reached the wall and vaulted over it, while Ashley and the others made their way around the barrier and crouched down. As they did, snowballs began landing on the ground nearby. "We're taking fire!" Harvey shouted. He started handing out snowballs. "Let's show them what we've got!"

He stood up and launched one at the other fort. It hit Bill just as he was standing up. He looked simultaneously disappointed and impressed as he walked to join Emma, Drew and David.

Ian grabbed a snowball in each hand and ran out from behind the wall. "Cover me!" he yelled. Ashley grabbed a snowball of her own and raised herself up just past the wall. Ian was making a dash towards the other fort, drawing the attention of Marc and Roger. Ashley chucked her snowball as hard as she could, adding in a guttural cry for good measure. They saw it coming and retreated behind the wall, allowing Ian to get close enough to throw both snowballs behind their barrier. A second later, Sally stood up and walked over to join the eliminated group.

The Frost Bites returned fire. Marc, Roger and Jack sprang up behind the wall and unleashed a volley of snowballs at the Ice Dinosaurs. Ashley threw herself against the snow as the icy balls rained down. Emma's daughter took one off the top of her head, while Carol was hit in the back. They both walked off the battlefield.

Ian grabbed another two snowballs, nodded to Ashley and ran out again. Ashley again covered him, though this time no one stood up from the other fort to try to hit him. As Ian got closer, Marc suddenly jumped out from the side of the fort and released a missile of a shot. It hit Ian in the shoulder. He swore and walked off, sulking.

"Hey, language!" Harvey shouted, throwing another snowball at the fort. It hit the wall, knocking a chunk of snow from it. Jack stood up and launched his own. It sailed through the air and landed a few feet away from Ashley.

Adam crawled from his spot along the wall to the snowball pile and grabbed a few of them. He ran out in front of the fort and threw them, though not a single one was able to make it all the way to his opponents. He ducked back behind the wall as another slew of snowballs came at him. These ones hit the fort and blew several pieces off of it.

This continued, the remaining fighters going back and forth, throwing and dodging snowballs and creating large gaps in each opponent's wall. After about five minutes without anyone being hit, Harvey ducked down behind one remaining section of the wall. "This is taking forever," he said. "I'm going on a suicide run. If I don't make it, the rest is up to you."

"Wait—" Ashley started, but Harvey had already grabbed a few snowballs and taken off running toward the other fort. His hat came off, causing his long hair to flow in the wind behind him. A loud battle cry erupted from his mouth. He looked like a Viking running into battle. His daughter ran behind him, each of her hands holding a snowball.

Jack stood up and threw a snowball at him. Harvey dove forward and, while in midair, chucked his snowballs at Jack. One hit Jack, the other hit his daughter behind him, while Jack's snowball exploded against Harvey's leg. Harvey hit the ground, then picked himself up and raised his arms in triumph. Jack walked over and patted his shoulder. Both men walked over to join the other eliminated contestants.

Harvey's daughter, clearly inspired by her father's bravery, kept going towards the fort. Marc suddenly sprung up and gently tossed a snowball at her. It hit her arm, and she simply swerved around without slowing down and ran to join her dad. Jack's daughter followed.

Marc stepped out from his half-destroyed fort, carrying several snowballs. "It's just us, Ash," he shouted. "I will accept your surrender at any time."

Ashley grinned and stood up. "Don't hold your breath."

She grabbed a snowball from the pile and ran out from behind the fort. Marc threw his first ball, which missed her by just a foot. His next one landed just in front of her. She had to duck to avoid the last one.

She cut back in front of her wall and took aim. As she did, her foot slipped and she fell forward, landing deep in the snow. She struggled to get up.

Marc slowly walked up to her. With her free hand, Ashley threw her snowball. It missed him by a few yards.

"Well, well, well," Marc said as he reached her. He crouched down and formed a snowball in his hands. "Still sure you don't want to surrender?"

He stood back up. The bright Christmas sun shone right behind him, silhouetting his frame. A large grin came across Ashley's face. "What's so funny?" Marc asked.

"I just realized something," Ashley said. "Also, I think you're about to realize something too."

A snowball hit Marc right in the stomach. Marc looked down at it, then over to the Ice Dinosaurs' fort, where Adam stood, looking equally shocked and amazed. Marc gasped, then dramatically grabbed his side and fell over into the snow.

"That's it!" Drew yelled. Loud, exuberant shouts came from Ashley's teammates. "The Ice Dinosaurs have won the Christmas Cup!"

Ashley stood up and grabbed Adam in a tight hug. "Good work," she said. "I knew you could do it."

They were joined by the rest of their team, who surrounded them in a big group hug. "Hey!" Carol shouted. "Let's hear it for the Frost Bites, for being strong competitors to the end!"

They all cheered and broke from their hug to walk over to their opponents and shake their hands. Paige lifted Adam up onto her shoulders, allowing him to high-five all of the adults. He was smiling so hard his dimples looked like craters.

When they were all done, Marc spoke up. "Congratulations to the Ice Dinosaurs. I had a blast competing with all of you, and I want to give a special thanks to David and Drew for stepping up and running these events. You did a better job than I ever would!" There was unanimous agreement from the others.

"Now, with just a few hours left in Christmas Camp, there are a few important things you need to know. First, dinner is at 5:30, and will be over by seven. If possible, please try to be out of your cabins by eight. I checked the road conditions and I'm happy to say that once you clear the hill you shouldn't have any issues getting on the highway. I'm sure you all have some packing to do and I'd suggest that now is the perfect time to do it. And as I always say at the end of camp, please make sure you return anything you borrowed from each other." He looked over at Ashley. She raised her eyebrows.

"That's all," Marc said. "See you in a few hours for Christmas dinner!"

Ashley said a few more congratulations to her teammates and then turned and walked briskly back to the cabins. There was a lot to do and not much time to do it.

She started at the Lodge, where she grabbed one of the gift boxes left over from Secret Santa. Then she went back to her cabin and began sorting through all her borrowed clothes and putting them into piles: one for Emma, one for Janice, one for Carol. There were a few things she'd need to keep on for the rest of the day, but those could be couriered to her friends once she got back to the city. She had a feeling they'd be okay with that.

When she was done sorting the clothes and then packing up her own things, she grabbed her last sheet of construction paper, wrote a quick note on it, and then folded it up and put it in the gift box. She slipped the box in her coat pocket.

She spent the next half hour returning the clothes to Janice, Emma and Carol, offering her profound thanks for their generosity. As she suspected, none of them complained about her asking to send them any outstanding items. Janice even suggested they meet up in person ("And, you know, maybe have a few drinks while we're at it," she added). Ashley could not agree more.

When the clothes were all returned, she walked over to Marc's cabin and put an ear to the door. Hearing nothing, she knocked, and when there was no response she entered. Ashley fished the box out of her coat and laid it on the easy chair, turning it so it faced the door. Then she darted back out of the cabin and closed the door firmly.

Her heart was racing, and not just because she had committed her first break and enter. She was about to take a risk, to try to redo something that had happened fifteen years earlier.

She was about to trust that maybe there was some Christmas magic after all.

Chapter 35

The sun was just inches above the horizon and glowing in a muted orange and red. Its diminished rays were quickly being overtaken by the dark sky, but they still cast a golden tinge on the snow that covered the lake. Despite the cold and increasing wind, it was still a beautiful scene. Comparable to a painting, perhaps.

Ashley stood on the frozen lake, shifting nervously at every creak and crack she thought she heard in the ice below. Even after walking on it with Adam and sliding over it on the tube, she still didn't fully trust it to hold her. It could have been twenty feet thick and she still would have worried.

It occurred to her that this was the first sunset she'd seen at Cedarwood in fifteen years. Up until now, she had been too busy — and, really, too scared — to go out on the lake to watch it. Now, though, it seemed like the right place to be. Possibly the only place to be.

There were heavy crunching footsteps behind her. Marc came down the steps to the side and walked out onto the lake. He wore his grey jacket with a plaid scarf that blew behind him in the wind. There was no hat on his head, so his golden-blonde hair shone in the dying sunlight. Ashley felt her heart rate pick up and her hands started to shake.

He smiled as he walked up. "You know, I need to take in these more often. It's amazing how they're beautiful no matter what time of year it is." He stopped beside her and watched as the sun touched the horizon. "Good evening, Ash. I hope I'm not late this time."

"You're good," Ashley said. "You must be used to being second now. How's your ego doing? A bit bruised?"

"Oh, for sure." He rubbed the back of his head. "Amazing how I just forgot that Adam existed for a minute, huh? Gosh, do I feel foolish for standing there out in the open for him to hit me."

She couldn't help but grin. Of course, she thought. How completely typical of him.

"What?" he asked. "What's so funny? Don't tell me you're upset I threw the game."

"Of course not. It's just... I just..." She took a deep breath, still keeping her eyes on the setting sun. "You know what I was supposed to do today? I mean, before a blizzard forced me off the highway?"

"Um, no. Did you have plans?"

"Big plans. Wear my pajamas, make popcorn and watch Netflix." He scoffed and shook her head. "That's how I was going to celebrate Christmas Day. And instead I'm here, and I just had the best four days in who knows how long, and I just... I'm mad at myself, you know? I'd forgotten what this place was like. I'd forgotten what it was like to meet new people and eat tons of food and do wild activities and, really, just have fun." She looked away from the half-covered sun and looked at Marc. "And I'd forgotten about you."

"Ash..." he started.

"We were right here, Marc." She pointed at the ice with her still-trembling hand. "I remember it. We were right here, and you asked me to stay, and I didn't. I did what I thought was best for me at the time. And you know what? It's worked out pretty well for me."

He nodded. "Of course it has. It's you."

"But we lost touch. It was my fault. and I'm sorry. It's the one thing I regret. I wish I'd replied to your emails, I wished we'd stayed in touch, I wish there hadn't been a fifteen-year gap between then and now because I was so focused on school and work and putting this camp—this amazing, wonderful, incredible camp—out of my life."

He grinned and looked at her with those crystal-blue eyes.

"But I'm back here now." Her hands were shaking even harder. "And you and I, we're standing here again, fifteen years later, and this time I don't want to throw any of this away."

Marc nodded. "So what you're saying is, you'll be back next year?"

"Honestly," Ashley said. The shaking in her hands stopped. "I'm hoping it will be a lot sooner."

She leaned in and, once again, brought her mouth up to his. This time there was no interruption. They connected, and Ashley felt his warm, soft lips against hers. She kissed him, gently at first and then with more power as she brought her hands around his head. He hugged her back and pulled her in closer, taking in deep breaths between each caress.

She had kissed guys before, but she could not remember the last time a first kiss had felt so deserved, so meaningful. They held the last one for a few seconds before Ashley pulled away. She took a second to collect herself and then started laughing. "I bet you think you're so smart, don't you?"

"What?" Marc asked jovially. "I'm not sure what you mean."

She looked back to the setting sun, catching it just as it dipped completely below the horizon. "Peppermint," she said. "Your breath tastes like peppermint." She looked back at him and smirked. "You knew this was going to happen, didn't you?"

He beamed and scratched the back of his head. "I had a gut feeling." He took another deep breath and sighed. "So what now?"

"Now I believe we have dinner."

He gave her some side-eye. "I mean, with us. You don't strike me as the sort of person to kiss and run."

"Well, not when the guy I'm kissing is particularly handsome," Ashley said. "What are you doing for New Years?"

Marc shrugged. "Resting, mainly. Normally a bunch of locals set off fireworks on the lake."

"Who'd want to miss that?" Ashley deadpanned. "Or you could come down to the city and spend it with me. I've been out of my element for the last few days, I think it's time for you to do the same."

Marc offered his hand and Ashley grabbed it. "Sounds like a date." They leaned in and kissed once more. Marc laughed and looked over across the lake. "I've been waiting fifteen years for this."

She squeezed his hand. "I hope it was worth it. Now let's go, I'm starving for some Christmas dinner."

Hand-in-hand, they walked back up the stairs and headed to camp.

*   *   *

The sky was dark and the moon was out in full force as Marc and Ashley reached the Lodge. They let go of each other's hand and walked in to find just about everyone seated. Marc felt a swell of pride as he looked at the layout for their final meal: he had put all the tables together, running from the stage to halfway down the hall, to create one massive communal table for everyone to sit. Each table was covered in a red cloth and featured a small antique Christmas tree—a gift from a former guest— as centerpiece. A dozen large red candles flickered, providing illumination under the dimmed overhead lights. The camp's fine China and silver cutlery had been broken out for this special event. It looked amazing, if Marc did say so himself. Like something out of a movie.

But the pride he felt in putting this meal together was nothing compared to how he felt as he looked to the woman next to him. It was an utter, heart-leaping, fist-pounding, jump-up-and-down-like-a-kid-on-Christmas-Day joy at the idea that this was the beginning of something new. Ashley Tidings, the girl who'd broken his heart, had found her way back to Camp Cedarwood and was ready to pick up where they'd left off.

Actually, no, Marc thought, it was better than that. They weren't picking up where they'd left: they were starting from a much better spot, when they were more mature and established and knew who they were. That made it even better.

There were two free seats opposite each other at the far end of the table. They sat down, Marc sitting next to David and Ash next to Adam. The kid made a few teasing remarks about how he hoped Marc wasn't too hurt from the snowball he'd hit him with. Marc just stuck his hand out and rubbed Adam's hair.

When the final guests had arrived and taken their seats, Gunter walked out, carrying a massive turkey on a silver platter. A chorus of gasps erupted from the patrons, followed by loud clapping and cheering, and then a standing ovation as they all pushed their seats back and stood up. Gunter just nodded politely and put the bird down in front of Marc. Gunter's wife walked out next with a large tray of mashed potatoes and put it in the middle of the tables. Steamed vegetables and multiple bowls of gravy and cranberry sauce followed.

When everything was in front of the guests, Marc invited Gunter and his wife to join the two remaining seats, right in the middle of the table. "You are, without question, our guests of honor tonight," he said, with more applause coming from the others. "And now, before we eat, I think it's appropriate that we say a quick grace."

Heads bowed, and Marc recited the poem he'd read at every Christmas meal for the last seven years.

"Be with us at this table, Lord,

As we celebrate Your birth,

Bless us all and our time here,

Your children on this earth. Amen."

Marc picked up the carving knife—easily the camp's biggest one—and fork. "Merry Christmas everyone! Let's eat!" He started carving the meat and putting it on each plate as they were passed to him. Despite the twenty people he had to serve, he was able to cut and plate quickly and soon they were all taking part in the Christmas feast.

The food was spectacular. The turkey seemed to taste juicier, the mashed potatoes creamier, and the vegetables fresher than any Christmas meal Marc had had before. It undoubtedly had something to do with the beautiful, intelligent, super-kissable woman sitting opposite of him. New Years could not come soon enough.

"What are you so happy about?" Adam asked. "Did you forget that we beat you earlier today? 'Cause I'm happy to help you remember."

Marc stuck his tongue out. "It's Christmas. Aren't I allowed to be happy?"

"No, Adam's right," Ash said, her eyes twinkling at him. "Marc's too happy. Hey Adam, remind me again, what team was Marc on?"

"He was on the Frost Bites," Adam said.

"And what team won the Christmas Cup?"

"The Ice Dinosaurs."

"And just one last question, how did they win the Cup?"

"I hit Marc with a snowball to win the game." Adam waved his hands mockingly.

"That's right. Marc, are you unhappy now?"

Marc grabbed his chest. "Just crushed. Thank you for putting me in my place."

A few plates were passed back down for seconds, and then thirds. Marc sliced generous amounts of turkey onto each. The bird was big enough to feed a small army.

When the meal was over, the campers all cleared their own plates and stacked them in the kitchen window. Gunter and his wife disappeared into the kitchen and emerged with multiple pies — pumpkin, berry, pecan and meringue — as well as two large chocolate cakes, with intricate icing patterns around them.

"If it's okay with all of you," Gunter said, "I'd like to play a few festive pieces on the piano."

There was no objection. Gunter sat on the bench, hovered his fingers over the keys and began playing "Silent Night" while everyone else enjoyed their desserts. It transitioned into "Angels We Have Heard on High" and then "Hark! The Herald Angels Sing." By this point, the guests had all stuffed themselves and were enjoying coffee and tea from the side table. They joined in singing along to "Santa Claus is Coming to Town," "Deck the Halls" and "Jingle Bells."

Marc looked up at the clock above the fireplace. 6:45. It was time to wrap things up. "Hey Gunter," he said, "one more song."

Gunter nodded. "I know the perfect one."

He started playing the Camp Cedarwood anthem. Marc stood up and sang along, as did Ashley, Adam, Paige and David, and Drew and Sally. At the end of the first verse, Gunter kept playing, and all eyes fell on Marc. They clearly wanted a repeat of his performance from a few nights ago. Who was he to deny them it? He sang, loudly:

"And when the skies are dark and the moon is full and white,
Look up for me to guide you on until the morning light,
I point and reach, continue home, until I speak to you,
For where you find my lasting wealth, your treasure will be too."

Gunter tinkled the keys a few times and then finished. They all clapped and cheered. Marc walked up to the stage and grabbed the microphone. "You know, I've been doing Christmas Camp here for seven years and I still always find myself at a loss for words now," he started. "I can safely say that this has been the best one yet and I have all of you to thank for that. You all come here from across the country to spend your time with people you barely know, and yet we all feel like family. Especially this year, the way we've been able to celebrate with each other in our joy and support each other in our pain, it really is incredible. So, from the bottom of my heart, thank you for coming here and making this the most magical Christmas.

"Now, speaking of Christmas magic, in that I still think their win was physically impossible, I am proud to present this year's Christmas Cup to the Ice Dinosaurs! Will their captain please join me up here to collect their prize?"

He reached into the dark box on the stage and pulled out a copper trophy with the words "Camp Cedarwood Christmas Cup" engraved on it. On the trophy's wooden stand were miniature plaques with each year's winners listed, going back to the first one six years earlier. Carol walked up to the front, shook Marc's hand cordially, and then grabbed the trophy and held it above her head. All of her teammates cheered, except for Ash, who sat at the table staring out blankly, clearly in deep thought.

"And now, there is one last thing I need to tell you," Marc said. The others quieted down quickly as the tone in his voice dropped. He couldn't avoid this any longer. It wouldn't be fair not to tell them. "This has been such a great time here, and as they say, all good things must come to an end. Unfortunately, for Camp Cedarwood, that means that we might—"

"Wait." Ashley suddenly stood up. "Don't say anything yet." He pointed at Marc. "Your metal detector. Do you still have it?"

"Y-yeah, it's in the shed." Marc looked at her, confused. "Why?"

"Grab it and follow me." Ashley took off running for the door. "Campfire Point. C'mon, we need to save this camp!"

Chapter 36

Ashley ran outside and down the path, Carol's boots stomping loudly in the snow with every step. She could hear people moving behind her but did nothing to slow down and let them catch up. Her target lay just ahead. She was going to solve this mystery.

She crossed over the small path that led down to the lake and ran through the trees to reach Campfire Point. She stopped and caught her breath.

"Ash!" Paige caught up to her, with Adam right behind. Carol and Janice were about twenty feet back. "What's going on? Are you okay?"

"Yes," Ashley said. She walked down the snow-covered steps, to the arch between the two cedar trees. Standing right beneath it, she looked up at the moon. It was obscured by the snow in the tree branches. "Help me get this down."

She reached to the ground and rolled up a snowball, then threw it at the branch. It hit and knocked down some of the snow.

Adam ran down and joined in, followed by Paige, Carol and Janice. After a few minutes of chucking snowballs at the branches, they managed to clear them all off, and while only getting a drops of snow and ice on their heads. By this time, the rest of the guests had made their way to the Point and stood at the entrance, watching with a mix of confusion and curiosity.

Ashley brushed herself off and went back under the arch. She looked up again. The roof of the arch began to sparkle as some of the stones glowed in the moonlight. "Well I'll be," Carol said, joining her and looking up. "These stones — they must be clear enough that they reflect the moon's light."

"But under the sun you'd never be able to make them out," Janice added, also looking up at them. "It looks like they say something."

They seemed to form letters and numbers, but Ashley couldn't make them out. Was that a 2? A 7? An upside-down F? She slowly turned around until she was facing the snow-covered benches. The numbers and letters became coherent.

35' F. 21' R.

"Carol, what's your boot size?" she asked. "Would you say these are about a foot?"

"Maybe a bit smaller. Why?"

Ashley put one foot right in front of the other and began to walk forward. She counted aloud. "One, two, three..."

As she hit 35, Marc ran into the Point, carrying a large metal detector. "Ash!" he shouted. "What's going on?"

Ashley held her hand up, took another step, and then pivoted 90 degrees to her right and started counting again. At 21 she stopped. "Here! Marc, try it here!"

Marc walked over and put the metal detector down. He flipped it on and began waving it back and forth over the ground. A light buzzing noise came from it. "What is this?"

"It was the song," she said. "That second verse, when it says 'I point and reach, continue home,' that sounded so weird to me. Until I realized that it's a message."

"A message?" He moved up and to the right. Still nothing but buzzing came from the detector.

"Point refers to Campfire Point. And then take the first letter of 'and reach, continue home,' A-R-C-H. And then the first two lines, about looking up when the sky is dark and the moon bright—there were stones in the top of the arch that spell out coordinates in the moonlight. 35 feet forward and 21 feet right. I think that's where we are now."

Marc gave her an uneasy look. "And the final line, about 'my lasting wealth' and 'your treasure.' You think that will be here?"

He took two steps forward and moved the detector to the left. It began to beep. He moved further up the benches and the beeping got louder. "Yeah," Ashley said, her mouth wide. "I think I do."

The metal detector emitted a loud, prolonged beep. Marc brought a hand to his mouth. "There's something here! There's something big here!" He dropped the tool and fell to his knees. "If this is... if it's what I think it is, then we're good. Camp Cedarwood is saved!"

"It's saved?" Harvey shouted. "What do you mean? Was it in trouble?"

"Who cares?" Janice replied. "You heard the man, it's saved! It's a Christmas miracle!"

There were some cheers and some confused "huh?"s. Marc stood back up and faced the rest of the guests. "As I was saying, all good things must come to an end, but Christmas Camp isn't ending yet. I will see you all back here in a year—if not sooner!" He raised his hands above his head and then threw them forward. "I officially declare Christmas Camp over! Let's head back to our cabins and say our goodbyes!"

The crowd at the Point's entrance turned and began to leave. Ashley walked over to Marc. "Speaking of saying goodbye, I still need that gas canister from—"

Marc grabbed her and planted his lips on her. She squeaked in surprise and then kissed him back, but unlike their first kiss on the lake, this one had much more passion. Marc kept opening and closing his lips and at one point Ashley was sure she felt his tongue.

Marc pulled back and looked at her like she was Santa Claus himself. "I am forever in your debt. You have saved this camp."

"I'm glad I could help." She once again grabbed his hand and they started walking towards the entrance. "But I'm still going to pay for my stay here."

"Uh huh? You sure are committed to that."

"And I don't want any discounts, either." She leaned her head against his shoulder. "In fact, I think I may even include a tip."

*   *   *

Ashley took one last look around her cabin to make sure she hadn't forgotten anything, then faced her bed and felt a twinge of sadness that she wouldn't get any more sleeps in it. Somehow it was more comfortable and restful than her Queen mattress with memory foam and her weighted blanket. Go figure.

She left the cabin and walked past the others, now dark on the inside and barren on the outside, and headed to the parking lot. The guests were all gathered there to say their goodbyes. Open trunks were stuffed with suitcases and presents, windshield wipers swished back and forth to remove the snow and ice, and fog lights lit up the trees around the lot, all as the campers gave each other hugs and wiped away tears.

Ashley threw her gym duffle bag into her backseat and joined in with the group. She thanked Drew for his awesome work running the Christmas Cup and told him and Sally to take care of each other. She hugged Emma and thanked her for all the clothes she loaned her, and told Jack she admired their ability to stay together as a family despite the intense Christmas Cup competition. "Yeah, well, we'll win next time," Jack said. Ashley high-fived their daughters and wished them a Merry Christmas.

Harvey approached her and gave her a tight hug, with his kids joining in. "We won the Cup," he said. "And we couldn't have done it without you."

"Eh, you probably could have," Ashley said.

"But it wouldn't have been as fun!" Ian said. "Or funny!"

Ashley glared at him jokingly. "I hope you guys have a great year. See you next Christmas?"

"Without a doubt." Harvey guided his kids over to Marc to say goodbye.

Carol, Bill, Janice and Roger were all huddled together, saying their farewells. Ashley walked over just as they finished. "Ash, honey," Carol said, wiping tears from her eyes. "Y'all are the best thing to happen to Cedarwood since they started this Christmas camp. I know you din't expect to be here, but I can tell you that you made it great for everyone. Thank you so much."

"Thank me?" Ashley asked incredulously. "Thank you! I showed up here with nothing and you all gave me the clothes off your backs. Especially you, Carol. I know I'm still wearing your boots, but I promise I will send them to you as soon I as get to the city."

"Darlin', what am I going to do with those boots? You keep them and bring them back to me next Christmas, 'kay?"

Ashley laughed. "Deal." She gave Carol and then Bill a warm embrace. Then she faced Roger and Janice. "I expect that the three of us will be getting drinks in the next month."

"As long as they're non-alcoholic, I'm good," Roger said.

"And as long as you bring someone too, Ash," Janice smirked, her eyes darting over to Marc.

"We'll see." Tears that she had been trying to keep down started forming in her eyes. "I'm just so happy that I not only met you, but got to be here for such a special event. You two are going to be the best parents in the world." She sniffed loudly. "Well, until the kid turns 18 and goes to Harvard or Yale or something."

"Out of the question," Roger said, cutting the air with his hand. "There's only one school she's going to, and it's the one with the same colors we're going to use to paint her nursery."

Janice turned to her husband. "There's a lot to unpack with what you just said. Good thing we've got a few hours of driving ahead of us. But first..." She grabbed Ashley tightly. "You take care of yourself, okay? I know you're an amazing marketer-slash-mind-reader, but take some time for yourself."

"I will." Ashley rubbed Janice's back and few times and then hugged Roger.

The guests began getting in their vehicles and driving away. Ashley waved as Carol and Bill left in their pickup truck and Janice and Roger drove off in their sleek crossover. She walked back to where Marc stood with Adam, Paige and David. Adam had his face buried in his arm and was audibly sobbing. "Hey, buddy." Marc crouched down so that he was on eye-level with the boy. "I know it's hard to say goodbye, but summer is just a few months away. And we are going to have the best summer camp ever, okay?"

Adam raised his head up and nodded. "Okay. Promise you won't take down my fort in the forest?"

Marc shrugged. "What fort? I have no idea what you mean. Do your parents know what you're talking about?"

Paige and David both shook their heads. "Sounds to me," Ashley said, "like your fort is still a secret."

Adam wiped his face with his glove. "Good."

His parents faced Ashley. "I don't think we can thank you enough," Paige said. "What you did for us, for Adam, for the Ice Dinosaurs… it means the world to us, Ashley." She stepped forward and lowered her voice. "Especially now. We really needed some Christmas magic and you delivered it."

Ashley wrapped her arms around her. "It wasn't me," she whispered. "We're not the ones who make Christmas magic happen."

Paige stepped back from the hug and grabbed Ashley's shoulders. She opened her mouth, and then smiled and said nothing.

David came over and offered his hand. Ashley shook it. "There are a lot of things I'm not going to forget from these last few days," he said. "But you hitting the wrong ornament in archery? That's gonna be burned in my memory forever."

"Gee, thanks," Ashley said. "You'll be in my thoughts. All three of you. And if there's ever anything I can do to help, please don't hesitate to reach out."

"We know," Paige said. "And we will." She spoke a bit louder. "Hey Adam, come and say goodbye to Ashley."

Adam ran over and jumped right onto Ashley, like a monkey on a tree. "You're the best!" he said. "Thanks for distracting Marc so I could hit him with the snowball!"

Ashley shrugged at Paige and David. "If that's what sticks out to you, fine by me."

"That and like a million other things." He dropped off of her and looked up with his big hazel eyes. "I love you."

That was enough to break her. The tears flowed freely as Ashley knelt down and squeezed him as hard as she could. "I love you too. I'm sure I'll see you soon." She looked at his parents. "And I mean it. We're going to see each other really soon."

"Okay," Adam croaked. She let go and he took a deep breath.

"Merry Christmas," Paige said. She grabbed Adam's hand and the three of them walked to their silver SUV. David arranged all the stuff in the trunk to make sure it would close—Ashley saw her robot next to Adam's red bag. They got in and drove off, honking the horn a few times.

That left just Ashley and Marc. He walked over and put his arm around her. "So, New Years?"

"If you're up for it. And don't worry, I have a couch you can crash on. You're going to love it—my place has heat and cell service and everything."

Marc feigned shock. "Modern technology? I don't know if I'll be able to handle it." He leaned over and kissed the side of her head. "I suppose I should give you my contact info, huh?"

"It'd be helpful. Unless you were planning on ghosting me."

"That'd be kind of hard to do when you know where I live. I'll go get you a business card." He walked toward the office. Ashley followed, but stopped as he went in. She looked out at the area—the Lodge, the cabins, and the giant Christmas tree in the middle—and wiped away another tear. She was going to miss this place.

A gleam of light under the massive tree caught her eye. She walked over and saw the star that had been on top of it—the same one Adam had found in the chest inside the forest that may or may not have existed. She picked it up and examined it. It still shimmered in different colors.

She put it in her coat pocket and walked back to the office.

Marc came out a minute later, a small card in his hand. "This has my office number, email and cell phone, though that last one works about one percent of the time."

She took the card and put it in her jeans pocket. "I'm just glad you can be contacted at all. I was afraid I was going to have to hire carrier pigeons or something."

He chuckled. "It's funny, in some ways you're a totally different person from when we were kids. And in some ways, you haven't changed a bit."

They walked back to the parking lot. Marc opened his trunk and pulled out the gas canister, then used it to fill Ashley's car. "I feel like this is goodbye," he said, "even though I'll be seeing you in just a few days."

"It's goodbye to Christmas at Camp Cedarwood," Ashley said. "And that's kind of sad. There will be other camps and other Christmases, but there will never be this exact thing ever again."

He finished adding the gas and put the canister back on. "It's sad. But this was still the best camp I've ever done. All because you showed up." He walked over to her and put his arms around her shoulders. "Thank you, Ash."

"Thank you, Marc." She gave him a light kiss. "And I mean that. If you hadn't put that sign out on the road, I never would have even known the camp was here."

He cocked his head to the side. "What do you mean? What sign?"

"The one in the field, maybe a mile west of here. With the lights and everything."

"Ash…" he said, clearly confused. "There is no sign out there. There used to be one, like ten years ago, but it was hit by lightning and burned down."

"What?" she asked. "The one with the lake and the trees —"

"And the cabins, yes. It hasn't been there for over a decade."

Ashley stepped back and put a hand on her forehead. "But I — it was — how could…" Her hands fell to her sides. "Christmas magic."

"Christmas magic." Marc repeated. He raised his hand in a half-wave. "Drive safe."

"See you soon." She gave him one last kiss and then got in her car. The engine roared to life. She backed up, then rolled down the window. "Oh, and Marc?"

"Yes?"

"Merry Christmas."

He grinned. "You too, Ash."

She put the car in drive and started up the driveway. It was much easier now that the snow had been flattened by a dozen vehicles. She slowed down at the archery range to glare at it, and then reached the sideroad and headed up the hill. Her tires skidded a few times, but she was able to make it to the top and onto a plowed, drivable road.

She turned left and headed back the same way she'd come four days earlier. The city awaited. Her own clothes, a hot bath, Wi-Fi. And, best of all, Marc. She was already thinking about what they could do to ring in the new year.

As she passed the empty field, with snow covering the remnants of a burned-down sign, she turned on the radio and scanned for a channel. After a few seconds, music began to play.

"Chestnuts roasting on an open fire..."

She cranked up the volume and sang along.

Epilogue

The drive to Cedarwood, Ashley decided, was a million times easier in the summer.

With a bright sun shining above her and not a speck of precipitation in the air or on the ground, it was easy to motor down the highway, windows open and wind whipping against her hair. The turnoff was visible from a mile away — this time she didn't need police to shut down the road and divert her.

She slowed down as she hit the dirt road and drove past the farms. The last time she had seen them they had been covered in three feet of snow. Now, there was nothing but row after row of green crops, with the occasional tractor going through them.

Ashley passed a pond that had several kids swimming in it, and then orchards that were sure to be ready for harvest in a few months. She checked her fuel tank. Nice and full. It was hard to believe that seven months earlier she had been scared for her safety as she'd tried to traverse this route.

She passed through a small forest, with the overhead trees creating a canopy of leaves that nearly blocked out the sun entirely. Two minutes later she was through it and looking out over a vast field of golden grains. It looked so much nicer when it wasn't being buffeted by snow and wind.

At the end of the field, a large plastic sign, supported by a plank of wood on either side, had been erected. In big, black letters it read "Camp Cedarwood: Next Right."

"It's a start," Ashley mused.

She turned down the large hill. It wasn't nearly as scary when her tires were able to grip the road. At the bottom she continued into the camp's driveway, where she joined a line of cars coming in. She followed it to a busy parking lot. Nearly every space was taken. Kids and parents alike pulled suitcases and sleeping bags out of trunks, ran to greet each other, and gathered around a blonde-haired man who was somehow managing to carry three clipboards.

Ashley parked along the forest and walked over to the group. "Right, Samantha," Marc said, consulting one clipboard and then another. "You are in the Pawnee cabin. Your counselor is Grace and she's the best we have. You're going to love it."

The girl he was speaking to leapt in the air and started running towards the cabins, with her parents walking behind.

Marc helped the last boy with his cabin and then wiped the sweat from his forehead. "Excuse me," Ashley said. "I'm trying to find my cabin. It has a wooden stove, two comfy chairs and a very handsome man."

Marc looked up and smiled. "Hey beautiful. I'm happy to say that cabin is always available for you."

She put her arms around his neck and they kissed. "How'd the presentation go?" Marc asked.

"Even better than the one I did in December. They're hiring us to do even more work."

"Awesome. I guess that means you'll be driving past these parts a lot, huh?"

"Looking like it'll be every week." She playfully jabbed him with her elbow. "Maybe this camp will become my second home after all."

A couple with a smaller, crying boy walked up. "I should probably handle this," Marc said. "You in any rush? Want to stay for dinner? There's definitely going to be someone who wants to see you."

"You know I do. I'll see you in a bit." She walked back to her car as Marc knelt down and told the sobbing kid about all the cool things he was going to experience.

Ashley opened the passenger door and grabbed a small plastic bag off the floor. She locked the car and headed into the woods.

The forest was a lot harder to navigate in the summer, with every branch full of leaves and no footprints in the snow to follow. It took her a bit of wandering, as well as a few scrapes from branches and some mosquito bites, before she was able to recognize a few of the trees that she'd passed seven months earlier. With those landmarks established, it wasn't too hard to follow them to the small, teepee-like shelter behind a pine tree.

Aside from a few of the sticks having fallen over, the shelter still stood firm, looking just as it had when she'd last been there. She crouched down at the entrance and began digging away dirt, until she'd formed a small hole. She reached into the bag and pulled out the glass star. In the afternoon sun, it reflected a bright green light. Ashley smiled to herself, put the star back in the bag, and then put the bag in the hole. She covered it back up with dirt.

"Hey!" a squeaky voice shouted. "What are you doing?"

A boy, maybe ten or eleven years old, ran up to her. He wore a t-shirt with alternating blue and light-blue stripes that was somehow already covered in dirt. His light-brown hair fell over his eyes as he ran. "That's our fort!" he said. "We built it last year!"

Ashley stood up and held out her hands. "I know. I was just checking it out. A friend of mine helped build it. His name's Adam."

The boy nodded. "Yeah, he's my friend too. But my parents said he won't be able to come to camp this year." He frowned and then asked, "How do you know him?"

"I met him here last year at Christmas Camp," Ashley said. They started walked back towards Cedarwood. "We were on the same team for the Christmas Cup. He ended up winning it for us when he hit Marc with a snowball."

"Really? What happened?"

As they walked, Ashley told him about the final snowball battle, and then all the other events that had led up to it. The whole time, the kid stared up at her with wide eyes. "That's amazing!" he exclaimed when she was done. They reached the parking lot, which was now a bit emptier. "I'll have to go this year. It sounds incredible."

"It's more than incredible," Ashley said.

A loud horn blared near them. A familiar silver SUV came down the driveway and into the parking lot. Before it had even stopped, the backdoor opened and a boy with a red bandana over his head popped out. "Ash! Jeremy!"

Ashley looked over at Marc, still scanning through his different clipboards, then back at the car, and then finally to Jeremy. She grinned. "It's magical."

Author's note

Thank you for reading Christmas at Camp Cedarwood--I hope you enjoyed it as much as I enjoyed writing it! This is my first-ever novel and I truly appreciate everyone who has bought and read it.

I'm hoping this won't be the last Ashley Tidings story, and let's just say that Ash's interest in mysteries and detective work will be at the forefront of future novels. If you'd like to see more, please recommend this book to your friends and leave a rating and review on Amazon.

The more people who read about Ashley and her adventures at Cedarwood, the more likely there will be more to come!

Thank you again, and Merry Christmas!

-HW

Made in United States
North Haven, CT
28 November 2024

61100953R00143